ZERO ONE

**OTHER BOOKS IN THE
DANIEL BYRD ADVENTURE SERIES**

MOUNTAIN JUSTICE

A LITTLE BIT KIN

SELF RESCUE: PART 1 OF THE TEXAS TRILOGY

ASPHALT BLUES: PART 2 OF THE TEXAS TRILOGY

A DANIEL BYRD ADVENTURE

ZERO ONE

PART 3 OF THE TEXAS TRILOGY

PHILLIP W. PRICE

Alpharetta, Georgia

This is a work of fiction. Names, characters, businesses, places, and events are either the products of the author's imagination or are used in a fictitious manner. Any resemblance to actual persons, living or dead, or actual events is purely coincidental.

Copyright © 2025 by Phillip Price

All rights reserved. No part of this book may be reproduced or transmitted in any form or by any means, electronic or mechanical, including photocopying, recording, or any information storage and retrieval system, without permission in writing from the author.

ISBN: 978-1-6653-1091-8 - Paperback
eISBN: 978-1-6653-1092-5 - eBook

These ISBNs are the property of Lanier Press (a Division of BookLogix) for the express purpose of sales and distribution of this title. The content of this book is the property of the copyright holder only. BookLogix does not hold any ownership of the content of this book and is not liable in any way for the materials contained within. The views and opinions expressed in this book are the property of the Author/Copyright holder, and do not necessarily reflect those of Lanier Press/BookLogix.

Library of Congress Control Number: 2025924913

Printed in the United States of America

∞This paper meets the requirements of ANSI/NISO Z39.48-1992 (Permanence of Paper)

112625

DEDICATION

In our culture, the greatest wrong one can perpetrate is the murder of another human being.

In the lexicon of the Georgia Bureau of Investigation, any case involving the investigation of a death—whether accidental, suicidal, or homicidal—is designated as a "zero one" case. These are the cases where countless hours, resources, and emotions are expended in the pursuit of justice.

Each agent assigned to a murder investigation has a single goal: to speak on behalf of the victim. The result of a murder investigation should never be vengeance, but rather the impartial administration of justice for the wrong done.

PROLOGUE

Judge Jerry Mason walked briskly into the courtroom and took his seat behind the bench. He placed a folder containing several documents on the desk in front of him, then glanced around the room. People awkwardly took their seats after briefly standing for his entry. A Gulf War veteran, a former cop, and most recently, the District Attorney for the Appalachian Judicial Circuit, Mason had been appointed to the bench a year earlier when Judge Reginald "No Chance" Lance retired. He was still getting acquainted with the other side of the bench.

Omar Warren was seated beside his attorney, Lane Sims, who had been a defense attorney in the circuit for many years. Warren looked uncomfortable—his face was drawn, and his hands gripped the arms of his chair. He was in a Pickens County courtroom to enter a plea for crimes he had committed when he was much younger. He was now a family man, a businessman, and a changed man. But for Daniel Byrd, this day had been a long time coming.

Twenty years earlier, Omar and his father—a contractor for the CIA—had worked with Mexican drug traffickers to smuggle large quantities of methamphetamine into the United States. Now, all these years later, what Omar once saw as a great adventure was coming back to haunt him.

Before Judge Mason's clerk could call the first case of the morning, a medium-height woman with curly blonde hair dressed in western attire stepped into the quiet room. The woman held a white western hat in her left hand, her right hand resting on a Colt .45 semi-automatic pistol tucked into a hand-tooled leather holster.

Omar Warren was even more surprised to see the woman he had once known as Stacey Carter stride into the courtroom. He stared for a moment as she approached the railing.

Judge Mason stared at the intruder, unsure of her intentions. "Madam, do you have business before this court?"

The woman dropped her chin, chagrined by the judge's tone. She pulled her jacket to the side, revealing a sheriff's star pinned to the left side of her blouse.

Byrd turned to Mason. "Judge, this is Sheriff Raelynn Michaels of El Paso County, Texas. You might say she's an interested party in this matter. I made her aware of the hearing, but I didn't think she'd come."

Sheriff Raelynn Michaels had been Agent Raelynn Michaels of the El Paso Sheriff's Office when Byrd first met her. In 2005, she was undercover, using the name Stacey Carter, as a load of six tons of methamphetamine oil was trucked from Presidio, Texas, to Georgia. She met Omar Warren while he brokered the transportation of the meth. Raelynn, along with Texas Rangers Adeline Riley and Clete Petterson, broke the case with Daniel Byrd's help.

Mason leaned forward and looked her over as she walked toward the bench. Omar continued to stare as Raelynn came to a stop in front of the judge.

"Apologies, your honor. I just landed on a red-eye flight and got here as quickly as I could," Michaels said.

Judge Mason nodded solemnly. "Thank you for making the journey out here to Georgia." Then he smiled. "As a young lieutenant in the Army, I was assigned to Fort Bliss in El Paso. We called it Fort Blister."

Sheriff Michaels chuckled. "It can get hot back home!"

Mason pointed to the front bench. "Well, Sheriff. Relax and have a seat. Our district attorney was about to throw the opening pitch on this case. I'm guessing that Agent Byrd here was just about to explain to the court why Mr. Warren should not suffer the full brunt of the charges he faces. I guess you'll have something to offer on the matter?"

Sheriff Michaels nodded. "If you'll permit it, I will."

Michaels took a seat on the hard wooden bench as Geneva Whitmire organized her notes. Whitmire was a young, hard-charging prosecutor appointed to fulfill Judge Mason's term. At thirty-five, she was among the youngest of Georgia's fifty district attorneys.

Mason looked toward the prosecutor. She wore a business suit with a white blouse and low-heeled shoes, and her brown hair hung down over her shoulders. Geneva Whitmire stood and addressed the judge. "Your honor, the government is ready to proceed. I ask that Agent Daniel Byrd take the stand."

Mason pursed his lips. "Let's get this hearing underway."

Daniel Byrd strode to the stand, climbed up, and raised his right hand. He wore his best navy-blue suit with a medium blue tie. He stood perfectly still as he waited for the prosecutor to approach.

Whitmire had Byrd remain standing as she administered the oath.

Byrd responded with "I swear," and lowered his hand.

"Please take a seat," Whitmire continued.

Byrd sat in the uncomfortable wooden chair and leaned forward. While the prosecutor flipped through her yellow legal pad, he cleared his throat.

"For the record, please state your name, title, and assignment for the court," Whitmire said.

"I'm Daniel Byrd, Special Agent in Charge with the Georgia Bureau of Investigation. I'm assigned to the GBI Regional Investigative Office in Cleveland, Georgia."

"And SAC Byrd, you have direct and indirect knowledge of the circumstances surrounding the investigation of the man you know as Mr. Omar Warren, is that correct?"

Byrd proceeded to enumerate Mr. Warren and his late father's involvement in a methamphetamine smuggling organization that spanned from southwest Texas to Georgia. He testified about the shooting that resulted in Adam Benjamin's death and the cross-country undercover operation involving Raelynn Michaels. Then he described Warren's movements based on information he'd recently received from the US Marshals. Byrd explained to the court how Omar had managed to slip through international borders and, at last, seek refuge in England.

"And I believe," Whitmire added, "we're expecting confirmation of that from the British government? I understand the Consul General has asked to address the court."

Judge Mason leaned forward. "When do you expect the Consul? This hearing was scheduled with adequate time for them to appear."

Before Judge Mason could finish, the back door to the courtroom opened, and a smartly dressed woman of about fifty stepped inside. She was of average height and slim. At her arm was a man of the same age. He, too, wore a navy-blue business suit. He stood six feet tall and had an athletic build. The only clue to his age was a full head of gray hair.

Judge Mason checked his wristwatch. The time was well past when he had planned to begin the hearing.

The woman approached the bench. Mason scowled at her.

"Please forgive my tardiness, your honor. We hadn't anticipated so much traffic," the woman said. "I'm British Consul General Gail Rahway. I'm accompanied by the Director of British Special Forces"—she motioned to the man—"Major General Jaco Carleton-Smith, late of the Grenadier Guards. We believe we can offer information regarding Mr. Warren and his contributions to the British and American common good."

Mason leaned back and crossed his arms. "Such as?"

Omar nudged Lane Sims. "Must he explain this in open court?" he pleaded.

Before Sims could stand to object, Byrd turned to the judge and said, "Judge, I think we should go into those matters in chambers. The British government has asked for—maybe I should say, have insisted on—secrecy in this matter."

Mason looked to Sims, who stood behind the defense table. "Your honor, my client has asked that I make the same request—that this testimony be taken in chambers."

Mason looked to Whitmire, who shrugged and said, "The people have no objection."

Mason stood. He addressed the security deputy standing beside the bench. "Deputy, make sure the jury room is clear, and then station someone at the door. Once we're in there, no one comes in or out without my approval."

Then Mason motioned to Byrd. "SAC Byrd, please escort the Texas sheriff and the British government officials around to the jury room."

Byrd stepped down from the stand and walked to Raelynn.

He saw her eyes were red. He sighed. "I could have handled this, you know."

She wiped a tear from her eye. "I had to be here, Danny. I wanted you to know I had your back." She threw her arms around Byrd's shoulders and held him.

Judge Mason turned away from the pair and headed for his chambers. He stopped mid-stride. "Sorry to interrupt this little homecoming, but I'm guessing you don't want a court reporter in this meeting?"

Byrd looked back, red-faced. "That's correct."

He motioned for the sheriff to go first. "How's the family? I think Montana told me you had a couple of boys?"

Raelynn grinned. "A couple of hellions. They'd tear up concrete if you gave them a chance." She stopped and turned back. "I hate that we didn't stay in touch."

Byrd shrugged. "You've been busy. Being a sheriff is a big deal. You've come a long way from being an undercover narc."

Raelynn's chest heaved as she tried to avoid Byrd's eyes. "You know why I came. It's still raw, even after all these years. I guess that's why I haven't tried to reach out."

Byrd held the door to the back corridor of the courthouse and pointed to one standing open. They crowded into the jury room.

The space was barely big enough for such a large group. Everyone managed to find a place around the small conference table piled high with legal documents. Once seated, Judge Mason cleared his throat. He knew it would be a while before he could have a cigarette. "Would you and the sheriff here bring us all into the story?"

Byrd felt hollow as he watched Raelynn. Her eyes were red, but her jaw was firmly set. She placed her hands on the table and looked down, keeping her gaze fixed on them.

"Tell the story, Danny. I'm a big girl, so don't leave anything out."

Byrd glanced at Raelynn, then turned to face Judge Mason. "It seems like everything started in Texas in December 2007. But to give this story full context, I need to go back to Christmas 2005."

Mason steepled his fingers. "Tell it all, Danny."

Byrd said he would. But he knew he *wouldn't* tell it all.

CHAPTER 1
ON THE LAM

Omar Warren stepped out of the taxi. Twice in his life, he had fled across the world to escape American law enforcement. *Not bad*, he thought, *for a twenty-year-old*.

He had landed at Budapest Ferenc Liszt International Airport just over an hour ago. The airport was crowded, and Omar was thankful he carried only a single bag. The night before, he had left Woodstock, Georgia, and driven directly to the Atlanta airport after the failed attempt to smuggle six tons of methamphetamine oil across the country.

His father, General Mitchell Warren, had advised him months ago of the best exit strategy and where they could meet. Mitch Warren, a former CIA contract officer, tapped his old contacts to arrange an escape route for his son. Once he landed in Budapest, Omar texted his father: "out." Then he destroyed his phone.

He used a French passport to board the first flight to Hungary. Omar never got over how easily his father produced new identity documents. He'd been in the air for nine hours when the flight landed in Frankfurt for a brief layover. Passport control in the German city was crowded with tourists headed for the Christmas markets along the Danube River. The customs inspectors were overworked and gave his documents only a cursory glance.

He spent a few restless hours waiting for his final leg. While he waited, a middle-aged woman dressed as a flight attendant sat beside him long enough to pick up his counterfeit French passport. It would be used by someone else—Omar didn't care who—to fly to New Zealand. Once the passport was flagged, it would lead law enforcement to a dead end.

Now inside the European Union, Omar planned to resume the identity of William Kleinman of Midland, Texas. He knew the GBI, Texas Rangers, and a host of federal agencies would do their best to track him before he fled the EU and went underground.

His father's connections with the CIA had gotten him through a similar route a year ago. That time, the journey ended in Cambodia. This time, the destination was far less tropical.

He flagged down a taxi and asked to go to the Buda-Castle Pier, officially known as the Budapest International Cruise Terminal. The pier sat on the Buda side of the city. Exploring its hilly, cobblestone streets and historic architecture might've been a charming way to take in the city—but tonight wasn't the night.

Holiday travelers were everywhere he looked, rushing to make last-minute purchases before heading home. The taxi let him out near the pier where a dozen long, low riverboats took on tourists who would leave Budapest in luxurious style—at least compared to the room Omar had waiting.

Nearby, the Christmas Markets were slowly winding down with the holiday just around the corner.

Omar was bundled up, but the air was cold and damp. He hustled to the bank of the Danube River and searched for the ship he was meeting. The Danube was a romantic destination, drawing tourists from around the world, but Omar barely noticed the lights and the festive atmosphere.

He had seen enough on the taxi ride to know that Budapest was still recovering from its decades behind the Iron Curtain. The buildings were bleak and boxy, even with the holiday decorations.

He had walked nearly half a mile when he spotted the name painted in white block letters on the stern of the freighter: Der Holländische Junge. The boat was long, low, and flat, typical of ships designed for Europe's inland waterways.

He glanced over his shoulder as he climbed onto the gangway. A man in dark thermal coveralls stepped into the light and motioned him forward. "Quickly, Herr Kleinman. We must be departing soon." His English was heavily accented. Omar hadn't spent enough time in Europe to guess the man's country of origin, but he assumed German. It didn't matter.

The man led Omar to a cabin in the rear of the freighter. The little room was cold and, based on the throbbing sound, over the engine. Omar dropped his small bag on the cot and looked around his new quarters.

"How long to Amsterdam?" Omar asked the man.

"Depends on the river and the rain. Maybe three days, maybe five. We've had much rain this week." The man turned to leave.

"Do I pay you?" Omar asked.

The man shook his head. "I've been paid. Stay below

decks and rest. I'll have food brought to you twice a day. The toilet is up the hall. You'll not be bothered."

Omar extended his hand to shake, but the man had already left. As the door closed and latched, Omar pulled a novel from his bag. It was a mystery he'd picked up at the Atlanta airport.

Budapest airport had been his last major hurdle. His passport had cleared inspection twice in two days. Now that he was inside the EU, Omar could travel uninspected all the way to London.

As Omar stretched out on the bunk, he wondered what his dad would say about the latest debacle with Rojo. The thought made him smile.

The engine roared louder, and the boat rocked as they pulled away from the docks.

FRIDAY, DECEMBER 23, 2005
10:22 P.M. CET
COLOGNE, GERMANY

Omar heard a knock on his door and turned as the man he'd met two days earlier poked his head in. "There is much rain, so be careful. We're not near any other traffic, and you may walk on the deck for a while. Just keep your hood up. I don't want any of the crew to be able to describe you later."

Omar had spent hours watching through his porthole as tourist ships and service boats—like the one he was on—crossed from the Danube to the Main and finally to the Rhine. The river was as busy as an interstate highway. At times, their little vessel had to sit idle for hours, waiting to pass through locks that brought them to the next level of the river.

He grabbed a heavy, hooded raincoat and climbed the slick stairway to the upper deck. Containers in a dozen colors were lashed down with turnbuckles along the wet surface, but there was room for him to weave around to the bow. He stood for a while, watching a tourist boat glide past. Through its wide windows, he could see passengers in what looked like a lounge—drinking, laughing, relaxed and happy. Under different circumstances, he could imagine feeling the same.

He sensed someone beside him before he heard them. It was the man—his host. "We are passing Cologne," he said, pointing toward the lights of a large city on the river's northern bank. "Do you see the spires of the church?"

Omar squinted. He could just make out two open-work spires topped with crosses. "Yeah, I see them."

"That is still the tallest cathedral in the world. In the Great War, Allied bombers used it to mark the city. As a consequence, Cologne was the most heavily bombed city in Germany." The man turned and faced Omar. His face was drawn but not sad. "It is my home. It is where I met your father."

"What was he doing here?" Omar asked.

"Working for the US government—so he claimed. For all I knew, he might've been working for Moscow." The man grinned. "He was a good man. The Berlin Wall still divided our country back then. Your father was tasked with establishing a network that could pass intelligence about the East to the West. He recruited me in 1980. The last time I saw him was in 1990, just before he left for Kuwait City."

Omar realized he hadn't gotten a good look at his host

yet. He tried to get a better look at the man in the dim light on the dark deck. "So, you knew my father pretty well, then?"

The man laughed. "No one knew your father—only parts of him. He was an exceptional operative. Ran operations without a budget. Didn't care how the job got done—he enjoyed the game. And he played it well." He looked over at Omar. "Some say he worked for MI6 at the same time he was being paid by the CIA. *That* was your dad."

"So, he was already in the intelligence game?" Omar asked.

The man smiled. "We called him the *freundlicher lügner*. I believe that loosely translates as 'the seller of the used cars.' No one ever really knew what game he played."

Omar laughed—maybe his first real laugh in days. It felt good, hearing about his father from the early days. There was still so much he didn't know.

The man pointed again toward the church. "Your father once claimed his grandfather had been mayor of Cologne during the war—and that he'd done all he could within his power to preserve the cathedral." He snorted, "We later discovered he was a *lügner*—a liar."

Omar nodded. The rain began falling harder. He wiped his face, trying to memorize every detail of the city disappearing behind them.

The man pulled his coat tighter and turned away. "You should head below. We'll reach Amsterdam tomorrow night."

Omar stepped off the high-speed train and dragged his bag onto the platform. He walked past the silver train with the swooping yellow nose and wove around construction equipment parked at odd angles for the station's nearly billion-dollar expansion. He had traveled from Amsterdam to Brussels on a local train and then caught the high-speed line to London the same evening.

The station lights were bright, and his eyes were heavy with fatigue. He glanced around the atrium and saw people eating at food kiosks and shops on the level below.

There were few people in the station this late, and Omar didn't expect his dad to come running up to him in front of even a small crowd. He trudged along the concrete platform and passed through the turnstiles into the public area.

Omar scanned the space, looking for any sign of his father. As he adjusted his grip on his bag, a tall, well-dressed stranger touched his elbow. Without making eye contact, the man guided Omar toward a bench and motioned for him to sit.

Omar had been sitting for too many hours, but he collapsed into the seat beside the stranger.

"My name is Steve Loftus. I was a friend of your father's." The man looked around for anyone who might be watching.

Omar frowned. "Was a friend? What's he done now?"

Loftus turned to face Omar and let out a long sigh. "He died."

MONDAY, DECEMBER 3, 2007
10:35 A.M. EST
GEORGIA PUBLIC SAFETY TRAINING CENTER
FORSYTH, GEORGIA

Daniel Byrd stood at the twenty-five-yard line of the pistol course. His hands were sweaty despite the cold. He was making a second attempt that day to shoot a qualifying score. The first time through, he'd dropped a single round off target and put six rounds into the lower abdomen of the human-shaped board—enough to drop his score below the required eighty points.

Off to the far-right side of the range, he avoided the other shooters as he struggled to regain his composure. He'd missed the range day for his office in Gainesville and was required to make up the training before the end of the year.

The winter air bit at him as he hovered close to coming up short. If he failed to qualify, he'd lose his arrest powers, the ability to perform law enforcement duties, and his pay. No pressure there.

He had qualified easily with his Remington 870 pump shotgun and issued M4 rifle, but the rifle had caused a sudden hearing loss. After reporting the issue to the range master, an inspection revealed a faulty seal on his hearing protection. The .223-caliber rifle had a notoriously loud report.

The chief firearms instructor for the day, Lamont "Monty" Davis, offered to trade his full-length M4 for a short-barreled version with an attached suppressor. Byrd knew Davis better than most instructors and appreciated the gesture. Davis handed over the heavy, AR-15-style rifle. Byrd examined the sausage-shaped attachment on the barrel.

"That's a .223 suppressor. It won't silence the shots, but if you have to use it, it'll do less damage to an unprotected ear. Don't get the idea it works like Hollywood," Davis pointed out. "But it will mitigate the sound for the shooter. The bullet, traveling faster than the speed of sound, creates a small sonic boom that isn't normally an acoustic problem behind the gun."

Byrd hefted the rifle and brought it to his shoulder, aiming down the length of the weapon. "With the suppressor on the end, it's about the same length as a normal carbine," Byrd noted.

Davis nodded. "I can add an EOTech sight, if you're interested."

Byrd had accepted the offer and had run through the rifle qualification course without issue. He liked the feel of the gun with the additional hardware and enjoyed shooting it on the range.

Then, on an open range with the temperature hovering near freezing, he rushed through the pistol course—only to fail.

Now, at the twenty-five-yard position, Byrd waited for the targets to turn. His head was beginning to ache from the tight hearing protection clamped over his ears. His pistol stayed holstered until the command came over the public address system. The instructions echoed in his mind: using the angular search technique, on command, the shooter will assume left-side cover, pointing their weapon at the right target. When the targets turn, the shooter will fire one round at the right target in four seconds and then return to cover."

Byrd took a deep breath and waited. The two targets turned and clattered as they stopped. The other shooters to his left fired. Byrd exhaled and fired, waiting until the last second to get the best sight picture he could. Then, just as suddenly as they had turned toward him, the targets turned away.

He continued through the course and finished with an 84. Not stellar but acceptable. He thanked the instructors and shook their hands, aware they would record both the failure and the passing score in his training record. Then he made his way toward his car. Some of the agents, acquaintances from narcotics and even one from the Special Agents' School, made small talk. Byrd opted out of lunch and the chance to catch up with his friends. "I need to run by headquarters and sign for this new rifle," he said, not meeting their eyes.

He locked his new M4 in the trunk of his Crown Victoria, slid the shotgun into a scabbard in front of the bench seat, and sat in his car. He wanted to escape the range and the feeling of failure. He fired up the Ford police car and turned up the heater. Then he held his hands low in the car and drove a loaded magazine into his pistol before racking a round into the chamber. It was a major violation of GPSTC protocol to load a weapon in the parking lot, and Byrd knew the staff watched for breaches on the security cameras around the range. Today, he was willing to take that risk to get out of the facility as fast as possible.

Byrd pushed his government ride through the Southside of Atlanta and swung by GBI Headquarters. He needed to sign for the new rifle and turn his old one in to Supply. He snuck in and out of the building as quietly as possible, not wanting to see any of the bosses to get dragged into any lengthy conversations.

By 3:30, he was pulling into the driveway at the Georgia State Patrol Post in Canton. He maneuvered his car into a parking slot in the back and jogged up the steps into the back door.

Trooper Frank White was pouring a cup of coffee, getting ready for his evening shift, in the kitchen of the post. White stood at six feet and was built like a boxer.

"What's up, Frank?" Byrd asked.

White took a first sip from his coffee cup. "Doing my best to work like the State pays me; as little as I can get by with twice a month."

Byrd smiled. "Ain't that the truth. Has anybody been looking for me?"

White shrugged. "I just got here, myself."

Byrd nodded. "I've been down in Forsyth this morning."

White rolled his eyes. "GPSTC?" White pronounced it "jip-stick." "If I never had to go back there, I'd be fine."

Byrd grunted. "Not a stellar day for me. I took two tries to qualify. I've got to get more trigger time." Byrd poured himself a cup of coffee.

Byrd took his cup of starter fluid and walked to the radio room as White followed. The State Patrol still used a bound logbook for each trooper, radio operator, or DPS employee to sign in and out of the Post. Visiting command staff also had to sign in and out. White took his silver mechanical pen and wrote his time out, patrol route for the night, and patrol car number.

While White filled out the archaic record, Byrd checked his mailbox for messages. Finding none, he turned and marched to his office.

The wood-paneled room, a holdover from the building's 1964 construction, was as comfortable as home to Byrd. He spent hours each week dictating reports, reviewing them, and examining evidence before it was submitted to the Gainesville office evidence room. He sat at his desk in the worn office chair and logged in to the GBI computer system.

Discovering nothing of consequence, he logged back

out and looked at the office clock. He'd gotten on the road at 6 a.m. to get to Forsyth on time. He was technically into overtime—if he bothered to report all his hours for the day.

Byrd pushed back from the desk and turned off the lights. Home early for a change, he thought. Time to head into the woods behind his house to the range he'd built but barely used. Maybe he could get off a few rounds before sunset and then clean all his weapons before bedtime.

CHAPTER 2

I'VE GOT A PRESCRIPTION FOR THAT

TUESDAY, DECEMBER 4, 2007
7:19A.M. EST
HOTHOUSE COMMUNITY
MINERAL BLUFF, GEORGIA

Jerry Rutledge rested the loaded syringe on the edge of the bathtub. He pulled his TV with the broken face over and put it in a chair beside the tub. He had already dropped his pants and underwear in the living room, and they joined the fast-food wrappers and other trash strewn on the floor. *That bitch, Joyce, was probably going to be late coming home from her shift at the Dine and Dash.* But that was fine with him. Having her out of the house during the midnight shift made his life easier.

Jerry and Joyce lived in a mobile home Joyce's family had moved onto a half-acre lot near Hothouse Creek. Joyce told him the trailer had been pulled onto the scenic lot shortly after the war. She wasn't clear which war, and Jerry figured it must have been the Civil War.

The living quarters didn't matter much to Jerry. He had spent almost his entire adult life in one prison or another, with short respites in a county jail here and there. At forty-six, he probably wouldn't ever know any other life.

Satisfied that everything was ready, he lowered himself into the bathtub and prepared to shoot up. He tied his arm off with a shoestring he managed to pull tight with his teeth. He found a spot near the inside of his forearm where the needle mark wouldn't be as obvious, and as the vein bulged, he inserted the needle into his left arm.

The moment he pushed the plunger, the surge hit—lightning in his veins. He leaned his head back and let his body come fully alive, every fiber humming with electricity.

After a few moments, he shoved the video cassette into the player and waited for the porn to start. He sat back and started stroking himself, already half-hard. He liked the way meth made everything feel sharper, more electric. His body hummed, and his penis quickly sprang to attention, one of the things he loved about using meth. As he found a rhythm, the muscles in his butt clenched, and he began to work in earnest. It crossed his mind that he probably would've been more comfortable with some water in the tub. *Might have to try that later*, he thought.

Jerry thought he heard his dog rustling around in the front of the trailer, but wasn't concerned. The dog was allowed to roam freely in the house, earning his keep by barking and threatening any unwanted visitors—like cops—who tried to get into his home. He stretched his neck and worked the muscles in his back as he started getting into the video.

Suddenly, a man stepped into the bathroom. "Well, looks like you're having a good time!" He was big, all facial hair and a dirty baseball cap, with a pistol held loosely in his right hand. The big man squeezed into the bathroom and sat on the toilet. "Just like always, you're having to beat yo'r meat instead of fuckin' an actual human bean." Then he laughed hard at his own joke.

Jerry's eyes had been big as saucers, but he didn't stop stroking himself. "I know you, don't I?"

"I guess you damned well do. I'm Brandon Fisher. I'm kin to you on your momma's side, and we served some time in Jackson together when you first went into the system."

"Oh, yeah. I remember you now. What are you doing here, though?"

The big man stood up with a groan. "How about you stop jacking and put on some pants. I want to talk to you about a job I might have for you."

Rutledge reluctantly stood up and found his jeans. He stuffed his still erect penis into his pants and found an unoccupied part of the couch in the living room. Fisher sat in the lounge chair Rutledge usually occupied in front of the TV.

"Good to see you, man. What have you been up to?" Rutledge asked.

Fisher grunted. "Making money, how about you?"

Rutledge shrugged and slumped forward, deciding to say nothing.

"That's what I figured. Letting some woman keep you up?"

Rutledge pulled on the collar of his shirt. "It ain't been easy to find a job since I got out. I guess you've done found the pot of gold?"

Smirking, Fisher pushed the pistol into the front of his pants. "I might have a way for you to make a dollar or two if you was to want to get out of this trailer and stop tuggin' your pud."

Rutledge squirmed. "I'm on intensive prohibition." He held up his leg to show the ankle monitor. "I ain't allowed to go nowhere but to my prohibition office and to work. And I can't afford to get in no more trouble, man."

Fisher nodded. "You can go to the doctor if you need to, can't you?"

Rutledge considered the question. "I guess so. I ain't been in a long time, though."

Fisher looked Rutledge over. "What do you weigh?" he asked.

He couldn't remember the last time he'd weighed. "I guess about a hundred and thirty pounds."

"How tall are you?" Fisher asked.

"'Bout five nine."

Fisher scrunched up his face, thinking hard. "That should work."

"What are you talkin' about?"

"I got an MRI out in the car. You'll need to take it to a doctor I know, and he'll prescribe you some medicine for your bad back." Fisher stood up.

"Right now?"

Fisher nodded. "Now is as good a time as any. Get a shirt and some shoes. Let's get going."

"How'd you know I got a bad back?" Rutledge asked.

"Get your ass in gear. Time's wasting. I'll have my girl-friend take my car. We'll go in yours."

Rutledge did as he was told.

WEDNESDAY, DECEMBER 5, 2007
6:07 P.M. EST
DAHLONEGA, GEORGIA

Daniel Byrd was slumped in a chair, listening to former Georgia Governor Arnold Ellis explain the complexity of government administration. Byrd was attending his first night class of the week and second-guessing his decision to pursue a master's degree.

He had graduated from North Georgia College in 1994 with a bachelor's degree in Criminal Justice. Now, more than ten years later, he was attending night classes again.

When his work phone vibrated in his pocket, he quietly slipped out of the classroom and answered the call. He noticed the governor frowning at him as he eased the door closed.

"Byrd."

"Danny," Byrd recognized the voice. "It's Rick Arlen with Georgia Drug and Narcotics."

Byrd smiled. He'd worked cases with Arlen years ago, and the two had enjoyed a great relationship. "What can I do for you, Rick?"

"We need to meet up. I'm working a case up in Blue Ridge involving a crew boosting scripts all over North Georgia. And the ringleader's a friend of yours—at least, according to his criminal history."

Byrd stepped away from the door. "Who are you talking about?"

"Does the name Brandon Fisher ring a bell?"

Byrd knew Fisher well. He'd arrested him more than once on drug charges. Almost four years ago, Fisher had tried his best to drown Byrd on Valentine's Day.

"He's out of jail?"

Byrd could sense Arlen was smiling as he replied, "You can't keep a good man down."

"I'm in class right now. Can we get together tomorrow?"

"Sure," Arlen said. "What are you in class for?"

"I'm working on a master's in criminal justice."

"Do y'all get more pay for that?" Arlen asked.

"Not a dime," Byrd admitted ruefully.

Arlen chuckled. "You've got to love working for the state."

"How about we meet up at GSP Blue Ridge in the morning?" Byrd offered.

"Is nine thirty too early?" Arlen asked.

"Works for me." Byrd broke the connection and tried to sneak back into class. He wasn't successful.

When the class broke up, he headed for his car, a dark blue police package beast. It was shipped to the GBI by mistake, built to State Patrol specifications, and the Bureau intended to return it. He had been in headquarters the day the car arrived, and he pleaded with the supply clerk who issued cars to let him have it. The agency staff relented, and Byrd couldn't wipe the smile off his face for days.

The car had the most powerful engine Ford had produced to date in the Crown Victora Police Interceptor, capable of 250 horsepower, and the highway patrol version came with heavy-duty brakes, a more robust transmission, and heavier suspension. The dark blue exterior and interior suited Byrd, who had used adhesive remover to take the Police Interceptor logo from the trunk and installed a covert antenna in place of the ubiquitous whip found on law enforcement vehicles.

Byrd relished the drive as he took the hour trip from the college to his home. He parked the car in the rear of his ranch house near Canton. The property and one hundred-year-old house had been willed to him by his uncle when no one else in the family wanted it. Byrd valued the privacy the ten-acre parcel provided.

He stepped out of the car into the darkness and headed for the back door. The landline rang just as he flipped on the lights, and he hustled to the wall phone in the kitchen.

"Byrd," he said.

"Hey, Danny. This is Marilyn Hunter." Marilyn, a Cherokee County deputy sheriff, was someone Byrd had plans to take to dinner Friday night.

"Hey, Marilyn. What's up?"

"I need a rain check on Friday," she said. "I had to switch shifts with another deputy. So sorry for the late notice."

"I understand," Byrd remarked. "It sucks having a job. I guess it works out for the best, though. I got stuck with catching call for the office this weekend. You never know what you'll get pulled into this close to Christmas."

"How many counties do you cover when you're on call?" Marilyn asked.

"Our regional office covers fourteen counties. My responsibility is Cherokee up to Fannin, but when you're on call, you have all fourteen."

Marilyn let out a low whistle. "Dang, that's a lot of ground to cover."

"Can be," Byrd said. "Sorry you have to work this weekend, but I understand."

"I have a backup plan." She sounded tentative. "I could come over tonight. We could hang out for a while, if you're interested."

"Won't you have to leave about as soon as you get here? I thought your shift started at 7?"

"When I switched shifts," Marilyn said, "I ended up with tomorrow off. So, I don't have to get up super early."

Byrd pulled his gun from his belt as he talked. "Sure, but I may not be able to stay up too late. I need to hit the door by about 7:30. I've got a meeting in Blue Ridge at 9."

"I can lock the house up on the way out," Marilyn said.

"Oh!" Byrd realized what she had in mind. "I'm a little slow on the uptake. Sure, come on. I got the hot tub on the back deck up and running last weekend. It needs a grand opening."

"I'm on the way."

9:26 P.M. EST
CANTON, GEORGIA

By the time Marilyn came up Byrd's driveway, kicking up a trail of dust, she'd changed out of her uniform. She parked her Beetle and jogged to Byrd's back door.

"Come on in, darling," Byrd said. "I've got the hot tub turned up and drinks poured. You look like you're ready to unwind."

Marilyn Hunter was a tall, muscular brunette with a cop's attitude. She wore heavily worn jeans and a flannel shirt under her winter coat, finishing the look with tennis shoes.

Marilyn made a face. "Not that vodka and Kool-Aid, again."

Byrd frowned. "Proper drinks. Martinis—for both of us."

Byrd motioned toward the drinks, glasses beaded with condensation, the slightest hint of olive juice dirtying up the vodka.

"What do you put in a martini?" Marilyn asked.

Byrd smiled. "Vodka, since these are vodka martinis."

"What else?"

"An olive."

"Hmm. Serving me straight vodka," Marilyn said with a sly smile. She picked up one of the glasses and sipped. "Let's take these out to the deck and get comfortable."

Byrd offered her a terrycloth robe. "Want this for before and after?"

"You mean the hot tub, I hope." Marilyn laughed, warm and infectious.

They were out of their clothes and in the hot tub within seconds. She slid into one corner; he took the other.

She sipped her martini as the hot water took hold. "This is pretty close to heaven, right here."

Byrd reached over and turned on the spa pumps. "This kicks it up a level."

Bubbles erupted as the water shimmered in the moonlight. Byrd sipped his drink, letting the bubbles and heat strip away the day's tension.

Marilyn laughed. "Wow, that hits the spot, doing a tired girl good. I might have to rent time in this thing."

The heat and booze were making her tipsy fast.

"Why would you need to rent it?" Byrd asked.

"Because if Sheriff Nelson finds out I'm involved with you, he promised to fire me."

"What?"

"Okay, not you specifically. Just cops in general. No intra- or inter-agency entanglements. Makes things awkward as hell for me. I rarely meet anybody else."

Byrd exhaled. "Yeah, I'm in the same boat."

"The sheriff fired a couple of folks over relationships with other cops. He put out the word to all his deputies that running around with other officers—even from different agencies—was a fire-able offense."

Marilyn watched Byrd over the rim of her martini glass.

"I don't work for Willie. I've known him since his DNR days."

Willie Nelson, a former game warden and now Cherokee County sheriff, had helped Byrd with a corruption case in Gilmer County when Byrd first joined the regional office in Gainesville.

"Danny, I'm not after entanglements. Just a good time tonight," she said, shaking water from her hair.

Byrd felt both disappointed and relieved.

Marilyn brightened. "But speaking of being in the same boat, several cops I know are planning a three-day cruise to Mexico. You should come along. We'll have a great time."

Byrd shook his head. "Nope. Not a good idea for me to go back to Mexico."

Marilyn giggled. "So, you've been before. Did you end up locked up after a night of tequila and senoritas?"

Byrd looked away. "I didn't get locked up, but I'm not going to take a chance on going back. Some of those folks have long memories."

Marilyn wasn't sure what to make of the cryptic response. "Are you making something up to avoid the trip? It's not that expensive."

Byrd hung his head for a moment. Then looked up and said, "When I was out in Texas on a case, something went down that hangs over my head. A group of smugglers meant to trap a couple of Texas officers in Mexico. It was set up by a drug runner named Rojo. A DEA agent and I went into Mexico to get them out."

"Daniel Byrd, ambassador for the United States?" she asked.

"I was practicing détente. Texas détente. A lot of shooting. A couple of people died on the other side. So, as far as I'm concerned, Georgia is as close as I want to get to Mexico."

Marilyn seemed skeptical of the story.

"How come I've never heard that story. Seems like that would've made national news." Marilyn pressed with a smile.

"I know this may sound like some spy movie bullshit,

but officially, it didn't happen. I don't know if the Mexican government was fully on board with that resolution."

He dropped his head back and stared up at the moon, which was peeking around the darkening clouds that hinted at rain. The view of the moon, even more than the soothing hot water, relaxed Byrd.

"Don't look so sad, Danny. The cruise would've been nice, but we can still hang out together at your house. We just have to keep it secret."

Byrd slid over beside her. "I'm pretty good at keeping secrets." He leaned in and kissed her. "My lips are sealed."

Marilyn giggled. "No, they're not."

Byrd leaned back in the hot tub and watched the steam rise into the night. Crisp air whipped across the back deck of his small house.

"This will be a good weekend to be on call," he said.

"Why?" Marilyn asked.

"Cold, wet weather. People stay inside and don't seem to argue as much this time of year," Byrd said, eyes closed.

Marilyn chuckled. "Have you looked up lately?"

Byrd's eyes shot open. He shook his head as the full moon slipped behind a cloud. "Damn!"

No on-call weekend ever went smoothly when the moon was full.

WEDNESDAY, DECEMBER 5, 2007
6;59 P.M. CST
PYOTE, TEXAS

Rudy Grant was finishing his shift at the West Texas State School, a euphemism for a youth detention center, located at the old bomber base in Pyote. He didn't look forward to the twenty-mile trip from the school to his dusty trailer in Monahans.

Rudy despised the job—watching over underage punks who'd committed crimes more heinous than some adults. He spent his days watching the clock and ignoring all but the most grievous of problems. His motto was "leave it for the next shift."

To make an already bad job worse, the facility was in turmoil. The problems didn't come from the inmates—they came from management. Last year, the Texas Rangers and the FBI investigated the place after allegations of sexual abuse by one of the bosses. The facility was now being evaluated for potential closure.

Rudy felt like he couldn't catch a break. Rudolpho Tienda Grant had been named by his mother when she had mistakenly thought his father was a Guatemalan factory worker she had spent a drunken night with. By the time she realized her son had red hair, the birth certificate had been executed. Rudy hated the name in school, fighting boys more than once when they derisively used his name. It wasn't until he joined the military that he discovered his middle name was the Spanish word for "store."

Miserable as a child, he joined the military as soon as he was eligible. The Navy sent him through boot camp, where he learned self-discipline and organization. The three-year hitch produced a different person. He learned skills he thought would translate into a high-paying job as a jet mechanic.

He met a nursing student while assigned to Carswell Field in Fort Worth. Rosalind Michaels, a couple of years older than Rudy, was a pretty young Texan studying nursing at Texas Christian University. She loved to see Rudy in his uniform, and the romance blossomed into marriage four months before Rudy left the Navy to seek his future.

Turns out that the future was bleaker than Rudy expected. As a nurse, Rosalind had her pick of jobs. Rudy's skills, working on airplanes, were harder to market. He had several jobs over the years, but none were particularly lucrative. After being fired from his job at the Odessa Schlemeyer Field Airport for damaging a customer's turbine engine, he was looking for a change. The pay at the West Texas State School was higher than average, but the job was both boring and dangerous.

Now, fourteen years after the wedding, Rudy was served with a Temporary Protective Order. He could no longer see his wife or daughter. He and Rosalind had married young, and their daughter, Madison, was now twelve—at the age when a girl looked up to her father and needed his affirmation.

He climbed into his old SUV, fired up the engine, and considered his options for the night. At the first gate, he waved to the guard on duty, who returned the gesture and opened it. Once through, the old man waited for it to close behind him before moving to the second, which followed the same routine. By the time he hit the access road to I-20, he'd been off the clock for nearly twenty minutes.

Rudy decided he needed a twelve-pack and a bump of meth to get through the night. He knew just the place to get both.

Pyote was a small town, largely dependent on the correctional facility for its survival. With a population hovering around 130 and not a single fast-food joint or bar in sight, Pyote was dying on the vine. The new truck stop, practically the only new thing in the town, might help the bleeding, but it wouldn't stop it. So everyone in the little town knew about Moe's Hole in the Wall.

Moe's, an aptly named metal building less than a mile from the correctional institute, served up cold beer, marijuana, pain pills from Mexico, and meth of the highest order. Moe ran the grungy business in what had been an oil change shop. He sold, on the record, sex toys, lingerie, and snacks. He had no license to sell or serve beer or any other alcohol, but everyone in town knew you could get almost any kind of mood-enhancing substance in the old metal building on the edge of town.

Moe, a small, rotund man of sixty-one whose real name wasn't Moe, had served time for molesting his own daughters. He was at once one of the most disliked and liked people in Pyote.

Rudy wheeled into Moe's and parked his Jeep. He felt under the seat for his stash of cash. Since he separated from Rosalind, he kept all his money in a natural void under the seat of his rusty vehicle. Rudy climbed out and walked through the front door.

Moe greeted him warmly. "Hey, Rudy. How are the kids doing?" Moe always found it funny to call the juvenile inmates "kids."

Rudy ignored Moe and made a beeline for the huge refrigerator in the back corner. He took a twelve-pack of beer and walked up to the counter. "I need a bump, Moe. Can you help me out?"

Moe shook his head. "That shit is getting harder and harder to get. I'm gonna have to get fifty dollars for a taste."

Rudy dropped the twelve-pack on the counter. "That's bull shit, and you know it. I can get a bump over in Monahans for half that."

Moe crossed his arms over his husky chest. "Then do it. I ain't in business to lose money."

Rudy turned to take the beer back to the refrigerator. "There are damned sure cheaper places to buy beer."

Moe held up his hands. "Alright. I'm losing money on the deal, but I'll set you up for twenty-five. And I'll cut you a break on the beer."

"You're a charmer, Moe. I think I can do that." Rudy pretended to count his money, keeping Moe from seeing his stash, then dropped four ten-dollar bills on the countertop.

"Will that do it?" Rudy asked.

Moe shrugged. He pushed the cash into his jeans pocket. "Close enough for government work. I'll just keep this little transaction between the two of us. Uncle Sam sucks enough blood from me as it is."

Moe tossed the corner of a sandwich bag, twisted and held shut with rubber bands, across the counter. Rudy examined the gritty-looking substance in the bag. "How do I know this ain't sand from the parking lot?" Rudy asked.

"Get your taste outside, no using in my store." Moe cautioned. "But if it don't blow the top of your head off and splatter your brains all over the inside of your old Jeep, I'll give you your money back."

Rudy gathered up his beer and meth. He was turning to leave when Moe asked, "You and your wife still on the outs? She still got a TPO against you? That don't sound temporary."

Rudy stopped and turned. "How do you know that? I didn't tell you."

Moe smiled. "One of the Constables is a customer. Him and his girlfriend like to experiment with my stuff."

"Your dope?" Rudy was surprised.

"No! The sex toys. He says his wife don't like to try anything new, but his girlfriend sure does.' Moe slapped his knee as he laughed at his own joke. "The old bastard says he's gonna leave his wife one day, but I figure that's just talk."

Rudy nodded. "Well, you heard right about my ex. She had me served, and now I have to jump through all kinds of hoops just to see my daughter. That shit ain't right. A man deserves to see his kid whenever he wants to."

"Damn straight. The cards are stacked against a man when it comes to custody of your kids. I probably won't never get to see my kids again, that's for sure," Moe said. He stood from his chair and stretched.

Rudy frowned. "You molested both your daughters. I imagine you're lucky not to still be sitting in prison."

Moe bristled. "Both them girls led me on. Since they was big enough to wear a bra, they prance around in front of me like strippers at the club over in Thornton."

Rudy turned back to Moe. Rudy's eyes narrowed. "How about I take one of these beer bottles and beat you to death? Or use it some other way? Maybe I'll give you a colonoscopy with it."

Moe reached for the revolver he kept under the counter. "Rudy, I consider you a good customer, but don't act like that. I bet you and them other guards are tapping some of those young boys. What you got to say about that?"

Rudy held his breath. He tried to control his breathing to calm down. It was a technique he learned in his corrections training. "I'm out of here, Moe. Sorry about starting a commotion between us."

Moe raised his eyebrow. "My offer is still out there. You drop one of them boys by here one day, and I'll give you five hundred for the hour. And I'll take care of the kid, too."

Rudy shook his head. "Even if I wanted to, the Texas Rangers are all over that kind of shit. They've been looking at some things going on inside." Rudy tucked the beers under his arm and pushed the worn wooden door open. "You stay out of trouble, Moe," Rudy offered as he turned for the door.

"Ain't no fun in that, Rudy," Moe said to his back.

Rudy kept walking, not looking back, as he responded with the middle finger on his left hand.

CHAPTER 3

SCRIPT BUSTERS

THURSDAY, DECEMBER 6, 2007
9:13 A.M. EST
BLUE RIDGE, GEORGIA

Rick Arlen stood in the kitchen of the Georgia State Patrol barracks in Blue Ridge. He traveled the state for work and had been in more patrol posts than he could count. Many of them, built in the 1960s, were based on the same floor plan. No doubt, the state had a single architect draft the plans and contractors adapted them to each site. Cutting corners to save a dime was the state's default.

Arlen stood a couple of inches over six feet in a dark, tailored suit. When he entered the state patrol facility, the first trooper who saw him assumed he was a defense attorney fishing for information.

"This area is for law enforcement only. You'll need to go back around front if you're looking for an accident report."

Arlen stopped and faced the trooper. "Actually, I'm an officer."

"You'll have to forgive me for thinking you were a lawyer," Trooper Troy Clifton said. Clifton was a big, raw-boned man who had earned a reputation in the North

Georgia Mountains as a tough customer. "What agency did you say you worked for?"

Arlen smiled. With his glasses and neatly combed hair, he looked more like a lawyer or a college professor than a cop. "I work for the Georgia Drug and Narcotics Agency. People call us drug inspectors. We audit pharmacies and medical facilities, among other jobs."

Trooper Clifton was intrigued. The big state lawman eyed Arlen with skepticism. "But you're a gun totter?"

Arlen nodded. "The law requires us to be fully certified peace officers and be fully licensed pharmacists."

Trooper Clifton shook his head. "I've never heard of such a thing. Why would a man like yourself, with a pharmacist's license, want to turn around and become a cop? There can't be much money in it."

Arlen had heard this same question from many other officers. "This job may not pay as much, but you get a real sense of satisfaction arresting some script busters or a doctor overprescribing. And I don't have to stand up all day to do it."

"What's a script buster?" Clifton asked.

"Someone who uses fake identities to obtain prescriptions from multiple doctors. They travel around, sometimes in groups, and visit doctors who don't ask a lot of questions. They do their best to get pain medications—opioids—and then sell them on the street."

"I guess you're here to meet Danny Byrd then?" Clifton asked.

"How'd you know?"

"He just pulled into the back lot," Clifton said.

The two men watched as Byrd hustled up the back stairs of the old brick building and pushed the door open into the kitchen. "Hey, Rick. I see you've met Troy."

Trooper Clifton turned to leave. "I'll let you super sleuths get after it. Y'all probably have some big case you're getting ready to break."

Byrd nodded. "Rick here is helping me arrest Mr. Brandon Fisher again."

Clifton didn't recognize the name. He stopped and waited.

"Remember I told you about the guy in Blue Ridge who dragged me into a creek? I had to fight him off while he tried to drown me," Byrd said.

Clifton nodded. "The meth cook?"

"Yep, and dealer. Probably a flunky for my old friend Judge Pelfrey."

"That would be Justice Pelfrey, now," Arlen corrected Byrd.

Byrd shook his head in disgust. "Right. Now she sits on the Georgia Court of Appeals."

Clifton shrugged. "Ain't that the way in government? Fuck up to get up?" Then he turned and left the two investigators alone.

Byrd slumped into a chair as Arlen poured himself a cup of coffee from the always-ready coffee pot. Coffee was more central to law enforcement than radios or guns.

"What's my man Brandon been up to that would bring the GDNA all the way up into the mountains?" Byrd asked.

"One of the drug agents down in Canton, at the Cherokee Multi-Agency Narcotics Squad, actually tumbled to this case," Arlen began.

"We call them CMANS," Byrd offered.

"Right," Arlen continued. "A CMANS agent who focuses on prescription cases called me. Do you know Janice Griffin? She's their birddog on scripts?"

Byrd nodded. "We've met. Wally Demopolis, the Commander of CMANS, speaks highly of her."

Arlen grunted. "CMANS may be the only agency in North Georgia that takes any interest in prescription fraud. Janice came across several names as she was working another case, but most of the activity was outside Cherokee County. She called me and gave me the tip."

Byrd sat up in the chair. "It must be a good tip."

Arlen agreed. "Yes, and she's done a lot of the legwork. I'm not sure if you know this, but Georgia is the only state in the US without a prescription drug monitoring program. In the other forty-nine states, doctors are required to log prescriptions for often-abused drugs and confirm that the patient isn't seeing multiple doctors. These folks travel all over, hitting as many doctors as they can for pain pills."

Byrd raised his eyebrows. "How many pills are we talking here?"

Arlen shook his head. "A couple hundred. Enough to kill every man, woman, and child in this county."

Byrd shook his head slowly. "I guess I can see how they can do that. Where do I come in?"

"This crew—Fisher's group—hits doctors Monday through Wednesday to stock up on oxy scripts. Then on Thursday, they make the pharmacy rounds and cash them in. Friday's for selling."

Byrd nodded. "Today is Thursday."

"It is," Arlen agreed. "And Fisher has started using a drugstore here in Blue Ridge. He likes to avoid the chains. One of the stores he's been going to is a small drugstore in town, but he didn't realize the pharmacist is the father of a cop. That's where Janice got the tip."

"CMANS isn't available to help?" Byrd asked.

Arlen shook his head. "They're tied up with surveillance in Cherokee County. And, after looking at Fisher's record, figured you might want another chance at locking him up."

Byrd stood up, rubbing his hands together. "Oh, I'm more than happy to take another swing at him."

THURSDAY, DECEMBER 6, 2007
6:52 A.M. CST
PYOTE, TEXAS

Rudy Grant brushed his hands through his hair. He gunned the SUV along the rough asphalt track toward the juvenile prison's front gate. He was running late for work. He waited impatiently for the first set of gates to open and close, then pulled forward and repeated the drill at the second. After he cleared the gates, the guard at the gatehouse motioned for him to stop.

"What up, Ralph?" Rudy asked.

Ralph leaned on the side mirror of the Jeep as he stuck his head through the window. "The main office called. They want you to report to the assistant superintendent."

The message set Rudy's nerves on edge. He'd never been called before the newly appointed second-in-command at the youth detention center. "Hell, I'm not that late, am I?"

Ralph shrugged. "You ain't the only one getting called on the carpet."

"Thanks, Ralph," Rudy said as he pulled off, wheeled the Jeep around, and found a parking spot.

He entered through the west side of the administrative building and threaded his way through the corridors to the suite housing the superintendent's office. The old building—where Rudy figured the administrators hid out—was built in 1965. The inside walls had been painted countless times by the inmates. Today, the hallway leading to the superintendent and assistant superintendent's offices reeked of fresh paint. Rudy wondered if the paint helped mask the stink of the place—sweat, filth, piss, and shit—the reek of confinement.

Rudy stopped outside the door marked "Claire Trevor, Assistant Superintendent." He still thought it was stupid that the bosses were called superintendents instead of wardens. Figured it was all part of the fallacy that the "children" were students—not inmates.

Rudy stood before Trevor's secretary. His voice quivered as he introduced himself. "I'm Rudy Grant, a guard on the second shift."

The gray-haired lady ran her finger down a list and checked his name off. Then she looked up at Rudy. "Have a seat. Ms. Trevor is with someone else right now, but she'll see you in a moment."

Rudy had a bad feeling. He couldn't sit, so he paced the front office, studying the pictures of the old Army Air Corps base where the facility was built. The black-and-white photos in the office documented the lines of bombers waiting to join the US effort in World War II. He wondered what had happened to the men—smiling, ready to go to war—and how many came back.

He heard the inner office door open and saw Frank Cramer, a fellow guard, coming out. He looked pale and sick. Rumors had been flying for months about layoffs in the guard staff after the Texas Rangers and FBI investigated the sexual abuse claims. Seeing Cramer's face, Rudy knew the meeting was just a formality.

Byrd and Rick Arlen sat outside the City Retail Pharmacy, a couple of blocks from the Blue Ridge Police Department. The old brick-and-cinder-block building, with its fading sign and drooping awning, was a fixture in the mountain town. They were parked across the street in Byrd's GBI car, engine off, and the interior was growing cold. Byrd knew the condensation from the exhaust would alert a crook as seasoned as Fisher.

"How are you so sure what time they'll show up, anyway?" Byrd asked.

Arlen checked his watch. "Every prescription a store fills has the date and time stamped on it. I checked last month, and they never show up before noon."

"I hope they show up sooner rather than later. All I've had to eat today is a cup of coffee," Byrd said.

Arlen nodded. "They usually get to the pharmacy around lunchtime, if they can. They don't want the pharmacist calling the doctor's office. At noon, the office is wrapping up with morning patients, grabbing a bite to eat, and getting ready for the afternoon crowd. It's hard to reach most doctors by phone this time of day. By the time the doc calls back, the deed is done."

Byrd was tempted to fire up the engine and turn on the heat, but knew the space was too tight for even the dumbest criminal not to notice two men in suits sitting in a running car. Instead, Byrd crammed his hands into his overcoat pockets.

"I wish I knew what Fisher was driving these days," Byrd muttered, more to himself than to Arlen.

"Actually, he's been riding with some kid from Morganton named Justin Carder. Fisher is afraid to drive. He's scared he'll get stopped and have to go back to prison."

Byrd rolled his eyes. "And yet he violates half a dozen drug laws like it means nothing."

Arlen frowned. "The drug laws in this state don't mean much. Fisher's been in and out of jail more often than most guards."

Byrd perked up. "Maybe you can recommend a good doctor around Canton? You probably know most of them."

"What's going on?" Arlen asked.

"I had a bout of gout," Byrd grumbled. "So, when I went to get it looked at, the doctor told me my blood sugar was high. Said if I didn't make some changes, I'd end up with type 2 diabetes."

"Both of those problems are what medical folks call 'lifestyle issues.' So, are you going to make any changes?"

"Yeah. I want to change doctors."

Arlen shook his head. "That's a terrible idea. You could cut back on red meat and wine. Both are bad for you."

"It was a joke, Rick. Lighten up."

"Easier to recognize jokes when they're funny," Arlen fired back.

Byrd listened while keeping a careful eye on the street. He saw an old, worn-out Toyota sedan pull to the curb. The car was filthy, with dents covering nearly every panel. As the car pulled to the curb in front of the pharmacy, Byrd recognized Fisher and felt his pulse quicken. "Here they are."

The lawmen watched as a tall, skinny meth-head crawled out of the driver's seat and looked around. He was tweaking, his mouth twitching in the telltale way of a meth user. Without noticing the two cops, the man bounced into the pharmacy.

They gave the skinny guy five minutes, then Arlen climbed out and ambled into the pharmacy.

Byrd saw Fisher make Arlen and lock onto him, tracking his every move as the big guy in the suit ducked under the pharmacy's porch and disappeared inside.

Byrd stepped out of the government car and sidled up to the Toyota. He could see Fisher in the rearview mirror, still focused on the front door of the pharmacy.

Byrd reached the passenger door and tapped the glass with the barrel of his Glock. Fisher shoved the passenger door open, trying to knock the gun from Byrd's hand, but Byrd slammed it back, pinning Fisher's leg and leaning his weight into it.

"Hands where I can see them! Out of the car—now!" Byrd barked.

Fisher did as he was told, stepped onto the sidewalk, and started to turn. Byrd caught the flex in his knees and, in one swift motion, grabbed his left arm, swung him around, and slammed him onto the hood of the rusty car. "I'm not in the mood to run after you today."

Byrd grabbed a handful of greasy hair, knowing Fisher

could ditch the winter coat if he tried to grab it. He pressed Fisher's face against the hood and kicked his feet apart.

"You're an asshole, Byrd. You know that?" Fisher spat.

Byrd locked the cuffs and hauled Fisher up by his left arm. "Hmm. That's what my mom wrote on my birthday card."

Arlen led the skinny guy out to Byrd's car and put him in the back seat while they waited for a deputy to transport Fisher. Climbing in beside him, Arlen kept one foot on the ground. The car wasn't getting any warmer. "What's your name, son?"

"Jerry Rutledge. My friends call me Jerry."

Arlen glanced over sharply, thinking Rutledge was being sarcastic. After studying him for a couple of seconds, Arlen knew Rutledge didn't have it in him.

Arlen started writing. "Where are you from?"

"Hothouse, sir."

Arlen set his pen down. "Is that a town, a state of mind, or where you plan to spend eternity?"

Rutledge looked confused. "No, sir, it's a town up near Mineral Bluff."

"In Georgia or Tennessee? That area's right at the state line."

"I ain't sure, sir. The probation officer who comes to my house for piss tests is from Georgia. And the cop who came by the other day looking for my live-in girlfriend was Georgia State Patrol."

Within a couple of minutes, a Fannin County Sheriff's patrol car pulled up. The young deputy recognized Fisher on sight. "Gentlemen, I'll be glad to take him off your hands. We got about three warrants out on him right now."

Byrd helped the deputy push Fisher into the back of the

marked patrol car. As they slammed the door, Fisher said, "I ain't got nothin' to say to you."

Byrd shook his head and leaned down to the window. "Brandon, just for the record, saying you have nothing to say is saying something."

Fisher grunted and leaned back in the marked car seat as the deputy carted him off to jail. Byrd watched with satisfaction, then turned to search the sedan. Fast-food wrappers and assorted trash littered the floorboard, but something else caught his eye—a faux-leather valise on the passenger side, crammed with medical documents. He crouched to inspect the papers spilling from the top.

Byrd closed the door and went to tell Arlen about the find. When he saw Arlen glance up from the back seat of his car, he motioned for him to step out.

As he walked up to Byrd, Arlen asked, "What have you got?" checking that Rutledge couldn't hear them.

A sudden burst of cold wind made Byrd shudder. Through gritted teeth, Byrd said, "That satchel sitting between Fisher's feet should be enough to wrap him up. There's a list of pharmacies, fake names, and blank forms for making Georgia driver's licenses."

Arlen nodded. "That's their MO. Fisher would take the picture when he hired them to boost scripts—I'm guessing—then he'd print the form, laminate it, and rub it all around with fine sandpaper. A busy pharmacist is going to accept as real nine times out of ten."

Byrd nodded toward the skinny man. "Who's he?"

"Name's Jerry Rutledge. He's been locked up a few times for meth."

"Is this his first time showing up in Fisher's operations?"

Arlen nodded. "Yeah, and based on the way Einstein tried to spell 'pharmacy' on the forged script, probably his last. What do you want to do with him? Lock him up or let him go?"

Byrd rubbed his chin. "A little of both. I think I'll sign him up as an informant."

THURSDAY, DECEMBER 6, 2007
7:12 P.M. CST
PYOTE, TEXAS

Rudy Grant prepared to head home from his last shift as a correctional officer at the West Texas State School. He dumped his gun, belt, badge, and identification card on his boss's desk.

"We're going to miss you, Rudy," Sergeant Monique Horton said as she emptied the chambers of the government-issued Model 10 revolver. Monique was a mother of four who, Rudy felt, worked to get out of the house.

"Fuck you, Monique. I got canned for nothing," Rudy snapped.

"You might have been able to fuck me if you weren't such an asshole, Rudy," Horton shot back.

Rudy started for the door.

"Wait," Monique said. "I've got something for you."

Rudy turned back. "What?"

She extended an envelope. "Your last check."

Rudy ripped it from her hand, turned, and stalked out of the office.

He jumped in his Jeep and gunned it toward the gates. The gesture was wasted as he waited for the first gate to open and close. Once the second gate set him free, he gassed the rough-running SUV again and tore down the access road.

He knew it was too late to get the check cashed. Then he remembered Moe. Moe's business, by nature, was all cash. Rudy navigated to the old steel building with the wooden doors.

Moe was seated in his usual spot behind the counter full of sex toys. He looked up from a skin magazine as Rudy came in. "Hey, Rudy. How's it hanging?" Moe asked.

Rudy did his best to ignore the cabinet full of dildos, vibrators, and ticklers of every kind. He was always sexually conservative and had zero interest in the novelties.

He ignored the stupid question. "Can you cash a check for me? It's from the school."

Moe laid the magazine on the counter. "Three cents on the dollar. That's what it costs to use a credit card or a cash machine."

Rudy stopped in his tracks. "Moe, that's nearly a hundred bucks. I'm hurting for money right now. Could you do it for me as a favor?"

Moe shook his head. "I ain't in business to do favors, Rudy." He picked the magazine back up and resumed ogling the pictures.

Rudy caught a clearer look at the cover and saw it featured boys who looked disturbingly young.

He didn't want to beg, but he needed the money. The plan he'd developed on the ride over was to take his daughter, by force if necessary, and leave town.

"Moe, I'm in a pinch. I just got laid off from the school. I promised my daughter I'd take her on a trip over Christmas, and I need the cash to keep my promise—every dime."

Moe didn't look up. "Maybe you should sign her up for Make-A-Wish."

Rudy frowned. "That's for kids who are dying. Madison ain't dying."

Moe flipped the page without looking up. "She's dying a little bit every day she lives in this county."

Rudy's temper flared. He jumped over the counter and grabbed the revolver Moe kept for protection. It was a single-action Colt revolver, the kind cowboys carried. Moe backed away, but not before Rudy took a one-armed swing and hit him on the left temple with the Colt.

Moe fell over his chair and curled up in a ball. Blood was running from a deep cut on his left cheek. Rudy absently figured the revolver's front sight had torn Moe's flesh.

"I'm sorry, Rudy. I'll cash your check. So sorry."

"My life is over, Moe. I got laid off, and I know my wife is screwing somebody over at the hospital where she works at. She's keeping me from seeing my daughter, too. I've got nothing left." He hefted the gun and looked at Moe on the floor. Moe raised his hands to protect himself as he looked down the barrel of the western gun.

"Listen, I won't say anything to anybody about this. Just let me cash your check, and we can forget all this," Moe pleaded.

"Moe, ol' buddy, I'm afraid that ship has sailed. I'm one of your best customers and I tried to be reasonable when I came in here. You just can't be a friend to anyone, can you?"

"Rudy, I'm not an idiot," Moe retorted. "I like to have sex with children. I can't help myself. Nobody likes me. Hell, my own family don't like me."

Rudy looked at the gun one more time. He couldn't afford to use the old pistol; the sound would bring neighbors running, and there was no way to know if it worked. "I reckon you're right, Moe. I don't like you, and I doubt if anyone will mourn for you."

After examining the blood-covered gun for a moment longer, Rudy swung with both hands and hit Moe in the center of the head. Moe tried to roll away, kicking at Rudy as he did. Rudy swung the gun again with all his strength, and Moe lay still.

Rudy bent over Moe's inert figure and searched his pockets. He found a wad of cash and a baggie of meth. Moe was still breathing as Rudy used his foot to turn him onto his back. "You won't be perving on any more little kids now, will you?"

Rudy turned to the cash drawer under the counter. There was over three thousand dollars inside. He grabbed the cash from Moe's pocket, then from the drawer, and crammed it into his coat. Glancing back at Moe, Rudy pulled a handwritten sign from under the counter that said "Closed" and hung it on the shop's door.

Rudy grabbed a twelve-pack of Moe's best beer and returned to the counter to check on Moe. The shopkeeper's breathing was labored, and a pool of blood was growing around his head.

Rudy hefted the gun and gave Moe one more swing. He let out a wet gasp and went still. Breathing hard, Rudy stood over him, watching to make sure he was dead. The smell told him Moe had soiled himself.

Then Rudy bent down to examine Moe's lifeless body, realizing he felt a tremendous sense of relief. He felt a dark, almost sexual satisfaction in the act of "putting Moe in his place." He wasn't ready yet to refer to it as killing.

He wiped the gun off and put it back under the counter. Then he tucked the beer under his arm and left, closing the wooden door behind him.

CHAPTER 5
SUNRISE/SUNSET

Raelynn Michaels pushed the gear lever of her truck into park. She waited for the dust to settle, then climbed down and looked to the east. She was just in time to see the sun peeking over the horizon. *A cold West Texas sunrise was second only to its sunset,* she thought.

She leaned on the truck as the sun's rays crept across the fields. She'd parked miles off the interstate on a dusty farm road—the kind of place that let her think. Today, it was about the sunrise—and what came next for her at the El Paso Sheriff's Office.

When she came home from a successful undercover operation almost a year ago, her boss, Sheriff Jim Hallman, had been ebullient. He'd offered her any job she wanted—anything but staying on the drug task force under her best friend, Texas Ranger Adeline Riley. Her undercover work—delivering almost twelve thousand pounds of methamphetamine oil to a warehouse north of Atlanta—led to the arrest of Reyes Acosta Hernandez. Reyes, the cousin of the notorious drug kingpin Rojo, acted as his US "fixer." On Christmas Eve last year, just days after Reyes's arrest, Rojo was assassinated by an old man with a grudge. Even so, Raelynn knew she'd never work undercover again—too many cartel members wanted revenge. So the sheriff assigned her to the Detective Division.

She let out a slow breath, watching it vaporize around her face. Applying to the Texas Department of Public Safety could lead to a job in the Texas Narcotics Service—or even the Texas Rangers.

Adeline Riley, had worked her way up through the ranks of the DPS. But Raelynn's heart was in local law enforcement—serving the community she'd grown up in. And El Paso was a good place to live—unlike some of the backwaters the highway patrol could assign her to.

She was about to climb into the bed of the truck and stretch out on her back when she heard the engine of another vehicle coming her way. The shallow draw she'd parked in kept the other truck hidden for several minutes as it approached. She pushed her western hat back on her head and waited with her hands on her hips as the other truck came into sight.

It was a beater, an old truck marred with dents and worn paint. What once had been green was now more primer than paint. She could see two men in the front seat.

Initially, she thought it might be the landowner coming to check on her and ask what she was up to. He had stopped by to talk with her one of the first times she had parked here. As the truck approached, she decided both young Hispanic men were too young to be the landowner.

She stood near the door of her truck, using it as cover in case the two men meant trouble. She squinted, trying to make out the features of the two men as the vehicle came to a halt. Dust swirled around the old pickup as the two men opened the doors and climbed down.

"Morning," Rae shouted.

"Hey, lady," the driver said. "We've been watching you since you left the highway. What are you doing out here?"

Rae frowned. "Minding my own business. Something you should consider."

Both men were dressed in jeans and boots. Each wore a red flannel jacket, like a uniform of some kind. The driver brushed his long black hair from his face and stopped, smiling at Raelynn.

"That ain't too kind of you. We just wanted to take a look at this new truck you're driving out here. And maybe get to know you better." He laughed dryly.

Rae shook her head as she tossed her cowboy hat onto the seat of her truck. Her curly blond hair fell around her shoulders. "You know me better right now than you want to. You boys need to get back in that truck of yours and head back to wherever you came from."

The two exchanged glances. In unison, the men revealed switchblade knives—blades glinting in the sun. "Maybe you'll want to be kinder once you get to know us," the driver said with a smirk.

Rae leaned into her truck and grabbed the Remington 870 police shotgun from its scabbard in front of the seat. She brought the gun up to her shoulder and aimed it toward the men. Once she had a bead on the driver, she racked the mechanism, loading a double-aught buckshot round into the chamber.

The two men were frozen in place. There was no sound more distinctive or terrifying than the racking of a police shotgun.

"I'm a deputy sheriff with El Paso County. I'm going to give you boys a chance to get the fuck out of my sight, or I'll feel compelled to lodge you in the common jail of this county on criminal charges." She slowly pointed the shotgun from one to the other. "What'll it be?"

The two men started to back up.

"Drop the knives."

The driver got into the truck first, dropping the knife at his feet. The passenger was moving more slowly. He glanced over his shoulder sullenly as Rae kept a bead on his head.

"You give me a little more time, and I may have a change of heart. I might decide that you fellows could have done this sort of stupid mischief before. Maybe I should run you in and see if any other women have met up with you two out here." Rae knew there hadn't been any problems, at least in her county. But she figured the pair didn't know that.

The driver smiled a lopsided smile. "We ain't hurt nobody, lady."

"El Mayo sent a couple of boys to put a scare in me?" Raelynn asked. El Mayo, whose real name was Ismael Luis Salazar, had stepped in when Rojo was killed.

The two men looked at each other. Raelynn realized she'd been a target of opportunity. The men, more punks than toughs, didn't know who she was—until now.

The driver shrugged. Raelynn thought it looked like he was considering the potential for currying favor with El Mayo. "El Mayo is an important man. Maybe we do him a favor. Maybe not. Who knows?"

The two teenage boys climbed into the old truck and fired it up. The driver turned it around and slowly headed back toward the main highway. Raelynn watched them as she grabbed her radio mic. "X-ray sixteen to Central. Can you have an SO unit check on an old green truck coming out of the draw out near Clint? They should be coming out of a wash right at mile marker 57 on I-10. I need both of them IDed."

The night shift dispatcher recognized her radio call sign. "Will do. I have two units that can be there in less than ten minutes. Do I need to send more help?"

"That should do it. I want field interview cards on both." Rae climbed into the truck, laid her shotgun along the console, and turned to follow the two men.

When her work cell phone rang, she assumed it was dispatch following up on the men she had called in. When she answered, she was surprised by the voice of Sheriff Hallman's secretary. "Deputy Michaels?"

"Yes, Miss Martha. What can I do for you?"

"The sheriff needs you to meet him. Where are you?" Raelynn noticed an odd tone in Miss Martha's voice.

"I'm out past Fabens, north of I-10. Is something wrong?"

"Hold on."

Raelynn listened to canned music as her call was put on hold. She tried to remember anything she could be in trouble for. The sheriff wouldn't have had time to hear about the run-in.

Then Miss Martha came back on the line. "Can you meet the sheriff at the Fabens airport?"

Raelynn was puzzled. "Sure. I can be there in about twenty minutes. Is that okay?"

"The sheriff is on his way. He'll be in a DPS chopper. Look for him when you get there."

"What's going on?" Raelynn didn't like the sound of all this and stepped on the gas.

"The sheriff will explain everything."

"I'm on the way." She pulled to the right of the old pickup and flew past the two teenagers.

As she was disconnecting the call, Raelynn thought she heard Miss Martha say, "God bless her."

FRIDAY, DECEMBER 7, 2007
7:51 A.M. MST
FABENS AIRPORT, TEXAS

Raelynn hit the airport property hot. She flew past the red and white striped gate; dust billowed from her tires as she tore down the access road toward the DPS helicopter in the parking area.

Raelynn saw the sheriff standing outside the aircraft watching her pull onto the property. She saw a second man, also in an El Paso sheriff's uniform, waiting with Sheriff Hallman. The other man was in his late fifties, broad-shouldered with a big head and almost no neck, and he was wringing his hands.

She parked the truck and hopped out. In a few long strides, she was standing beside the sheriff. Raelynn was surprised to see the sheriff, a robust outdoorsman, looking ashen. He shouted to be heard over the roar of the rotors.

"Deputy, does your mother live near Monahans? Off of North Main Avenue?" he asked.

Raelynn felt her heart stop. She didn't answer—only nodded slowly.

The sheriff motioned the other man over. "This is one of our chaplains. Reverend Albert Broadnax."

The burly pastor nodded to Raelynn with a forlorn look on his face. He was the county's newest and only Black chaplain and still looked uncomfortable wearing the uniform. But the uniform was the least of his concerns,

Raelynn assumed, as the word was out within the agency that he hated his first helicopter ride. He stepped closer to Raelynn.

Raelynn shook her head. She felt unsteady, a hollow ache forming in the pit of her stomach, and her hands tingled. "Tell me what's going on, please," she pleaded. Raelynn knew Sheriff Hallman as a twenty-six-year veteran lawman. He was big and gruff and occasionally rude. But he loved and took care of his people.

The sheriff's eyes were red. He struggled to speak. "There's no easy way to tell you this. Your mother has been murdered."

The chaplain grabbed Raelynn around the shoulders as she sank to her knees. She was crying harder than she had in a long time. The sheriff leaned down to her.

"We are going to get you to Monahans," Sheriff Hallman said. "The house is still an active crime scene, but the sheriff and the rangers are on the case. They want to talk to you as soon as we can get you there."

Raelynn tried to stand. "Murdered?"

Her legs felt like they couldn't bear her weight. Slumped over, she turned and asked her boss, "What about my sister and niece? They live with Mama."

Hallman shook his head. "We don't know much right now. Let's get in the air. The sooner we get there, the sooner we'll be able to answer your questions."

Sheriff Hallman took one arm, and Reverend Broadnax took the other. The men were helping her into the back seat of the helicopter when the sheriff grabbed his phone. He must've had it on vibrate, Raelynn thought—there was no way he could've heard it over the noise of the helicopter's rotors. She focused on the phone to avoid thinking about anything else.

She watched the sheriff as he listened to the call. She saw him glance at her, then look away.

As the helicopter started to take off, the sheriff leaned into the cabin and shouted in Raelynn's ear. "We'll know more once we're on the ground."

Reverend Broadnax held her hand in his big paw. He didn't try to speak. Raelynn figured he knew there was nothing he could say.

CHAPTER 6

HOME SWEET CRIME SCENE

FRIDAY, DECEMBER 7, 2007
10:11 A.M. CST
MONAHANS, TEXAS

Raelynn sat silently in the back of the helicopter as the highway patrol pilot nosed the aircraft toward Monahans. The ride had been smooth in the cold December air. Raelynn tried not to think about what she was about to experience. In many ways, she only felt numb.

She had seen it in the victims she had met. They all said it didn't seem real. She knew it was hard to wrap your head around the sudden death of a loved one. Raelynn knew, on an intellectual level, the people who settled the West lost children and loved ones on a level that would be catastrophic in today's world. She tried to remember that she came from the same stock, the pioneers who had settled the West. The memory didn't help.

As the helicopter raced toward her mother's home, Raelynn felt as if her ears were filled with cotton, and her perception of reality was skewed. She shook her head and tried to clear the cobwebs.

Six years ago, while Raelynn was a jail deputy with El Paso County, her father died unexpectedly. Eva Gene Michaels had been desperately in need of a reason to continue living. Raelynn's sister had provided that purpose. Miss Eva moved to Monahans to help her other daughter with child care. Miss Eva had bought a house to get her daughter and granddaughter out of the double-wide trailer her sister's husband, Rudy, had them living in.

Raelynn visited her family in the little city along Interstate 20 a dozen times in the last year. Monahans was founded around a water well, the only one for many miles in any direction, which had attracted the Texas and Pacific Railroad. In 1926, the discovery of oil in the dry earth around Monahans cemented its place in West Texas.

Ward County Sheriff Robert Sinclair radioed the pilot to say that his office had cleared a section of North Main Street for the DPS helicopter to land. Raelynn heard the pilot acknowledge the information, then tilt the helicopter back north. Raelynn watched, detached from her emotions for the moment, as she identified her mother's house. She had never seen it from above.

After the two-hour flight, Raelynn sat forward in her seat as the pilot dropped the Eurostar AS350-BA model toward the asphalt highway, dust swirling all around, and watched the sheriff and his deputies hold their hats in place, their heavy coats flapping open.

There were law enforcement cars, fire trucks, and ambulances scattered in the roadway, with a sprinkling of other government vehicles, blocking access to Raelynn's mother's home. *Or, more accurately*, Raelynn thought, *her house. That building would never be a home again.*

Raelynn leaned back in the seat and closed her eyes. In her career, she had been on the other end of what was about to happen to her a few times. Each time, she had tried her best to console devastated family members at a moment when their world had been upended. She felt bad for both the sheriffs and the chaplain. And that helped her keep it together.

She reached for the chaplain's hand again as the helicopter settled firmly on the ground. Before she could get her seatbelt unbuckled and work the door handle, the pilot was pulling the door open for her. She used the step on the skids to climb down to the ground.

The pilot stood awkwardly. Raelynn assumed he wasn't sure what to say to her. Then he leaned in, shouting in her ear. "I have to go back west and pick up Major Crosby. I'm very sorry for your loss."

Raelynn grabbed the pilot's hand and shook it. "Thank you."

Sheriff Hallman stood hunched over, holding his hat in place until the helicopter was safely in the air. Then he motioned for the Chaplain. "Albert, can you stay here with Deputy Michaels until I see what's going on?"

Hallman spotted Ward County Sheriff Robert Sinclair striding toward him. Sinclair was Hallman's age and height, but he had the look of a runner. Sinclair had finished a full marathon last year at age sixty-six, an event covered by the *Sheriffs' Association of Texas* magazine.

Sinclair looked grim as he stuck out his hand to greet Sheriff Hallman.

The two men quickly shook hands and stood together near the back of a Ward County Volunteer Fire Department truck parked among the mass of government vehicles at the scene. Both were hoping the fire truck would block some of the wind whipping across the landscape, making the air seem much colder than it was.

The fire truck had a stainless steel-covered rear step, and a large insulated coffee dispenser sat next to a box of foil-wrapped biscuits. A large, molded coffee dispenser with an inset faucet and two handles—common in detention centers—was manned by an inmate in an orange jumpsuit and an ill-fitting down jacket.

"What have we got, Sheriff?" Hallman asked.

Sheriff Sinclair took his white cowboy hat off and wiped his forehead. "It's bad—worse than anything I've ever seen. We've got two women dead in the house."

"Two?" Hallman interrupted.

Sinclair nodded. His jaw was tight. "We found out enough from a neighbor to piece things together."

"Who's the other victim?" Hallman said as he glanced back at Raelynn.

Sinclair exhaled slowly. "It's her sister, Jim."

Hallman sighed. "Good lord in heaven! Both killed?"

Sinclair spat in the dust. "Jim, it gets worse. The mother and sister lived with the sister's twelve-year-old daughter— who's now missing."

"I can get more help out here if we need it," Hallman offered. "This is bad."

Sinclair shrugged. "I think the whole company of Texas Rangers is either here or on the way. But I sure do appreciate you coming with your deputy. This is going to be a rough day for her, unfortunately."

Hallman looked at the scene—yellow tape strung along the front of the little white house set back from the road. The Christmas lights outside were twinkling incongruously in the morning sun. There were small groups of people working out- side; one group was devoted to marking and cataloging evidence while others examined the area and talked with neighbors.

"Can we get a ride to your office? I don't think my deputy needs to be here. And maybe you, or someone else, can help me answer her questions." Hallman asked.

Sinclair nodded to Sheriff Hallman. "One of the rangers will want to interview her for background on her family. The lead ranger is Chandler, out of Midland. He can run y'all into town."

"That's good," Hallman said.

Sinclair frowned. "Jim, do you need me to break it to her? About her sister and niece?"

Hallman sighed deeply. "No, Bob. I need to take care of my people. Could you wait right here, though? I want to get her some coffee and have something for her to lean on if she needs to. This truck's about the only thing out here that's not part of the investigation."

Sinclair put his hands on his hips as Hallman walked toward Raelynn.

Hallman motioned to Raelynn and Chaplain Broadnax. "There's coffee and food over here if you need it."

Broadnax shook his head and licked his dry lips. As far as Hallman knew, Raelynn hadn't eaten today. He waited for her to answer. "Coffee would be good," Raelynn said, then followed Hallman toward the red truck.

Hallman saw Raelynn's hand shaking as she pulled a white Styrofoam cup from the sleeve on the truck. She filled it halfway and took a sip of the black liquid. The coffee was bitter, strong—and exactly what she needed.

After Raelynn sipped her coffee for a moment, Hallman pushed his hat down firmly on his head and reached for her hand. He held her left hand in both of his and did his best not to cry.

"Deputy, there is no good way to tell you this. Your sister was killed along with your mother. And your niece is missing."

Raelynn nodded without looking up from her coffee. Even though the news was expected, her heart sank at the words. "I was worried that was the case. The word came too early for my sister to be at work at the hospital or for my niece to be in school."

Sheriff Sinclair stepped beside her. "One of the rangers is going to take you to my office to talk to you. Be sure to ask my staff for anything you need."

Sinclair turned to go back to the house.

Hallman watched as Raelynn finished the last of the coffee and set the cup on the tailgate. She took a couple of steps on the dusty roadway, looking toward her mother's home, and then collapsed in a heap.

FRIDAY, DECEMBER 7, 2007
10:22 A.M. CST
SHREVEPORT, LOUISIANA

Rudy Grant glanced over at his daughter, Madison, as his old Jeep pounded along Interstate 20. She sat quietly, staring out the front windshield. Rudy knew she was scared.

He had been driving since before midnight. He was tired, and his hand was throbbing where he had cut himself. He found out the hard way that people who stab other people end up with cuts on their hands. He had tightly wrapped his left hand, the one he cut several times, in a towel he'd pulled from a closet. Most of the towel was now red with his blood. He knew holding the hand up over his heart would help, but he couldn't do it for fear another driver might spot it and call him in.

He had to remember to keep his hand in his pocket when he got out of the car. They had stopped for gas once, and he had offered Madison a drink or a chance to use the restroom.

Madison refused to acknowledge him. She and Rudy hadn't had a stellar relationship since her mom had thrown Rudy out. Rudy hadn't spent much time with Madison in the past year, but she seemed like an average twelve-year-old girl—sneakers and jeans, sleepovers and gossip, and a growing awareness of boys.

Soon, Rudy planned to get off the Interstate and use back roads. He knew by now the cops would be looking for him. And for Madison.

Rudy also knew he was in big trouble. The fight last night had escalated beyond anything he thought he was capable of.

He had waited outside Rosalind's mother's house; the house they had shared until Rosalind kicked him out, waiting for her to come home from work. The house was trimmed in Christmas lights, and Rudy could see the outline of a tree in the living room.

For the last month, Rudy had parked down the street and watched as Rosalind had come home late several nights. When Rosalind came home late from her job at Ward Memorial Hospital, Rudy suspected a pattern was emerging. He knew in his heart she was cheating on him.

Last night, Rudy had watched the house for several hours after leaving Moe's shop. He could see his daughter, Madison, watching TV. His mother-in-law had fed Madison and was helping her with homework as they waited for Rosalind to get home.

Rudy had been drinking for over an hour by the time Rosalind parked her car beside the house. Rudy didn't want to confront his wife falling down drunk. It seemed like a good idea to shoot a little meth, enough to get him sober.

Rudy could see Rosalind come into the home and drop her purse and keys by the back door. Rudy had pulled his car closer and came into the house. Rosalind had sighed and stood with her hands on her hips.

"I'm tired, Rudy. I just want to get my shoes off and get into bed. They want me back in the morning early to help in the ER." She had tried to push past Rudy. "You know you're not supposed to be here. Don't cause any trouble for us."

Rudy had slapped her hard enough to knock her down. Her momentum took her into the Christmas tree she had decorated a week ago. Eva Gene had rushed up behind him and grabbed his arm as he swung again. "Stop it!" Eva Gene shouted. "Don't you hit her again."

Rosalind had stumbled back against the wall as she tried to stand. She held her red cheek as she got back on her feet. "Rudolpho! This is it. I'm calling 911."

As much as anything, Rudy's temper had flared because she used his given first name. She knew he hated that name. Rudy believed he had snapped. It was an excuse he used to comfort himself when the events of last night flashed through his mind.

Rudy had slapped at her again. Rosalind dodged his hand and went into her bedroom to get to the phone.

He turned to his mother-in-law and glared. "You need to stay out of this, or I'll beat both of you."

Eva Gene retreated to sit beside Madison. Rosalind stuck her head out of the bedroom. "I ain't playing with you. I'm calling the sheriff."

Suddenly, a knife was in his hand. He couldn't remember where it came from. The rage overpowered him, he thought, as he tried to rationalize an irrational action.

Looking back, he knew the meth was a bad idea. He had taken one more hit before he came inside his old house. He couldn't remember grabbing the knife. He did, however, remember the taste of blood in his mouth as he raged. He remembered that.

On the way out the door, he'd picked Madison up in his arms and ran from the house. He had carefully buckled Madison into the front passenger seat. Then he stood by the quiet road and pulled off his jacket and pants, which were soaked in blood, and pulled on a set of thermal coveralls he wore hunting.

Rudy glanced back at his daughter, staring straight ahead through the windshield. He knew she was angry. Then he remembered her favorite doll, a rag doll her grandmother had sewn for her. He ran back to the house, past the still-warm bodies of his wife and his mother-in-law, and grabbed the raggedy doll from the floor of Madison's bedroom. He tucked it under his arm and jogged back to the Jeep.

With a final glance back at his mother-in-law's house, he had fired up his SUV and headed east. Finally, he was out of Texas.

FRIDAY, DECEMBER 7, 2007
12:02 P.M. CST
MONAHANS, TEXAS

Sheriff Sinclair walked back to the house. The wind was making the yellow crime scene tape in front of the modest home jump and flop. He came to the deputy, keeping the crime scene log. His orders were to write down the name and agency of every person who entered the house and to note the time. Sinclair couldn't help noticing the peculiarity of the Christmas decorations, a symbol of peace on earth, blinking outside the blood-spattered home.

Sinclair watched as his deputy dutifully penned Sinclair's name, agency, and the time he walked back up on the stoop. The deputy nodded at the sheriff when he had properly noted his return.

Sinclair found that dealing with death was the least enjoyable part of his job. Sinclair had worked as a city police officer in Odessa before he ran for sheriff. He had dealt with the death of the elderly, victims of accidents, and the occasional suicide. This was only his third murder scene in his twenty years wearing a badge.

Sinclair pulled on cloth booties and rubber gloves. He didn't want to risk contamination of the scene. Then he carefully entered the front door. There was less blood in the living room than in the kitchen, the other entrance to the house. He didn't look forward to the kitchen. He could smell the mingled scent of blood and the early onset of decomposition from the threshold.

Two Texas Rangers were kneeling over Rosalind Grant's body. Rosalind lay on the floor on her back. Her right hand was out beside her, and her left was folded over her chest. There was a large puddle of blood, darkening as time passed, emanating from near her throat. Sinclair's eyes were drawn to the unnatural slit, no longer weeping blood, under her chin. Rosalind's sightless eyes looked to the ceiling. The eyes were already dull and dry. Sinclair knew there was no way to unsee this scene.

Miss Eva was slumped in the first two feet of the hall leading to the bedrooms. She sat with her arms in front of her, seemingly reaching out for something. The family's Christmas tree lay near her feet. Her blouse and dress were saturated with her blood. Sheriff Sinclair had known Miss Eva from visiting her church. Sheriffs who served small towns were often familiar with crime victims. She had stood out for her easy confidence and generosity to the needy in the county.

Sinclair found the man he was looking for, Ranger Steve Chandler, in the laundry room, examining the clothes hamper.

"No, obviously bloody clothes in here," Chandler said. "I guess we'll need to send the whole basket to the lab."

"That's your call, ranger," Sinclair said. "I want to be sure we cover all the bases. The victims are part of the law enforcement family. So, take all the time you need."

"Thanks, sheriff,"

Sinclair tried to keep some hope alive in his heart. "Are we sure the young girl was here? Have we seen any sign she could have spent the night with a friend or anything?"

Ranger Chandler was grim. "Her room looks like she was doing homework when the fight happened. Her books and some papers are scattered on the bed."

"But no sign of blood in the room?" Sinclair asked. Chandler shook his head.

Sinclair pointed toward the road. "The deputy from El Paso is outside. The DPS helicopter just dropped her off."

Chandler was impressed. "The highway patrol flew her out here? Is she something special?"

Sinclair nodded. "From what I hear, she went undercover after Rojo's bunch before he was killed. In fact, the work she did may be why Rojo was killed. I heard tell that a couple of rangers nearly got killed over in Mexico on that case."

Chandler looked out the front window to get a glimpse of the woman. "I've heard some stories about that case. That's the case where a couple of men tried to kill Lieutenant Petterson. That was a hell of a case, I'm told. I sure hope this is not the work of the Mexican mafia. Some kind of payback."

Sinclair glanced back to where Rosalind lay. "It can't be discounted."

Chandler wiped his forehead with the back of a gloved hand. "No, it can't."

Sinclair motioned with his head toward the road. "Well, she's waiting on you to interview her. I guess you can ask her about the other stuff when you talk to her."

FRIDAY, DECEMBER 7, 2007
12:20 P.M. CST
MONAHANS, TEXAS

Texas Ranger Steve Chandler helped Raelynn Michaels climb into his Ford pickup. Once she was strapped into the seat, he hustled around to the driver's side and climbed in.

"Are you sure we don't need to get you checked out at the hospital?" he asked Raelynn.

She shook her head. "I'm good. But I wouldn't mind getting away from here for a while."

He nodded. "The Sheriff's Office is just a little ways. Then we can get out of the cold and maybe get some food, if you want."

Raelynn slumped against the door frame. "Getting out of the cold would be good."

The pair made the drive in under ten minutes. The ranger parked in front of the tan building that served as the Sheriff's Office. The building was officially the Lee Russ Memorial Law Enforcement Center, named for a Ward County deputy stabbed to death while on the scene of a domestic dispute. The ranger couldn't ignore the irony of the situation, but he knew the deputy had killed his attacker before he died. In Texas, the community supported its fallen officers.

Chandler helped Raelynn into the building and took her directly to the sheriff's private office. The office was pure Texas with framed American and Texas flags on display. A handcrafted and engraved saddle was on a stand beside the sheriff's desk. An antique roll top desk, handed down from sheriff to sheriff, stood against one wall. A leather-covered couch was along the other wall. There was a private bathroom in the corner.

"Ranger, I'm going to duck in here for a minute," Raelynn said as she made for the restroom.

She switched on the light and pulled the door closed. After a moment, she examined her face in the mirror over the small sink. Raelynn didn't wear much makeup when she worked, but what she had applied was a mess. She ran cold water in the sink and used both hands to wash her face. The cold water and the vigorous massage made her feel better.

She took a moment more to gather herself and then stepped out of the little room.

Chandler watched as Raelynn sat on the worn couch and then slumped to her side.

"You'll have to excuse me, I'm worn out. Do you mind if I stretch out?" Raelynn asked with an embarrassed smile.

The ranger pulled off his heavy barn jacket and laid it across her shoulders. "I'm going to get some coffee and send someone for food. Then we can talk," Chandler said.

With a backwards glance, he went out to find the sheriff's secretary.

When Chandler returned to the sheriff's office, Raelynn was huddled under his jacket. She was shivering and wide awake.

Chandler set a bag of tacos and a couple of cups of coffee

he had brought onto a filing cabinet and stooped to comfort the El Paso deputy. "Let me get you over to the ER. You could use something to help you relax."

Raelynn shook her head. "My sister worked at that hospital. That's the last place I want to go right now. I want to give you as much information as I can. That bastard killed my whole family and took my niece hostage. I'll not be the cause of a delay in getting him behind bars."

The ranger took his hat off, laying it brim up, and pulled a chair close to the couch. "Eat a taco and sip some coffee." He pushed the coffee cup into her hand. "And then tell me who the bastard is. You say it like you have someone in mind."

Raelynn ignored the offered taco. "My brother-in-law. Rudy Grant. He and my sister split up less than a year ago. There should be a TPO on file in this county."

"Your sister took a Temporary Protective Order against him? Rudy?"

Raelynn sipped her coffee and looked at the ranger closely for the first time. He wore the standard ranger uniform, a starched white shirt with the Cinco peso badge pinned above the pocket. He had a tooled leather gun belt matching the belt that held up his pants. His boots were highly polished and looked well-worn.

Raelynn thought his face looked young. He couldn't be more than thirty-five; young for anyone to earn the badge of a Texas Ranger. His light-colored hair was cut short, and his face was recently shaven. Raelynn was beginning to enjoy looking into his eyes. They were a pale blue.

"You been a ranger long?" she asked.

Chandler blushed. "Yes. I was hired as a trooper when I was barely twenty-one. I worked my ass off to get into all the right schools and studied hard for the ranger test. I scored number five out of thirty-seven applicants. The Ranger Service was planning on promoting four. Then the top applicant left to go to the FBI. His loss; my gain."

"Have you worked a lot of murders, ranger?"

"Call me Steve," Chandler said with a comforting smile. "And yes, I've worked a few. Your family's case will be in good hands. Lieutenant Clete Petterson is on the way here to lead the investigation, and Major Stetson Crosby is coming to help out. Ten more rangers from the area are already combing through the crime scene, inside and out. As you know, child abduction is a top priority for any law enforcement officer. Anything we need, the Major will see that we get it."

Raelynn started to tear up. "I know the major. Clete and his wife, Montana, were planning to meet me at my sister's house for Christmas. They wanted to meet my mom and the rest of my family."

Chandler wondered if Raelynn would cry again. He studied her closely as her face seemed to harden in that moment. Raelynn's lower lip trembled as she turned to Chandler, but there were no tears in her eyes. "Let's get this son-of-a-bitch."

CHAPTER 7
MEMORY LANE

Daniel Byrd saw the comfortable chair he preferred in Anne Kuykendall's office. He dropped into the plush revolving armchair and leaned back. He picked up the marble nameplate on the desk. It said, "Anne Grace Kuykendall, MSW; Licensed Clinical Social Worker."

Kuykendall snatched the nameplate from his hand and put it back on her desk. Then she folded her left leg under her as she sat in her comfortable chair.

"I guess the GBI thinks I need a tune-up," Byrd said with an ironic smile.

Anne Kuykendall was dressed to impress, as always. "More likely they think you need an oil change," she quipped. She had on a green business suit, and her hair and makeup were immaculate. "I guess they should know. Have you done anything to get yourself into trouble lately?" she asked.

Byrd chuckled. "That's a leading question."

Anne nodded. "It's intended to lead you to opening up to me."

Byrd was hesitant. "Not that I know of. I guess they're worried about my old girlfriend overdosing."

Anne blew out through her lips. "Wow! That gives us something to talk about. How did you feel?"

Byrd shrugged. "We had broken up and I hadn't seen her in about a year."

"That's not a feeling. That's a chronology."

"I got over it," Byrd said.

Anne shook her head. "Danny, I want to know if you felt hurt? Maybe betrayed. An overdose connotes drug violations, the very thing you've spent a big part of your life dealing with."

Byrd threw a leg over the arm of the chair and turned his body so that his back was against the other arm. "I'm telling you, Anne. We had both moved on. I felt bad for her, but that's about it."

"At last, we get to a feeling. You felt bad? No more than that?" Anne was leaning forward now. Byrd recognized the technique. He had used it for interrogations.

"Anne, I'm over it all. I've moved on." Byrd was glib, and he knew it would push Anne's buttons.

"What about the killer who came after you? Are you over that?" Anne persisted.

"I'm still here. She's probably facing the needle in Texas for killing some good officers. I'd say she might need help more than I do."

"And the fellow agent who betrayed you? No issues with that?"

Byrd sat up. "Who the hell told you about all that?"

"This appointment was arranged and is paid for by your director's office. They gave me some background."

Byrd leaned back again. "I'm good."

"Are you in a relationship now?" she asked as she watched Byrd's face.

Byrd looked toward the ceiling. "Not right now. I'm between women. Lately, I've been on a three-month cycle."

"A three-month break?"

"No, it seems to work out that most of my relationships last about three months. Then we just drift apart. I see a couple of ladies, sort of an off-and-on kind of thing, but those aren't really relationships."

"What about friends. Do you socialize with anyone in particular?' Anne Kuykendall asked. She could see by the look on his face that she'd struck a nerve.

"I stay pretty busy. I hang out with a couple of agents from time to time. Jamie Abernathy, for one." Byrd struggled to answer.

"That's one. Who else?"

"Well, Doc and I work together a lot. We get together a couple of times a week."

"Your relationship with Doc would be defined as a co-worker. How often do you socialize with Jamie?" she asked.

"Well, not very often. We both have a busy case load, and she has a steady man in her life."

Anne pursed her lips. "So, no real friends. Your social life consists of work and some occasional visits by members of the opposite sex, and conversations around the coffee pot at the jail or the GBI office, or the State Patrol Post. Does that about sum it up?"

"You're making me sound like Howard Hughes, or somebody. I'm not a recluse," Byrd insisted.

Anne arched an eyebrow.

"What about drinking?" Anne asked. "Any issues there?"

"The GBI physical I had said my liver is great. So, there's that."

"If you're not overdrinking or day drinking, why do you see alcohol as a problem? I see people who function on a very high level who drink more than you do. Some of them, much more."

Byrd shrugged. "I'd never had a drink till I went undercover for the first time. I was nervous as a cat, and the liquor relaxed me. Now, the worry is about being available if something big happens. Two drinks is all I'll allow myself. But I do like them strong."

Anne was curious. "Why not beer? You went from nothing to hard liquor?"

Byrd nodded, happy to be talking about something he was comfortable with. "With a mixed drink, you let the ice melt and nurse the drink. The people you're with, the targets of the investigation, tend not to notice. You can order a second drink, if you need to, as long as you let it sit long enough for the ice to melt."

"Sounds like a control issue. A need to be in control, I mean."

"You don't want to be out of control when you're undercover. Too many things can go wrong," Byrd pointed out.

"Do you take the same approach to relationships. Don't let things get out of control for fear that something will go wrong?" Anne watched him closely.

"Relationships can be hard."

"No shit, Sherlock!" Anne exclaimed. "Danny, you're building walls around your heart. That's not a good thing. You don't want to experience the pain of loss if things don't work out, so you never connect. It's a part of life to mourn loss and to feel pain."

He hung his head. "I feel pain. I feel the pain of victims

and their families. I feel the pain of children abused and scarred for life. I feel plenty of pain."

Kuykendall frowned. "That's the closest you've ever come to expressing your honest feelings. Sit back in that chair. We're going to spend some time together today. You're going down a bad road."

Byrd sighed deeply, raised his eyebrows, and looked at his therapist. "I guess I see you more than I see any of the agents socially."

"Who do you trust?" Kuykendall asked as she leaned back in her chair.

Byrd thought the question over. He hung his head and examined his hands closely.

"That's what I thought," Kuykendall remarked. She shook her head. "We've got a lot to talk about."

FRIDAY, DECEMBER 7, 2007
1:51 P.M. CST
MONAHANS, TEXAS

Raelynn began to describe her sister's family. Ranger Chandler took careful notes of everything that was said. He was impressed with Raelynn's attention to detail. He attributed it to her undercover work. He had heard stories about her, a team of Texas officers, and a GBI agent working drugs along the border. Watching her now, as she sifted through her memory for every detail, he was convinced the stories were true.

"I talked to my momma, Miss Eva, is what everyone except me and Rosalind called her, at least once a week. She told me a few weeks ago that my sister's husband,

Rudy, had been coming around again. Mama didn't like telling me because she was afraid I'd come out here and confront Rudy. She said Rosalind had seen him parked down the street from their house a couple of times. So, she went down to the courthouse and got a TPO against him sometime in the last two months," Raelynn said.

Chandler nodded. "We talked to most of the neighbors this morning. They knew your mom as Miss Eva, too. And the lady in the house next door said she saw an old SUV parked out in front of her house last night. She started to call the Sheriff's Office right around midnight when she heard the Jeep start up and leave."

"Is that Mrs. Tanner you're talking about?"

"Yes, ma'am," the ranger confirmed.

Raelynn glanced up from her recollections. "Don't call me 'ma'am'. I'm Raelynn or Rae."

Chandler smiled. "Rae, it is. What's the back story on Rudy? Where are his people from, and where might he run to?"

Rae wiped her face with both hands. "Well, to begin with, he drives an old Jeep."

Chandler glanced up from his notes. "Damn."

Raelynn continued. "His mom lives in Spokane, Washington, if she's still alive. He's got half-sisters and half-brothers all over the Pacific Northwest." Ray made eye contact with Chandler. "We'd call his mother a 'rounder.' She got around a lot."

"If you know his cell phone number, I'll get someone to pull his phone records as we speak. The phone company security is giving us everything they can as fast as they can. The guy in charge used to be a captain with a sheriff's office somewhere in Georgia."

Raelynn recited the phone number by heart. Chandler

wrote it on a slip of paper and then stood up. She watched as he took careful notes and seemed overly concerned about her. At a different time, in a different place, she might have flirted with the handsome ranger with those big blue eyes.

Chandler stood uncomfortably. He glanced at his notes and then back at Raelynn. "I'll be right back. We've got people in the 911 center following up on leads. I'll move this to the top of the list."

Raelynn grunted. "Can we ping his phone?"

"I'll check on that, too." Chandler hustled down the hallway.

Raelynn took a moment to close her eyes. It seemed like no time had passed when Chandler came back into the office. Raelynn realized she had dozed off. The adrenaline was wearing off.

Chandler sat in a chair and flipped back in his notebook looking for his latest notes. "Things are crazy in Ward County today. The Sheriff's Office got called to a place called Moe's Hole in the Wall. Ever heard of it?"

Raelynn thought hard. "Seems like Rudy had mentioned he bought beer there after his shifts at the school. Why?"

"Looks like the owner was beaten to death last night. We've only gotten preliminary information, but one of the rangers is on the way over to Pyote to help out."

Raelynn shook her head. "Sounds like Rudy may have gone off the deep end."

Chandler leaned back in the chair. "It could be a coincidence, you know."

Raelynn looked him in the eye. "You've been in this job long enough. Do you still believe in coincidence?"

Chandler shook his head. "Nope."

Raelynn waited. "Did you find out anything else?"

Chandler had a list of information.

"Your brother-in-law's phone's an old model. The phone company said the last time it pinged was about six hours ago on the other side of Dallas. The phone company security guy thinks he's ditched his phone. We've got a lookout for his vehicle. It is an SUV, and it certainly matches the description the neighbor gave us. We've alerted the airports in case he tried to fly out of DFW or Love Field. If all his family is up towards Washington, can you think of anyone he might run to for help east of here?"

Raelynn shook her head. "Nobody comes to mind. He was in the Navy at one time, so he could have a friend from the service he might run to. I can't remember him mentioning anyone in particular."

"No childhood friends that he might have mentioned?"

Raelynn thought things over. Then, from the deepest part of her memory, a bell began to ring.

Chandler was watching her closely. "Did something come to mind?"

Raelynn met his eyes. "Nope. Just thinking about all the arrangements to make for my mother and my sister's services."

Chandler nodded. He wasn't convinced. "The rangers have activated our 'A Child is Missing' protocols. We'll have everybody we need and some we don't need, but they'll be here just in case."

Raelynn was familiar with the protocol. Every member of the state and local government had pre-assigned tasks to perform. They had each been trained to help with search and rescue, evidence preservation, and any other task that might contribute to a successful rescue of a child in danger.

"What can I do?" Rae asked.

Chandler shook his head. "We got this. And the State of Texas will do everything we can to get your niece home safely. But it was made clear to me that you can't get involved in the actual investigation. I'm sorry to have to say this, but those are my orders."

Raelynn nodded. "I understand. We've all got our orders."

Raelynn stood to stretch her legs. She was nearest the door when someone knocked. Glancing at Chandler for approval, she opened the door.

Texas Ranger Lieutenant Clete Pettersen and Texas Ranger Major Stetson Crosby doffed their hats as they entered the office. Pettersen spoke first, "Rae, I'm so sorry for your loss." After an uncomfortable moment in front of the other officers, Rae and Clete hugged.

"Thanks, Clete. It's rough, I'll admit. I just want to get Madison back safe and sound. And then I hope you folks can find that bastard who killed my mom and sister and put him in the ground."

The six-foot-six ranger major spoke up. "Deputy Michaels, we're turning heaven and earth to find your niece."

Raelynn nodded slowly. "I know, Major. And I appreciate it."

"Our helicopters and planes are busy flying evidence to the crime lab in Austin," Clete added. "You remember Deneen Scott from the crime lab? She's holding everybody in the lab to get DNA and blood typing processed. She has offered to work around the clock if we want."

"She's good people," Raelynn said. "I remember her when she was in Drug ID. She'll do it right."

The rangers stood awkwardly, not sure how to proceed. At last, Major Crosby took the lead. "Deputy Michaels, can we get you a motel room where you can relax? I'll have a female ranger stay with you. You know, there is still a chance this was an attack on your family from the remnants of Rojo's organization in Mexico."

Raelynn shook her head. "They haven't given me any details yet, but I'm putting my money on my sister's ex. Rudy Grant."

Major Crosby nodded. "Do you have any idea where he might be right now?"

Chandler spoke up. "We pinged his phone this morning. He was near the Metroplex. We're having rangers from Company B check both airports as we speak."

Raelynn wanted to follow up on her hunch, but her undercover instincts told her she'd have to go slowly. If anyone got wind she was planning to head to Georgia, they would head her off. But she also knew she had to be forthright with the rangers.

"Major, there is one possibility that I just thought of. He has a woman he thought of as his grandmother. She's not really, as far as I know. She's the grandmother by blood to one of Rudy's stepsisters. She lives around the Tennessee-North Carolina-Georgia border area. I'm not sure, but I think she lives in Georgia."

Chandler whipped out his notepad. "Do you remember a name or an address? Anything we might be able to track?"

She answered honestly. "Gazaway was the name, I think. Maybe the first name of Bea or something like that. He spoke of her a few times. His mother would leave the kids with this woman for a few weeks at a time when they were teenagers. As a matter of fact, I think she put them on a bus to see the woman. He talked about how much they hated riding the bus for three days. He said they'd meet her at some service station right on the Georgia/Tennessee line at, like, one in the morning."

Chandler nodded. "That's helpful. You don't happen to remember the name of the city she lived in, do you?"

Rae chuckled. "The place she lived in stuck in my head. It's called Bethlehem."

Chandler raised his cell phone and stepped out of the room as he dialed DPS intelligence. After a movement, he stuck his head back in the room. "Intel says there is a Bethlehem in Tennessee, North Carolina, *and* Georgia. None of them are anywhere close to the state borders."

Crosby frowned. "Tell them to dig deeper. This woman may be known to one of the state's Child Protective Services case workers. Clete, why don't you put a call in to the Georgia Bureau of Investigation, the North Carolina State Bureau of Investigation, and the Tennessee Bureau of Investigation, and see if we can get some help."

Clete Petterson nodded. "I can call Daniel Byrd right now. He'd be happy to help."

Crosby pursed his lips. "Byrd is a friend to you and Deputy Michaels. Could that muddy the waters in a murder trial?" Crosby rubbed his chin. "No, let's go through the regular channels." He turned to Ranger Chandler. "Chandler, reach out through DPS Intelligence and see if we can get anything from Child Protective Services in Tennessee, North Carolina, or Georgia to identify this woman."

Chandler glanced at Raelynn. Then he looked at Crosby. "On it, Major."

As Chandler turned to leave, Texas Ranger Adeline Riley stepped into the room. Adeline had been Raelynn's undercover partner before she was promoted to the Ranger Service.

Adeline tossed her white western hat on the sheriff's desk and hugged Raelynn hard. "I'm so sorry about Miss Eva and Rosalind. I came as fast as I could."

Raelynn leaned into her best friend. "I'm glad to see your face."

Adeline looked grim. Her eyes were squinting as she asked, "Was it Rudy?"

"I'd bet my life on it," Raelynn said with an equal determination.

CHAPTER 8
NIGHT OUT AGAINST CRIME

FRIDAY, DECEMBER 7, 2007
3:45 P.M. EST
ELLIJAY, GEORGIA

Daniel Byrd struggled in the gloom of the trendy restaurant off the city square. In the last year, Ellijay has become a tourist destination, and new eateries have been popping up everywhere. He guessed the owners were going for candlelit-romantic. To Byrd, it seemed gloomy and cave-like. He spotted Jackson "Doc" Farmer seated in the back.

Doc was the most senior, at least in law enforcement experience, in Byrd's office in Gainesville. Doc was in his late forties and had a fringe of gray hair around his bald head. He was dressed in a light-colored gray suit.

Byrd ambled over to the table and took a seat. Doc had managed to get a table in the corner where both men could sit with their backs to the wall. Doc had made himself comfortable, dropping his sports coat on an adjacent chair and stretching his legs out.

"Come on in, son," Doc invited. "You look hungry."

"That's 'cause I am. My stomach thinks my throat's been cut."

Doc motioned toward the chair with his sports coat. "Take your coat off and relax. You're not working dope anymore. It's okay if folks see the badge on your belt."

"Old habits are hard to break, Doc," Byrd said as he grabbed a menu. "What are you having?"

Doc chuckled. "Indigestion, probably. Everything I eat seems to make me burp lately."

"It's the crazy hours we keep. They work on you. Like having lunch in the middle of the afternoon."

Doc ducked his head and pretended to search the menu. "Speaking of things working on you. How are you doing?"

"Good," Byrd responded. "Why?"

"Your old girlfriend overdosed. For some folks, that might be tough to handle."

Byrd shrugged. "We had broken up, and I hadn't seen her in about a year."

"But, y'all were pretty tight before she got caught using."

"I got over it," Byrd said. He was becoming defensive.

Doc sighed. He decided to change the subject. "How's your kung fu training going? Is your body a deadly weapon yet?"

Byrd shrugged his shoulders. "It's judo. I should have stuck with judo after college. My shoulders and back stay sore. And I think I'm getting too old to be thrown on a mat."

"Well," Doc remarked, "your color's better. Exercise has got to be good for you. I'm thinking about taking it up."

"Judo?"

"No, exercise."

Byrd smiled. "Doc, as much as you run your mouth and jump to conclusions, I'd say you get plenty of exercise."

"Very funny! I guess if your shoulders are bothering you, it'll be hard to pat yourself on the back."

Byrd ignored the jibe. "Doc, you're the one constant in this job. Your jokes are always the same."

Doc didn't respond to Byrd. "Did you hear that Tina may be leaving us?" He was referring to Christina Blackwell, the Special Agent in Charge of the Gainesville GBI office.

Byrd nodded. "I haven't heard who'd replace her. Have you?"

"I heard they're bringing Gary Thomasson back. They think he might be able to keep you in line."

Byrd shook his head. Thomasson had been an agent in the Gainesville office who betrayed Byrd to a cartel assassin. Six months after Thomasson had entered a guilty plea, he would finally be going to prison. "You're a laugh a minute, Doc. You should be on TV."

Doc sat back and enjoyed his joke. "Seriously, I heard that Kay Fullington may be getting the job. She's the ASAC in Douglas. The two offices are almost three hundred miles apart."

Byrd frowned. "She wants to move to the mountains?"

Doc raised an eyebrow. "She wants to be an SAC."

Byrd nodded. "I guess that's right." Byrd pushed his chair back and folded his arms. "Another one we'll have to train. I wonder who she pissed off to get me as a subordinate?"

"I don't know, son. But if you find out, let me know. I want to steer clear of anyone with that much evil in their heart." Doc was still chuckling his full-bodied laugh when the waitress came over.

"I'm having the meatloaf," Doc announced.

Byrd shook his head. "I thought you were worried about indigestion?"

The two lawmen ate and gossiped about the local law enforcement community. Doc knew every officer in the North Central Georgia mountains and was a local legend. When their plates were cleaned and the two men sat back, Doc asked Byrd, "What are you needing, Danny? You usually don't offer to buy my lunch for nothing."

"That's not fair, Doc," Byrd protested. "I hadn't talked to you in a while, is all."

Doc arched his right eyebrow. "Son, I love you, but when you call me on a Friday, history says you need me to work late."

Byrd shrugged. "I have an informant who says he can buy an ounce of meth from a former Towns County deputy. But he said it had to be tonight."

Doc nodded. "I told you! Didn't I say that's what you wanted?"

"Do you know why fortune tellers don't have kids?" Byrd asked deadpan.

"I've got kids. They're both grown, but I like to see them every once in a while," Doc observed.

"They have crystal balls. Can you help me or not? We don't often get meth in that quantity this far north."

Doc stood up from the table. "I reckon I've got nothing better to do. I mean, why would I want to be sitting in my comfortable house with my wife and family when I could be running around the country with you on a cold winter night?"

Byrd patted him on the shoulder. "Thanks, Doc."

FRIDAY, DECEMBER 7, 2007
6:12 P.M. CST
WEST POINT, MISSISSIPPI

Rudy Grant pulled his old SUV off US Highway 45 north of West Point. He looked closely at the front of the rundown motel, sitting a dozen yards off the highway. The old place must have survived the highway widening, but was now in hard times. He had to look twice to see the "Vacancy" sign.

Rudy parked the Jeep near the office and turned it off. If the clerk saw him trying to get a room with a young girl in the car, they might call the local police.

He got out and locked Madison in. He ducked under the rusty awning covering the door to the office. When he opened the door, the heat hit him in the face. The office was at least eighty degrees.

He saw an old crone sitting behind the counter, which was the focal point of the office. She was rocking in an old armchair and watching black and white TV. Rudy didn't recognize the show but recognized Steve McQueen in it. He stepped up to the worn wooden counter.

The old woman turned toward him. "You wantin' more ice? This ain't the Ritz." Her voice was a blend of whisky and cigarettes. She stared up at Rudy.

"No. I want to get a room." Rudy watched her stare harder.

"I thought you were one of the regulars. I can give you a room for $15, but you've got to be out by noon tomorrow."

Rudy nodded. "That's fine. I plan to leave early."

The old woman spat in the trash can near the counter. "Don't plan, do. This shit-hole is closing tomorrow. They're planning to put a new place of some kind here. Prob'ly a name brand where folks come to stay all night. This place caters to the hourly customers."

She stood and looked Rudy up and down. "Where'd all that blood on your shirt come from?"

Rudy knew his face turned red. He pointed at the coveralls. "I killed a deer this morning."

The old crone could have cared less. "You paying cash?" she asked.

Rudy nodded. "Cash is king." He offered a twenty-dollar bill.

The old lady took the bill and stuffed it into the pocket of her apron. She frowned up at Rudy. "I forgot to mention the room taxes." She passed a brass key on a tag with a number almost faded away. "Room four is the cleanest one we've got."

She dropped back into the old chair and resumed staring at the TV.

"You wouldn't happen to have a first aid kit, would you? I cut my hand changing a tire." Rudy asked. He held up the blood towel.

The old woman snorted. "You ain't got AA?"

"That kind of stuff costs money."

She stretched to pull a first aid kit from under the counter. "I can't guarantee what's left in the box, but you can have it."

Rudy walked across the lot to his Jeep. He knew he would have to carry Madison into the room. Rudy glanced back at the office. No way that old biddy will see me out here, he thought.

He grabbed Madison, putting an arm around her

shoulders and under her knees. He grabbed the rag doll and held it in his left hand with the room key in his right. He negotiated the door lock and shoved the door closed behind him. She didn't protest as he took her into the dirty room and carefully laid her on the bed.

Rudy was uncomfortable with the situation, but couldn't think of an alternative. Madison would have to stay in his room. Much as he dreaded the prospect, he'd also have to bathe her tonight. He hadn't done that since she was four or five years old. She went limp, like a protester. If only she'd cooperate, he thought.

FRIDAY, DECEMBER 7, 2007
6:44 P.M. CST
MONAHANS, TEXAS

Adeline had talked Major Crosby into letting Raelynn stay at the Law Enforcement Center for a while longer. Raelynn had napped again while Adeline was briefed on the investigation so far. It would be up to her to decide how much her best friend should be told.

Adeline, Addy to her friends, knew that Raelynn was tough. She decided to hold back only the most gruesome details.

Adeline held Raelynn's hand in her own. "I'm going to give it to you straight, Rae. If it gets to be too much, let me know."

Raelynn stared into her eyes. "That's what I want, Addy. I can take it."

Addy took a deep breath and then exhaled. "Your mother and sister were both stabbed to death in the living room. Preliminary indications are that Rosalind had around twenty to thirty stab wounds and then a slashing wound to her throat. Your mother was stabbed much less, but one of the wounds to the chest was a fatal blow."

"What about Madison? Any signs to indicate what happened?" Rae asked.

"We can't be sure until some of the DNA results start coming in. I can tell you there wasn't any blood in her room. And we found a broken knife in the driveway. It looks like it will be the murder weapon."

"Just the one knife used?"

"Again, this is all preliminary. One of the rangers doing the crime scene examination told me it was probably the same knife. That number of wounds is real anger," Addy observed.

"That number of wounds is family," Raelynn countered dryly.

Addy wanted to caution her friend. "Rudy is a piece of shit, but he isn't locked in as a suspect right now. We have to keep an open mind."

"You know as well as I do that Rudy did it."

Addy nodded. "Of course he did. But we still need to follow the evidence, and the evidence is still being processed."

"Is anyone searching Rudy's house-trailer? You should be able to get his DNA from there. He had to have gotten cut doing all that stabbing. They always do."

"We have a team at his place now," Addy replied. "And we'll leave a few there just in case he were to come back home."

"He's in the wind. He won't be back there," Raelynn observed. "He'll head to one of his kin folks. My money's on his granny. She's somewhere around North Georgia or Tennessee. He hated his mother and seldom talked to any of his brothers and sisters."

"Did you know Georgia had three communities named Bethlehem? Well," Addy corrected herself, "two communities and a city by that name."

Raelynn locked eyes with Addy. "You know who we need to call on this."

Addy looked away. "The major says this is to be strictly by the book. He had one of the other rangers contact the GBI. The biggest places in Georgia are not far from Atlanta. The GBI is sending someone first thing in the morning to run down any leads they can find."

Raelynn didn't back off. "I'll call him. You know he'll want to help if Rudy's in Georgia."

"The major said by the book," Addy said. "He mentioned Danny by name. He said mixing personal feelings into this investigation would be a mistake. Told me and Clete both that he wanted us to keep back and let the rest of the rangers do the work. Said he's to be tried in a Texas court."

Raelynn was incredulous. "He thinks Danny would do something to mess up any prosecution?"

"He thinks Danny would do anything for you or me or Clete," Adeline said.

"Why would the major think that?" Raelynn asked.

"He had to sort things out when Danny went into Mexico to get me and Clete out! Hell, you were there. You know, Danny can be 'full speed ahead and damn the torpedoes' sometimes. Let's wait to see if there's any evidence Rudy is headed to Georgia." Addy tried to reason with Raelynn, "There's also a Bethlehem in Tennessee and North Carolina. We've got folks looking in all three places."

Raelynn wasn't happy, but she was willing to wait a little longer.

CHAPTER 9

CHASING A WILD GOOSE?

FRIDAY, DECEMBER 7, 2007
7:47 P.M. EST
HIAWASSEE, GEORGIA

Daniel Byrd hung up the phone in the Towns County Sheriff's Office. He and Doc Farmer had dropped in at the jail to get a free cup of coffee. The dispatcher had told Byrd that GBI Headquarters was looking for him.

Byrd called Headquarters and waited as the operator patched him through to Tina Blackwell.

"Danny, we got handed a rush job for the Texas DPS. Seems the Texas Rangers have a child kidnapping going on. They want the GBI to try to locate a family member of the suspect. She's supposed to live in Bethlehem."

"Over in Barrow County?" he asked.

"Yeah. The regional office in Athens is tied up on an officer-involved shooting that will take all weekend to sort out. Run the information down and let me know what you get. I'll forward you the email I got with the particulars."

"Doc and I are in Hiawasee trying to do a dope deal with a former deputy. Should I drop that?"

Blackwell thought it over. "Can you get on it first thing in the morning? Right now, Texas's lead is more like a hunch."

"Will do," Byrd said as he broke the connection.

"What was that all about?" Doc asked.

Byrd shook his head. "I'm supposed to find some family member of a kidnapping suspect from Bethlehem."

Doc frowned. "The city or the community? The city is in region 11."

"The Athens office is all tied up on a killing over in Lavonia. They asked that I run over to Bethlehem and check with the sheriff's office to run this woman down."

"On Saturday morning? A phone call won't do?" Doc asked.

Byrd shrugged. "They have a last name and maybe a first name. I guess the bosses figure a personal visit and some digging with the locals might turn up more than a phone call."

Doc smiled. "Sucks to be on call."

FRIDAY, DECEMBER 7, 2007
8:01 P.M. EST
HIAWASSEE, GEORGIA

Daniel Byrd waited as Jerry Rutledge slunk over to his car. He glanced over at Doc, who shook his head ruefully. "That's your informant?" Doc asked.

Byrd shrugged. "They can't all be gems."

Doc frowned. "He's no diamond in the rough, either. I'll tell you that."

Rutledge tried to climb into the back seat of the car as Byrd stood up. "Let's talk out here," Byrd said as he motioned toward the trunk. Byrd could smell the body odor even in the cold air. He didn't want his car to smell like that.

Doc got out of the G-ride, lit a cigarette, and then joined them.

"Were you able to get us a name for this guy, the ex-deputy?" Byrd asked.

Rutledge was desperate to please. "I shore did. His name is Laverne Middleton. He lives right across the hill from here."

Doc shook his head, trying his best to suppress a burp. "Danny, I know Laverne. He was never a deputy. He's a volunteer fireman. And he's as plain as white bread. It'll be hard for me to believe he's dealing meth."

Rutledge looked worried. "I was told he was dealing tonight."

Byrd looked at Doc. "We'll give him a chance." He turned to Rutledge. "You better not be feeding us a line of bull. If you're planning to pull something, I'll guarantee you'll spend tonight in jail."

"I know one thing for sure," Doc observed as he leaned on Byrd's car.

Byrd readied the body bug transmitter to place inside Rutledge's jacket. "What's that, Doc?"

"I've got to lay off that meatloaf."

FRIDAY, DECEMBER 7, 2007
8:13 P.M. EST
HIAWASSEE, GEORGIA

Byrd and Doc sat in Byrd's Crown Victoria parked down the road from the target house. Byrd had made Rutledge point out the house before they wired him up with a transmitter and sent him in.

Rutledge drove his old car up to the quiet-looking house south of Hiawassee. Byrd had noted the house was neat and well-kept. The grass was neatly mowed, and lights were on outside. None of these observations gave Byrd a warm, fuzzy feeling about where things were headed. Dope houses were rarely well-kept.

The GBI men could hear the rustling of the microphone as Rutledge's clothes scrubbed over it. Then his footsteps on the cement driveway were clear. The two state lawmen could imagine everything as it happened.

Next, there was the sound of knocking. It took a moment before the sound of the door opening followed.

"Hello, friend. Are you coming out here tonight to get some of my product?"

"That's Laverne," Doc said.

"Yes, sir. I need something to give me some energy. You know what I mean?" Rutledge sounded nervous.

"You've come to the right place, son. I've got some powder in here that will make you feel like you got a rocket up your ass."

Byrd glanced at Doc. Doc was still skeptical.

"Is it powder or crystal?" Rutledge asked.

Laverne said something that the microphone didn't pick up.

Right here you go. You can get a one-pound bottle of these vitamins for thirty dollars. I buy 'em wholesale. They'll give you energy for days.

Byrd closed his eyes and shook his head. "What an idiot!"

Doc laughed. "You sure know how to pick 'em, son."

Byrd groaned as he heard Rutledge on the body bug. "What about some meth to go with it?"

They heard Laverne say, "Boy, that shit will kill you.

You get out of my house right now. I don't want nothing to do with the likes of you!"

Doc shook his head in the dark car. "You need to explain to your boy what time it is."

"I'm about to tell him. I don't know if it'll sink in, though. I think if stupid was a disease, Rutledge would be terminal."

Doc burped again. "We can only hope. You got any antacids on you?"

"Go on home, Doc. I can handle the rest of this mess on my own."

Doc chuckled. "Give him hell, son. He ruined a perfectly good Friday night!"

SATURDAY, DECEMBER 8, 2007
8:22 A.M. CST
MONAHANS, TEXAS

Raelynn had insisted on spending the night on the sheriff's couch. She had dozed fitfully and gotten up often to check for any new information. She was sound asleep when Addy came into the office.

Raelynn heard the door open and sat up. "What's going on?"

"A friend of yours is here," Addy remarked dryly.

Raelynn frowned. "Who?"

"Supervisor Agent Ben Brown just parked out front."

Raelynn got to her feet. "You mean former Assistant Special Agent in Charge?"

Addy crinkled her nose. "That'd be the one."

Brown had done his best to ruin the undercover operation

Raelynn had been involved in. The feds didn't want the massive delivery of six tons of methamphetamine oil to be completed by local officers. Brown had intercepted the load in Louisiana, well out of his office's territory, in the hopes he would be promoted. He got the opposite result when his boss in El Paso found out.

Raelynn stretched. "He shows up like a bad penny."

Brown pushed his way into the Ward County sheriff's office. He looked absently at Raelynn, noted the lack of a law enforcement badge or uniform, then turned to Adeline. In her starched white shirt with the Cinco peso badge over her heart, she stood unmistakably as a Texas Ranger. "I'm from the FBI. I'm here to take over the investigation," Brown announced.

Adeline was a diplomat. "Let me get the local sheriff and our major in here. They're the folks you need to talk to."

Brown impatiently threw his notepad on the desk. "Fine. Get them in here, then."

Addy left the room. Raelynn sat quietly as Brown concentrated on ignoring her. She was sure he didn't recognize her.

In less than a minute, Sheriff Sinclair stormed into the office. He was followed closely by Sheriff Hallman and Major Crosby. Addy had delivered the message to the law enforcement leaders word-for-word.

Oblivious to the tension in the room, Brown extended a hand to Sheriff Sinclair. "Hello, Sheriff."

Sinclair didn't wait for pleasantries. "Who the hell do you think you are?"

Sinclair had hardly finished a sentence when Sheriff Hallman pushed forward. "Son, you need to get your ass back to El Paso if you know what's good for you."

Brown was unruffled. "A child has been kidnapped. That's FBI jurisdiction."

Raelynn saw Sheriff Hallman ball up his fists. He stepped closer to Brown. "This is a double murder with a parental interference with custody. None of this is federal," Hallman said gruffly.

Major Crosby tried to lower the temperature of the room. "We appreciate any help we can get." At six feet six, Crosby had a way of commanding attention. "But coming in here and trying to take over won't fly."

Brown looked around the room. He didn't see a friendly face in the crowd. He pursed his lips and grabbed his notepad. "I'll pass on your feelings to my SAC."

Brown took a last look at Raelynn as he left the office. Raelynn watched him as he walked out the front door.

Sheriff Hallman grabbed an office phone and dialed. "I know Pete Connolly, the FBI SAC. He won't like what just happened. He's new to the area, but he's a good guy and always looking to help." Hallman looked around the room, conspiratorially. "Even if he is from New York City."

Hallman turned away as someone answered the phone. "Pete, this is Jim Hallman. I'm out here in Ward County on this missing child and the murders."

Hallman paused as the person on the other end asked a question. "Yep, they are all family of one of my deputies. Sheriff Sinclair and his whole office are working around the clock, along with a company of Texas Rangers."

Hallman nodded as he listened to the phone. "We had a little, uh, run-in with one of your people. I wanted to explain the situation before you heard it from someone else. An agent named Brown."

Hallman listened again. "I wouldn't say he was an asshole, but he sure was full of himself."

Another pause. Stetson Crosby and Sheriff Sinclair exchanged looks.

"Right. I understand. I have problem children to manage, too."

Hallman nodded after another pause. "He was busted back from ASAC over that drug deal we did with the GBI? You'll have to tell me about that one night over a bourbon and coke."

A final pause. "Thanks, Pete. I knew you'd understand. We'll take all the help we can get."

Hallman hung up the phone and turned to face the room. "Pete was well aware of what kind of man he had. Agent Brown happened to be on call today, or he'd never have been here. He's sending a couple of his best agents who really *can* help out."

Sinclair bowed his head. "Lord, please be merciful and protect us from the bullets of criminals and the help of the FBI."

The comment broke the tension in the room.

SATURDAY, DECEMBER 8, 2007
9:27 A.M. EST
WINDER, GEORGIA

Daniel Byrd had been on the road this morning for an hour and a half when he crossed the line into Barrow County. After the late night, he'd slept later than he planned. This morning, he had rushed through his shower and grabbed a dark suit. On his way out the door, he had glanced at the mirror, only to discover he'd nicked himself shaving. He had rushed back to the bathroom, cleaning the blood and then applying a styptic pencil. One more glance in the mirror and then he jogged to his car.

On average, GBI agents drive about three to four thousand miles a month. Georgia, the largest state east of the Mississippi River, requires agents to cover large territories on a routine basis. The need to cover long distances, coupled with the responsibilities of all his active cases, meant that time was precious and driving time was always a race against the clock. Byrd pushed the Bureau Crown Vic as hard as he could without risking an encounter with a uniformed officer.

Daniel Byrd knew Bethlehem didn't have a police department but was served by the Barrow County Sheriff's Office. Byrd pulled into the Sheriff's Office lot behind the jail in Winder and parked his blue, unmarked sedan.

Byrd found a detective working on paperwork in the Investigator's Office. After Byrd introduced himself, Stacey Carter, the weekend detective, ran a name check on any Gazaway old enough to be a grandmother on the county file system. Carter came up empty. Byrd was mildly amused that Stacey Carter had been Raelynn Michaels' undercover name during their joint investigation last year.

Byrd spent an unproductive hour looking through old phone books. Detective Carter offered to check with the county tax office on Monday. Byrd took her cell phone number and email address and was closing his padfolio when she offered, "You know, there are a couple of other Bethlehem communities in Georgia?"

Byrd stopped what he was doing. "There are?"

Carter nodded. "There's a place down in Monroe called Little Bethlehem. Some said it was a cult, but we never had information to back up those claims. It was just a church where the worshipers seemed very strict. We never had a problem with them. I think I have a phone number for the property owner."

Carter rummaged around in her desk drawer. After a brief search, she discovered the card she sought. She dialed a number written in pencil. A quick call turned out to be valuable.

Carter asked a few opening questions about the church. She would nod her head as she said, "Uh-huh" or "Wow." After several minutes of listening to the wrong side of a one-sided conversation, Byrd stood and walked around the office, checking for nameplates he might recognize. He didn't want to break the flow of the conversation on the phone.

At one point, Byrd tried to read Carter's scribbled notes over her shoulder, but the handwriting was worse than his own.

Carter thanked the person on the phone and then hung up. "I may have something for you."

Byrd was curious. "Lay it on me."

"There was a Gazaway woman who lived in Little Bethlehem back twenty or thirty years ago. She had a reputation for having round heels, if you know what I mean," Carter said. "She was involved with several men while she was there—at least, that's the best my guy can remember. She had two kids out of wedlock, and the man in charge had to ask her to leave finally."

"Where did she go? Or do they know?" Byrd asked.

"She left on a bus going toward Seattle. But guess where she was from originally. In fact, they think her mother still lives there."

"I give," Byrd countered.

"A place outside of Blairsville. A little community there."

Byrd was making notes. "That's back up my way. What's it called? Do you know?"

Carter smiled. "It's called Bethlehem."

CHAPTER 10

ROAD TRIP

Rudy spent the morning driving through Alabama towns with names like Sulligent, Beaverton, and Gu-win. Rudy knew he was in the home stretch. His old Jeep was cold. Rudy decided Madison might not speak to him, but he could make sure she was comfortable. He wanted her to remember he was a good dad. He'd stolen a comforter from the piece of crap motel and wrapped it around Madison and her rag doll. Rudy wished he'd thought to bring the iPod he'd given her last Christmas—something she might find more distracting than a worn doll.

They'd spend one more night on the road before getting to Granny Gazaway's house. As far as he knew, Granny Gazaway was not Rudy's blood kin; she was the biological grandmother of two of his stepsisters, but Rudy had spent several summers roaming around her house in the North Georgia Mountains. He needed a place to go to ground and regroup, maybe get a little actual rest, and then get a clean vehicle to make the last part of his journey.

Rudy took time to dig through the glove box of his SUV. He found a baggie with the crumbs of some counterfeit hydrocodone tablets he'd bought as a package deal from his meth dealer. The pill remnants had helped the pain in his wounded hand.

Madison was still refusing to eat, and Rudy was taking advantage of the opportunity to drive as much as possible. Staying on the back roads was taking longer than he had expected, but they hadn't met a single police car since they got into Louisiana.

Rudy had taken the precaution of stealing a license plate off the back of another car in the parking lot of the grungy motel in West Point. He hoped he could get to Georgia without seeing a cop.

SATURDAY, DECEMBER 8, 2007
10:22 A.M. CST
MONAHANS, TEXAS

Most of the morning Raelynn had been alone in the sheriff's office. Her hair felt oily, and her clothes were wrinkled and dirty from the time she had slept in them. She needed a shower. More importantly, she wanted to get to Rudy's granny's house. She doubted that Rudy would hurt Madison, but she had no illusions about the hell the child must be going through.

She checked the hallway to make sure no one was listening in, and then she grabbed a phone from the desk. She had spent a few hours in the early morning looking for flights that would get her to Rudy before anyone figured out where he was. She had found a flight to Atlanta leaving that evening. She got the airline on the phone and reserved a seat. She used her undercover name and matching credit card to make the reservation, reasoning that the ruse might gain her a day or so before anyone figured out she'd left Texas. Once that was done, she needed to get a ride back to her truck in El Paso.

She looked out into the hallway and saw El Paso County deputy Greg Harris, a long-time friend. Raelynn explained her need for a shower and a change of clothes. "I'll be happy to run you back to your truck," Harris said. "I need an excuse to go home myself. I packed a bag for an overnight. I'd like to kiss my wife and son."

Raelynn made a point to avoid Sheriff Hallman as she gathered her few belongings and made a dash for El Paso.

SATURDAY, DECEMBER 8, 2007
11:45 A.M. EST
WINDER, GEORGIA

Daniel Byrd called the GBI Communications Center from the Barrow County Sheriff's Office, and Sophia Romano, a radio operator for the GBI, answered the call.

"Sophia, this is Danny Byrd. Can you look at the log and see who called from Texas asking for information from Bethlehem? I need a call-back number."

Sophia was upbeat. "Sure. Someone sent you to Bethlehem right before Christmas? Sounds like what my granny always warned me. Is Jesus finally coming back?"

"It would be if there were a happy ending. It's connected to a child kidnapping," Byrd replied.

"Oh, dang. Hold on a second. I've got the log right here."

Byrd could hear Sophia pulling the log over and finding the latest page. "Here it is. A Texas Ranger named Clete Petterson. He's a lieutenant with the Rangers in El Paso."

Byrd was surprised. "I know him. I wonder why he didn't call me directly?"

"No idea. Do you want his number?" Sophia asked.

"Thanks, Sophia. I have it."

"Stay safe, Danny."

Byrd hung up the phone. He immediately dialed the number he had for Clete Petterson.

The sound of the connection being made was hollow. Then the phone rang once before Petterson answered.

"Petterson."

"Clete. Danny Byrd. What's going on?"

Clete sounded tired. "Danny! Good to hear from you. I'm kind of pressed right now. How can I help you?"

"I got a request to run a name down in the Winder area. Turns out you made the request. Why didn't you call me directly?"

Byrd could hear Petterson moving around. "Hold on a minute," Petterson said.

Byrd could tell by the background noise that Petterson had walked outside. After several seconds, he came back on the line. "You still there, Danny?"

"Yep," Byrd responded.

"Listen, a lot is going on here. I'll try to give you the *Reader's Digest* version. Raelynn Michaels' mother and sister have been murdered in a town between El Paso and Fort Worth. They were brutally stabbed, and the sister's ex-husband is a prime suspect."

"Damn," Byrd said to himself.

"Double damn. If it's the ex, he took their daughter with him and is on the run. His family is all from the Seattle area, but he had a grandmother, or grandmother figure, anyway, he stayed with. Raelynn remembered her name and that she lived in a place called Bethlehem."

Byrd digested the information. "I may be on to her. Or

at least I've narrowed down the search. The short version is that she probably lives up on the state line in a community called Bethlehem. I'm not sure if she lives in Georgia or North Carolina."

"Great. Can you keep on the trail, or do I need to call North Carolina?" Petterson asked.

"I can run up that way. If she lives in North Carolina, I'll reach out to their State Bureau of Investigation. We work with them all the time," Byrd offered.

"Great. Thanks."

"So, Clete," Byrd started. "Why didn't you call me? You know I'd do anything I could to help y'all."

Petterson lowered his voice. "We looked at the map and thought Bethlehem was out of your area. And Major Crosby wants to make sure that this investigation is by the book. He specifically told me to get the on-call GBI agent in the area to run down this Gazaway woman."

Byrd was annoyed. "What the hell does he think I might do?"

Petterson chuckled. "You did cross an international border to rescue Addy and me. And the major had a front row seat."

Byrd shook his head. "Okay, I understand. I guess. Anyway, I'll head up to the state line and see what I can find."

"Thanks, Danny. I appreciate you." Petterson gave Byrd a description of Rudy Grant's Jeep, and then he was gone.

SATURDAY, DECEMBER 8, 2007
2:45 P.M. EST
BLAIRSVILLE, GEORGIA

Daniel Byrd pulled into a drive-thru and ordered a burger and tea to go. He had struggled with traffic all the way north as tourists roamed the North Georgia mountains looking at the last of the colorful leaves.

He gobbled down the burger as he pointed his G-ride down Fairview Church Road. He pulled into a gravel drive that served a small brick house. Byrd saw both Doc Farmer's government and personal cars underneath the carport.

Byrd climbed from his car and hustled to the door, cold in the mountain air after two hours in the warm car.

He knocked tentatively. The door was answered immediately by Doc. He was dressed in jeans and a flannel shirt. "Come on in out of the cold, Teddy," Doc said, using Byrd's nickname.

Byrd stepped through the doorway into the warm house.

"Thanks, Doc. Sorry to bother you on a Sunday, but I'm following up on a lead from that Texas kidnapping. I thought you might be able to help me out."

Doc looked toward his wife, sitting in the family room watching TV. "You're gonna cause me to get a divorce, Teddy."

"I don't need you to go with me, I just wanted to take a minute to pick your brain about somebody who might live up on the north side of the county," Byrd was quick to point out. "Have you ever heard of any Gazaways living around Bethlehem?"

"Up here? That's just a wide spot in the road."

Byrd nodded. "Supposedly, a woman named Gazaway,

who would be in her sixties or seventies, lives up here and has a connection to the suspect in the Texas kidnapping."

Doc turned and opened a drawer in the kitchen. He pulled out a phone book for the area. "Old investigator's trick. Look in the phone book."

Doc Farmer thumbed through the pages and searched the listings for anyone named Gazaway. After a moment, Doc gave a low whistle. "There is a listing for a Theral Gazaway up near Lake Nottely. That would probably be considered part of Bethlehem."

Doc wrote the address on a notepad by his phone. "Let me get a coat, and I'll ride up there with you," he said.

Byrd shook his head vigorously. "I'm not taking you away two days in a row. Hell, your wife might shoot me instead of you!"

Doc wasn't having it. "If you get in a jam up there, Tina will have my ass along with yours. You know you have a reputation for running off on your own."

"What? What are you talking about?" Byrd was offended.

Doc pulled on his heavy coat and pointed toward the door. "Go warm the car up while I kiss Doris."

SATURDAY, DECEMBER 8, 2007
3:17 P.M. EST
BETHLEHEM COMMUNITY, BLAIRSVILLE, GEORGIA

The ride to the Bethlehem community offered a spectacular view of the Blue Ridge Mountains as they took Murphy Highway north. The mountains were idyllic, like layers painted in different shades of blue—a reminder of why they were called the Blue Ridge Mountains.

Byrd followed Doc's directions as they turned off the main highway. They crossed over the south end of Lake Nottely and continued west into the afternoon sun. After a couple of miles, Doc directed Byrd down an old tar and gravel roadway that had more potholes than pavement.

Byrd slowed to avoid a deep pit in the road when Doc pointed at a small white house sitting near the road. There were no cars in view as Byrd and Doc examined the house. Byrd continued past the house and looked for a good spot to turn around. Once Byrd pulled off the side of the rough road, he turned to Doc. "What do you think?"

Doc shrugged. "The house looked dark. If you don't mind tipping your hand, we can go knock on the door and be sure."

"I don't know. This is a pretty long shot—more like a Hail Mary. Guess we don't have anything to lose, right?"

Byrd executed a three-point turn and headed back to the house. After hustling up to the door and knocking, he waited in the cold air for any sign of life. When no one came, he decided against leaving a business card. *Maybe I'll try again tomorrow*, he thought.

SATURDAY, DECEMBER 8, 2007
3:45 P.M. MST
EL PASO, TEXAS

Raelynn Michaels dragged her carry-on suitcase onto the airplane and waited to locate her seat as the single-file line of passengers crept down the aisle. She was in the back. That's what you get, she thought, when you book on the same day.

She left her handgun in her apartment. She didn't have

time to arrange bringing it onto the plane and preferred not to check a bag. And she thought, *I'd rather beat Rudy to death than shoot him.*

She found her seat in the last row, dropped into it, and buckled up. She shifted to let the passenger in the window seat scoot by her, then settled in for the long flight. Before the plane pushed back from the gate, she was sound asleep.

CHAPTER 11
HOMECOMING

SATURDAY, DECEMBER 8, 2007
7:11 P.M. EST
ELLIJAY, GEORGIA

Rudy Grant knew from the run-down look of the motel that the owners of the Mountain Vista Courts of Ellijay would ask no questions. After a basic check-in process, a card he penciled full of bogus information, he paid the clerk for a night in advance.

The clerk was a teenage boy with oily hair and a dirty T-shirt. Rudy needed pain medication and had nothing to lose by giving the boy a try.

"You ain't had nobody accidentally leave any pain medication in their room, have you?" Rudy asked.

The boy watched Rudy with hooded eyes. "You need a little something for the night? That's what you're saying?"

Rudy nodded.

"I can get you some oxys that I keep in the back for myself. I got disabled working at the farmer's market."

"How much?" Rudy asked.

"Hundred dollars."

"That's all I got left in cash. I need money for food for me and my daughter," Rudy was almost pleading. He didn't want to admit he had a stash of cash from Moe's. That was going to be his escape money.

The clerk frowned. "I'll give 'em to you for seventy-five."

"Done," Rudy said.

The boy pulled them from his hip pocket. The white pills were in a sandwich bag. "Go easy on these at first. They killed a friend of mine a couple of weeks ago. Maybe start with half of one."

Rudy grabbed the bag and pushed it into his jacket pocket.

He pulled his Jeep around to the rear of the neglected motel and took Madison into the room.

After locking Madison in, he went for drive-through food and then settled in for the night. He washed one of the pills down with tap water. He wanted to sleep, but the images of Thursday night kept coming back to him.

He looked at Madison, stretched out on the bed, and hoped that one day she would understand. He leaned over and kissed her on the forehead. "Good night, Madison."

He had washed his face and sat down on the other bed. He thought the pill was helping with the pain. He felt lightheaded as he tugged off his shirt. He leaned down to pull off his boots and collapsed on the floor.

SATURDAY, DECEMBER 8, 2007
9:01 P.M. EST
CANTON, GEORGIA

Daniel Byrd was walking into his little house outside of Canton when his Bureau cell phone rang. As the on-call agent for the weekend, he was bound to answer, no matter how exhausted he was.

"Byrd," he said into the phone.

"Danny? It's Raelynn Michaels. I need a ride. I'm at the Atlanta airport. I'm using one of the last payphones in America and didn't know who else to call."

SATURDAY, DECEMBER 8, 2007
8:33 P.M. CST
MONAHANS, TEXAS

Adeline Riley was exhausted. She threw her gun belt and hat on the motel bed. She dropped onto the lumpy mattress and began to tug at her left boot when her cell phone buzzed. She was tempted to ignore it until she had a chance to shower.

"Ranger Riley."

"Ranger, this is Mike Roach. I'm the on-call analyst here in Austin."

Adeline stopped trying to get her boots off and sat up on the bed. "Is this about the murders in Monahans?" she asked.

"I'm not sure," the voice on the other end of the phone sounded tentative. "I got an alert from one of the airlines. I thought it might connect up, but I wanted to check with you first."

Adeline was curious. "What is it?"

"I got an alert that one of your former task force officers used her undercover ID to book a flight to Atlanta. The airline didn't know it was an undercover license, but when it went through our system in Austin, it flagged."

Adeline began to work her boots back on. "Would the former agent be Raelynn Michaels?"

"Yes," Roach replied. "She used her undercover credit card and ID and boarded a flight about four hours ago. Aren't her family members the victims in Monahans?"

"Yes, they are," Adeline responded. "Can you email me copies of the information? I need to get my major on the line."

SATURDAY, DECEMBER 8, 2007
9:58 P.M. EST
ATLANTA, GEORGIA

Byrd nudged his Crown Vic up against the curb at the Atlanta airport less than an hour after the call. He turned on his blue lights and looked for Raelynn among the mass of travelers. He saw her waving and tugging her luggage toward his car. Byrd was surprised by how pale and tired she looked.

She ran up and threw her arms around Byrd. He took her bag, tossed it on the back seat of his car, and then jumped back inside. Raelynn was already buckling up in the passenger seat. "Thanks, Danny. I appreciate this."

Byrd pulled away from the curb, watching for traffic as he doused his blue lights and navigated the roads leading back to Interstate-75. "What are your plans? I'm guessing you think your brother-in-law is here in Georgia."

Raelynn stared straight ahead. "I was hoping to borrow a car and a gun. I know where he's going. I'm planning on getting my niece back and then putting some lead in Rudy's ass."

Byrd shook his head, keeping his eyes on the late-night traffic streaming north. "I can't help you do that. Despite what Major Crosby may think, I go by the book." Byrd glanced over, "Well, at least I try my best to keep it between the ditches."

Raelynn sighed deeply. "I know I'm asking a lot. And I wouldn't do it if there wasn't so much at stake. I just want to get Madison back safe and sound."

"Every law officer wants to do just that. I'm getting the Bureau involved. We'll activate the *A Child Is Missing* protocols. We'll have more help than we'll know what to do with."

Raelynn chewed her lower lip. "I guess that might be best. It may take more than me to get her back. Can you do that?"

Byrd shifted into the HOV lane. "It's already in motion. Addy called me."

"Well, damn!" Raelynn exclaimed. "I guess I'm going to need a job when I get back."

Byrd cut his eyes over. "Now you know how I felt when I got out of Mexico."

Raelynn crossed her arms and stared straight ahead.

"As of now, I'm the case agent for the GBI," Byrd observed. "Agents from my office are establishing a command post in Blairsville. The community of Bethlehem is a few miles north of there. We'll get up early in the morning and get to the command post about dawn."

Raelynn frowned. "Will I be allowed to observe, at least?"

Byrd kept his eyes on the road. "If I have any say-so, you will."

"Will you have any say-so?"

Byrd shook his head. "This thing is going to be big. I'll try, but no promises."

SATURDAY, DECEMBER 8, 2007
11:58 P.M. CST
MONAHANS, TEXAS

"Sheriff Sinclair, can we borrow two mattresses and some blankets from the jail?" Major Stetson Crosby asked.

"Sure, Major. What for?" Sinclair could sense something was going on. "Anything I can help with?"

Crosby frowned. "Deputy Michaels has run off to Georgia. I think she may know something she hasn't told us. I'm taking one of my people in the DPS King Air and heading to Georgia. Everyone else will stay on task. This may very well be a wild goose chase."

The sheriff made a call to the jail and ordered up the mattresses and blankets. "Anything else I can get you, Stetson?"

Sheriff Hallman approached the men. "I hear my deputy has run off to Georgia. Is that what y'all are talking about?"

Crosby rubbed his face. "Sorry, Sheriff. I should have briefed you. She has flown to Georgia, and I'm heading out to link up with the Georgia authorities. I should have called you."

Hallman exhaled. "No harm, Stetson. I know you've got a lot going on. And my deputy isn't helping."

Crosby turned to Sheriff Sinclair. "I guess we should make it three mattresses."

Sinclair nodded. "Anything else?"

"How about some sleep and a shower. I could use both." Crosby sounded weary.

"How much time before the plane gets here?" Sinclair asked.

"About thirty minutes," Crosby guessed after consulting his wristwatch.

Sinclair motioned for Crosby to follow. "We've got a staff shower in the locker room. Get on down there and rinse off. I can't help with the clean clothes. I don't have anything to fit the Jolly Green Giant."

As Crosby began to push on the door to the locker room, Ranger Lieutenant Clete Petterson came out of the shower. "Hey, Major. I thought I'd clean up. It sure helps."

Crosby nodded. "I got word to Addy Riley to do the same thing. She's going with me to Georgia. I want you to stay on top of this investigation. Whatever you need, I'll figure out a way to get it for you." Crosby paused and lowered his voice. "I want Addy to grab hold of Deputy Michaels and make sure she doesn't do anything rash."

Petterson nodded. "Rasher than running off to Atlanta without telling anybody? Addy will have her hands full."

Crosby paused on his way to the shower room. "I guess if I were in her shoes, I'd do the same thing. I really can't blame her."

"We're still Texans, no matter how civilized we've gotten," Clete remarked as he left the major to himself.

Crosby stood under the hot water and tried to stretch his stiff joints. The long hours in the operations center had worked on him. He had only napped a couple of times since the investigation had started.

Once he was dressed, Crosby rounded up Adeline Riley and Sheriff Hallman. The trio was driven to the airport by DPS troopers. Then the group of lawmen waited expectantly for the big state airplane to land.

They didn't have long to wait. The plane, huge compared

to the other aircraft at the Monahans airport, touched down with a squeak of rubber and taxied up to the group of highway patrol cars.

As soon as the big turboprop engines were stopped, the copilot dropped the access stairs and motioned the rangers on board. Troopers loaded the mattresses on the airplane. The rangers made beds on the available floor space. Sheriff Hallman opted for one of the reclining seats.

"Major, I reckon this is the first flight I've made for the great State of Texas where the passengers brought beds on board," the copilot remarked. Dean Powell had been flying DPS aircraft for over ten years. He shook hands with Major Crosby and then turned to return to the cockpit.

"We've been on the hunt for over forty-eight hours," Crosby observed. "It may be our only chance to get any rest for a while."

Powell looked the arrangement over. "I might mention to our Captain that we ought to get something like this to keep in the hangar. It might come in handy later."

"How long before we get to Georgia?" Adeline Riley asked.

Powell looked at his chart. Powell still relied on the old-fashioned style of navigation. "It should take us about six hours to get to Chattanooga, but there's a big weather front moving across that area. Nothing substantial, just the usual 'winter in the south' type front. If we have to divert, it could take us up to eight hours. We'll have to dodge around and hope we can stay ahead of the storms. When we get to Chattanooga, we'll need to quench the powerful thirst this beast will have by then. With any luck, we should be able to get to Blairsville around sunup."

Crosby stretched his six-foot-six frame along the biggest section of floor space. He tried to get his long frame on the jail mattress, but no matter how he scrunched up, his feet hung off.

"Just get us there. We have a different storm brewing up in those North Georgia mountains." Crosby pulled his hat over his face.

Powell climbed back into the right seat of the black and white airplane and gave the pilot a thumbs-up. The pilot had the big turboprop engines fired up, and within seconds, the airplane was headed for the active runway.

Crosby was asleep before they got in the air.

CHAPTER 12
THINGS HIT THE FAN

Daniel Byrd parked his government-issued Crown Vic next to his little BMW Z3. The carport was barely wide enough to take both cars. "Come on in," Byrd said. "I'll go make sure the bed in my guest room has clean sheets."

Raelynn tossed her bag into the room, doing her best to avoid bowling Byrd over as he changed the fitted sheet and made the bed, and then collapsed on Byrd's couch.

"I missed seeing your house last trip. It's nice, Danny." Raelynn observed. "Where are your Christmas decorations?"

"That's right, you had to rush back to Texas," Byrd said, ignoring her question. "Do you want to talk?"

Raelynn looked the house over. "How can you afford a place like this?" she asked.

"It was willed to me by my uncle. I figured the little bit that was owed on the house would amount to nothing compared to the rent I was paying."

Raelynn nodded. "That makes sense."

"Do you want something to drink? I can fix up something,

and then we can sit on the porch. The water running in the creek is peaceful," Byrd offered.

"Sure," Raelynn responded. "What kind of bourbon do you have?"

"Come take a look. People bring brown liquor to parties and whatnot. I'm a vodka drinker myself."

Raelynn found a brand she liked and poured a stiff drink on ice. Byrd mixed his drink and joined her as they walked to the front porch. They were bundled up against the damp cold of a Georgia winter, even if it was technically fall. There was a porch swing that Byrd's uncle had installed. "Take the swing. I'm in good standing," Byrd said. "I've been in the car all day."

Raelynn took him up on the offer. "Sure. I'm dead on my feet."

Raelynn swung gently. She sipped her drink and took in the sounds, smells, and sights of Byrd's home. "You're isolated out here. And the running water does make this place seem very peaceful."

"Tomorrow you can see the creek that's right down there below us," Byrd said as he pointed off into the darkness.

Raelynn quietly sipped her drink.

"How are you holding up?" Byrd asked.

Raelynn hung her head. "I guess, under the circumstances, I'm doing pretty good. I haven't had time to think about a service for Mama and Rosalind. I haven't processed everything. I just want to get Madison back, and then we'll start making plans."

"Are you and Madison close?" Byrd asked.

Raelynn sipped the bourbon again. "As much as you can be close to people in this job. I go over to Mama's as often as I can." She stopped. "I *went* over to Mama's, I should say.

It's hard to think of them in the past tense. And Mama's house was where Madison lived the last four or five years. She's a sweet girl, like *her* Momma was, and seems to love her Aunt Rae."

Byrd noticed that Rae was crying. "Sorry, I shouldn't have brought it up."

Raelynn shook her head. "Nope, you're fine. It's still pretty raw. I didn't get to say goodbye to Mom or Rosalind. I thank the good Lord the rangers kept me out of Mama's house."

Byrd grimaced.

Raelynn leaned back in her seat. "In our line of work, we see people every day living out the same circumstances. I know in my head that this kind of thing happens and the families have to deal with it while we investigate what is usually the worst day of their lives." She wiped a stray tear and looked off into the woods. "Knowing you're not unique doesn't make it hurt any less."

"Would talking about them help?" Byrd wondered.

Raelynn shrugged. "You know what hurts the worst?" She met Byrd's eyes for a moment before she glanced away. "I couldn't protect them. I wanted to protect people in this job, but I couldn't protect two of the people who mean the most to me."

Byrd nodded without speaking. He thought it best to let her talk.

Raelynn finished her drink. "Let's go back inside where I can fix another drink. It's colder than an Eskimo's butt out here."

Byrd held the door for Raelynn as she went back in the house and found the bourbon bottle. She poured herself a double. "I need to sleep tonight. And I tell sad stories better when I'm drunk."

"Wouldn't you be better off back home?" Byrd asked. "You have a lot of family things to deal with right now."

Raelynn raised an eyebrow and gave Byrd a look that stopped the conversation.

Byrd followed her into his living room. "Why don't you tell me about your family. I don't even have any idea where Monahans is?"

Byrd listened as she talked about her family. Growing up in West Texas, fighting with her sister who was close to her in age, and navigating the rough waters from teenager to adult. The liquor was having an effect by the time she got to her law enforcement work.

"I thought I could make a difference. Every crime I came into contact with was related to drugs. So, volunteering to work undercover seemed logical," Raelynn observed.

Byrd nodded.

"Somehow, I believed that, by committing myself to that job fully, I could keep my family safe. Turns out, I might as well have worked shoveling cow manure. Everything I've done, and they were still victims of a bastard who couldn't keep his life straight." Raelynn had begun to cry again. Byrd couldn't tell from her voice or her posture, but the tears were welling up in her eyes and quietly streaking down her face. "My sister helped people. My Mama helped people, too, in her own way. I haven't done much other than put people in jail."

Byrd put his hand on hers. "Working undercover can suck the humanity out of you. I know that. It's a good thing you're out of that world. But you helped people along the way. People you'll never know about who kicked drugs because of you. Parents who have a few more days or months with their addicted child. Kids who didn't suffer abuse because you put their parents in jail."

Raelynn looked into Byrd's eyes. "But did it change anything? Is the world better?"

Byrd sighed. "That's a question I can't answer. I don't claim to understand this world we live in."

"What kind of God would let Rudy kill my mother and my sister? Can you tell me that?" Raelynn asked.

"I don't know. But I do know that Satan is as real as God. Somehow, this fight between good and evil is the way this world works. And without evil, we wouldn't appreciate good. Without darkness, we wouldn't enjoy the light. That's why we fight the fight as cops. We know how evil evil can be."

Raelynn sipped the bourbon and then shook the glass of ice. "I guess that makes sense in the bigger picture."

Byrd leaned forward on the couch. He held his drink in both hands. "It hurts when it's close to home."

Raelynn hung her head. "The worst thing of all is the new name my mom and sister have."

Byrd looked up. "Huh?"

"Victim. They'll be forever known in the official reports as 'victim.'"

Raelynn finished her drink. "Danny, I really appreciate you taking care of me. I didn't have much of a plan when I got on that airplane in El Paso."

"Come on. Let's get you to bed. I'm going to let you rest." Byrd stood and helped her to her feet. "Tomorrow will be a big day, I hope."

Raelynn stretched out on the bed and flopped backwards. In seconds, she was snoring quietly. Byrd put her feet up on the bed, pulled her boots off, and covered her with a comforter. He pulled her door closed and got himself ready for bed.

SUNDAY, DECEMBER 9, 2007
9:01 A.M. EST
BLAIRSVILLE, GEORGIA

Daniel Byrd, dressed in a dark suit and tie, escorted Raelynn Michaels into the command post. He'd regretted ditching his overcoat in the trunk of his car, even if only for the short walk to the CP. After a late night of drinking and talking, Byrd felt sorry for not being able to let Raelynn sleep late. He had discovered that Raelynn had only slept a couple of hours, anyway.

As the case agent, the dubious distinction he would have in this matter as the first GBI agent to open an investigation, he knew he would need to be at the command post at dawn. He woke Rae at 5:30 a.m., and they had rushed through coffee and toast before getting on the road.

As Byrd and Raelynn looked over the command post, Tina Blackwell motioned Byrd over to the central table with the map.

"Is that Deputy Michaels?" Tina asked.

Byrd nodded. "She'll be okay. She's a tough one."

Blackwell pointed Byrd toward the pilot's lounge. "Find her a place to sit in the lounge and tell her she has the run of the CP—as long as she doesn't try to interfere."

Byrd shook his head. "She won't. She knows running off to Georgia was a mistake. She is just worried about her niece."

"Okay," Blackwell said. "I need to brief the director. Stay close in case he has questions."

Byrd nodded as he escorted Raelynn to the lounge.

SUNDAY, DECEMBER 9, 2007
9:17 A.M. EST
BLAIRSVILLE, GEORGIA

Tina Blackwell, Special Agent in Charge of the GBI Gainesville office, had been contacted by the Texas DPS shortly after Daniel Byrd had called. Using pointers gleaned by the Texas DPS Intelligence unit, Texas Rangers found several locations where Rudy had used his gas card. The trail was pointing to Georgia.

Blackwell decided there was enough information to activate the Child Abduction Response Team. The word had gone out as soon as GBI Headquarters got Blackwell's call. The CART was established to pull together individuals from various state agencies who are trained and prepared to respond to a missing, endangered, or abducted child. Agents from the GBI, troopers from the Georgia State Patrol, game wardens from the Department of Natural Resources, and officers from other state agencies with special resources would soon converge on the mountain town.

Blackwell had contacted the Union County Sheriff and asked for a location for a command post. The sheriff had recommended the Blairsville Airport. The Blairsville Airport offices, or fixed base operations as it was known, were housed in a brown building with a tin roof and stone accents. Inside the facility was cozy and functional. As it turns out, it was also an ideal location for a command post.

When Blackwell arrived at the airport, GBI Agents, Troopers, and game wardens were already arriving to receive assignments.

Blairsville, the county seat of Union County, sits about ten miles from North Carolina. The county has some of the most treacherous terrain in the State of Georgia, and Brasstown Bald, the highest mountain in Georgia, rises in southeast Union County, straddling the Towns County line. The central and northern portion of Union County is located in the Hiwassee River basin. The area could be as much as ten to fifteen degrees cooler than the rest of the state.

The Union County sheriff, Andrew Wayne Smith, rallied his department to support the GBI operation. Smith was a retired trooper who'd been in law enforcement his entire adult life. The long, lean man kept a spit cup handy for his chewing tobacco juice. At seventy, he was one of the longest-serving law officers in the state. He kept his head shaved after chemotherapy had taken his thick gray hair, and he found he liked the simple, clean look. His chief deputy had a different opinion on his hairstyle choice. The chief argued Sheriff Smith had embraced the baldness as a way to give cancer the middle finger.

Smith had arranged to use the airport offices for a command post and was busy helping set up the operations center. Civilian intelligence analysts, scientists from the GBI Crime Lab, computer support technicians, and people to provide any other kind of technical support were waiting patiently to help.

GBI Director Olie "Buster" Hicks, wearing his trademark dark gray fedora, was sipping his third cup of coffee for the morning as he pushed his way through the door of the temporary offices. Hicks found Blackwell hunched over a map of Union County, surrounded by uniformed officers. Blackwell looked up long enough to acknowledge Hicks. "Hey, boss. I'm putting some of these patrol cars out at some key points. Then I can bring you up to date."

Blackwell looked over the make-shift command post as she finished assigning the uniformed officers. The lights were sufficiently bright, and there were a couple of usable tables, including the one with the map. She knew Hicks would leverage his authority to have the phone company drop additional lines into the temporary offices. She had already discovered cell phones were useless in these mountains.

Technicians were busy installing radio consoles for the three primary channels needed to coordinate the operations. There would be a station for the GBI radio system, the Georgia State Patrol system, and the Union County Sheriff's Office radios. Each agency would assign a radio operator to man the equipment. Despite the mandates of the 9/11 Commission, individual officers from different agencies still struggled with talking to each other.

As the deputies and troopers filed out to take up their positions, Blackwell motioned the Director of the GBI over. "Here's what we have at the moment. This thing is, of course, very fluid." She pointed to the map. "This area up near Lake Nottely is where we think our suspect has family. It's a community called Bethlehem. Danny Byrd and Doc Farmer located a house yesterday afternoon that may be our suspect's grandmother's. They knocked on the door, but nobody answered. Both agents had been working overtime Friday and Saturday and were exhausted. They made the call to pull off and wait for more information." Blackwell glanced at Hicks. "That's a call I support, by the way."

"I concur," Hicks conceded. "As you mentioned, this is a fluid situation. Those are a couple of good agents. I won't be doing any Monday morning quarterbacking. What do Danny and Doc think about the house?" Hicks asked.

"It looked like a typical family house. It's old, probably around sixty years old from the look Danny got. Maybe a two-bedroom and single bath. There weren't any cars there at the time. Danny stopped short of looking in the windows or prowling around the yard."

"That's reasonable."

"He's here if you have any other questions," Blackwell offered. "At the time, we only had an indication the suspect might be headed this way." Blackwell looked grim. "Texas DPS was able to get records from his gas card purchases. He's coming our way like a homing pigeon. The house Danny and Doc found isn't a sure bet, but it's the best thing we have going."

"Any chance he's already here?" Hicks mused aloud.

Blackwell nodded. "Sure. He could have gotten in here yesterday or even this morning. We've kept all uniform cars away from the house. I've got agents trying to establish surveillance of the house as we speak. It's rough country, Director. We'll be lucky to get an eye on the house."

"What is our backup plan if we can't get a look at the house?"

"We'll have to rely on periodic drive-bys. I'll have the agents switch cars as often as they can. We're reaching out to a couple of the drug units we work closely with to access some of their cars."

Hicks nodded. "Good work. I guess that's why we're bringing you to Atlanta."

Blackwell grinned. "I'll not turn down a promotion, but being the SAC in a good office is a damned good job. I'm going to miss this kind of action."

"What about the victim's family member? The Texas deputy? Are we keeping her apprised of the situation?" Hicks asked.

Blackwell frowned. "She's here."

"Here? How did she get here?" Hicks asked.

"She called Danny from the Atlanta airport. It seems she snuck out of Texas and flew to Atlanta last night."

"Why did she call Danny? Do they know each other?" Hicks asked.

Blackwell wasn't sure if she was angry or amused. "They know each other. She was the Texas undercover on the liquid meth we picked off in Woodstock last year."

"Will that be a problem?"

Blackwell shook her head. "I'm having Danny keep an eye on her. She thought Danny would keep quiet, but he called me on the way to the airport."

"Good." Hicks raised an eyebrow. "With Danny, it could go either way."

Hicks took another sip of his coffee. "What do you think our chances of getting this man bottled up are?"

Blackwell pointed out the window. "The Rangers are sure enough that their boy is coming here that a plane will be landing any minute with some of their people."

Hicks nodded. "The Director of the Texas DPS called me as I was on the way up here. Before I lost cell phone coverage, he told me Major Crosby and another ranger are on the way. The El Paso County sheriff is along too. They'll be here to monitor the situation."

Blackwell pointed out the window at the airport ramp. "We've got a chopper from the GSP Aviation Unit waiting for a mission, and I got word Arlow Turner, the DEA pilot, is on the way up to help. He has a military-grade Forward Looking Infrared unit hooked up on his plane. We're hoping the weather doesn't ground all our air support."

Hicks looked at the steel gray, Georgia sky. "It's winter in Georgia. We'll be lucky if we don't get rain."

CHAPTER 13
A CHILD IS MISSING

SUNDAY, DECEMBER 9, 2007
9:21 A.M. EST
BLAIRSVILLE, GEORGIA

Rudy knew Granny Gazaway would be in church. She always went to Sunday school and then the regular Sunday service. She was a member of a "hardshell" Baptist church, fundamentalists short of handling snakes, and wouldn't be seen leaving early.

He pulled his Jeep as far around behind the house as he could. Then he covered the Jeep with a tarp he found in the carport. Rudy used his pocket knife to force her front door lock and invited himself in.

He sat Madison on the couch in Granny's sitting room, propped her doll up beside her, and turned on the TV. Madison stared at the TV without looking or even acknowledging Rudy.

Rudy turned the thermostat down before he rambled around Granny's cupboard searching for food. He settled for chicken noodle soup. After heating the soup in the microwave, he sat in the dark living room waiting for Granny to return home.

SUNDAY, DECEMBER 9, 2007
9:44 A.M. EST
BLAIRSVILLE, GEORGIA

Blackwell and Hicks watched as the black and white Texas DPS King Air dropped from the overcast sky and touched down at the Blairsville airport. The big airplane stopped effortlessly and taxied toward the FBO. Once the King Air cleared the runway, it was followed closely by a Rockwell Aero Commander piloted by Arlow Turner. The King Air taxied up to the Fixed Base Operations Center as the little, in comparison, Aero Commander bounced along the taxiway behind it.

Once the steps for the King Air were deployed, the Texas contingent climbed down and stretched their legs. Major Crosby stopped at the door. "You might want to get some accommodations. We may be here overnight," he told the two crewmen.

Dean Powell pulled the headphones off and hung them on the control yoke. "Our boss says that we should stay here as long as you need us. We'll hustle up a ride to the nearest motel and leave a number with the command post."

Crosby followed Adeline Riley and Jim Hallman as they headed for the FBO. Each of the Texans pulled their western hats on tight and bundled up for the short walk to the building. Hallman led the way into the main room.

Tina Blackwell extended a hand. She looked the group over as they circled the table with the map. "You must be Sheriff Hallman," she guessed.

Hallman smiled. "My reputation has preceded me?"

Blackwell smiled back. "Nope. Everyone else has a ranger's badge."

Hallman looked back. Amused at the obvious conclusion. "You got it. And the tall man is Major Crosby. Then," he pointed to the other ranger, "this is Ranger Adeline Riley."

"I've read all your names in reports filed on that smuggling group. Even yours, sheriff. I'm Tina Blackwell, the Special Agent in Charge of the GBI regional office for this area." Tina Blackwell shook hands all around.

Crosby, aware that he was wearing the same clothes he had on last Friday, pointed to the map. He was ready to get things moving. "Where are we on this?"

Blackwell gave Crosby and the other Texans a briefing on the situation. "Our director is here somewhere. You may want to meet with him. But we're committed to bringing this man in."

Crosby rubbed his chin as he asked. "Is there anything we can do to help?"

Tina hesitated. "Go ahead," Crosby said. "We can't fix it if we don't know what it is."

"I've been on the phone with the sheriff out there in Texas," Blackwell said. "He says the district attorney will not file charges until we have the DNA results back. That may be a couple of more days. Right now, if we catch Rudy, we don't have any charges."

"If he has the girl with him?" Crosby asked.

Blackwell shook her head. "He's violated a Texas TPO. That's something we can hold him for. And enough to get a search warrant to look for the girl once we find him. It would be cleaner to have a murder warrant in hand."

Crosby tipped his white hat back on his head. "I see what you mean. I can ask the lab, but I know they're doing all they can."

Blackwell was grasping at straws. "Anything one of your rangers could take a warrant for with the information they have in hand?"

"I'll get on a phone when we have service," Cosby promised.

Blackwell shook her head. "You'll have to have a landline up here. We're getting more phone lines as soon as we can, but I can find you one to use."

"What's the chance of getting some motel rooms?" Crosby asked. "We all need to freshen up."

Blackwell frowned. "We'll work it out. And I'll get a couple of uniform cars to shuttle you to the closest one. Local businesses are beginning to find out about this manhunt. We've already had motels and restaurants offer their service for free."

Crosby nodded. "Thanks, but make sure you take care of your people first."

Blackwell turned to find the Texans a driver or two. She looked back long enough to say, "We will. Most of these cops live close by. We'll have a few from out of the area needing quarters, but we'll work it out."

Adeline spoke up. "Has Raelynn Michaels made it here yet? She's one of my best friends, and it was her mother and sister who were murdered. She desperately wants to get her niece back before something bad happens.'

"Danny Byrd is with her in the pilot's lounge. She slept at his house last night." Director Hicks said. He stuck out his hand to Adeline. "I'm Buster Hicks, the GBI's director. We are at your disposal."

Hicks turned and shook with Major Crosby and the sheriff. "You just tell us what you need."

Crosby nodded. "Thanks, director. We appreciate the southern hospitality, but we plan to stay out of your way.

Once our boy is in custody, we'll fly his daughter back to Texas. And, once Mr. Grant is in custody, we'll wait for the process to get him extradited to Texas. Where, good Lord willing, we'll get him sentenced to death."

Hicks winked. "We see eye to eye. Once you're cleaned up, find a chair or a desk and join in. We won't turn down any help."

Arlow Turner ambled into the center of the room to join the crowd. He was known to the Texans after his help with the investigation of the Warren smuggling operations. He'd gotten considerable heat from his bosses at the DEA for helping out on a state and local operation. He extended a hand to Tina Blackwell.

"Arlow Turner with the DEA Airwing. I'm here to offer any help I can."

Tina recognized the name. "Great to have you here. Any chance you could put eyes on the target house for us? I know this weather is getting messy, though. You be the judge."

Arlow looked out the window. "I had to crash land a few weeks ago in weather way worse than this. Is there anyone who can point out the house for me?"

Blackwell pointed to a young agent drinking coffee in the corner. "Can you go find Doc Farmer. He's seen the house and he knows this county like the back of his hand."

SUNDAY, DECEMBER 9, 2007
12:15 P.M. EST
BETHLEHEM COMMUNITY, BLAIRSVILLE, GEORGIA

Rudy had dozed off. He blinked awake as he heard the carport door of Granny's little house opening. He heard the screen door slam and the wooden door as it was pressed into place with a shoulder and then locked. Rudy had seen Granny push that back door closed a hundred times, having to use her whole body to lean into it. She had told him it helped to keep the cold out.

Rudy knew she'd hear the TV and probably go for her old shotgun. He called her name preemptively. "Granny, it's Rudy. I know I ain't been here in a while. Me and Madison have come for a visit."

Stoop-shouldered, barely five feet tall with gray hair tied tightly behind her head, Granny came into the living room. She was wearing a dark colored dress with a white blouse, most of which was hidden by the bulky coat she wore in the winter.

"Lord, have mercy! I haven't seen little Madison in a coon's age. Come here, girl, and let me see you," Granny said. "Why is it so cold in here? Did you leave my door standing open?"

Granny stepped into the dark room where Madsion sat in front of the TV. She peered into the room to see Madison on the couch. After a moment, she turned to Rudy.

"Boy, what in the devil's name have you done?" Granny shrieked.

SUNDAY, DECEMBER 9, 2007
12:21 P.M. EST
BLAIRSVILLE, GEORGIA

Doc Farmer had no love of flying, particularly in bad weather, but he saw how important it would be to get a look at the house. If the girl were there, the agents needed to move quickly to save her life. The sky was still overcast, and the air felt colder to Doc as he hustled to the DEA plane.

Doc reluctantly climbed into the side door of the Aero Commander and crouched as he navigated the aisle and dropped into the second seat in the cockpit. "I figure you sit on the left-hand side?" Doc questioned.

"In this weather, I will. I'm going to give you a rundown on this box right in front of you." Arlow clicked a switch, and the screen in front of Farmer came alive. In seconds, Doc could make out images of the airplanes on the ground in front of them."

"This thing," Arlow explained, "is a military grade Forward Looking Infrared system. It'll let us see in the dark based on the heat a human body generates. It will also work in the daytime, to a certain extent. There is a chance we can see what's going on inside the house."

Doc frowned. "Wouldn't we need a warrant for that?"

Arlow shook his head. "The girl being in danger and the probable cause we have now gives us exigent circumstances."

Doc rotated a wheel, and the screen zoomed in. He clicked a switch, and the brightness level changed. He found a lever that moved the picture left and right as well as up and down.

"You're getting the idea," Arlow said. He turned back to Doc. "Hey, you're Danny Byrd's buddy. I've heard him talk about you."

Doc glanced over. "Don't believe anything he says."

Arlow started the two turboprop engines and taxied the high-wing airplane out onto the taxiway. He opened the heater vent all the way. "It's going to get cold up here. We'll be orbiting at about four thousand feet."

Doc wrapped his big barn coat around his chest and then tightened the seat and shoulder harness.

"Aero Commander November 355 to Blairsville traffic. Departing runway 26." Arlow announced on the aviation radio.

Arlow deftly pointed the plane toward runway two-six and worked the throttles through their paces. Then he took the pressure off the toe brakes, lined up on the runway, and let the big engines launch the plane into the sky.

The heavy airplane bucked as it picked up speed on the small runway. On the fifth bounce, the airplane left the ground. Doc was surprised by how low the cloud cover was. "I hope this mess doesn't drop any lower," Doc said.

"Me, too. If the clouds get down on the deck, we'll be wasting our time and the government's money."

CHAPTER 14
FAMILY SECRETS

"Boy, you've done got yourself into a world of do-do. What are you wantin' from me?" Granny asked. She was pacing in the kitchen while Madison sat on the couch in the living room.

"I've gotta ditch my car and find somewhere to hide, Granny Gazaway. I was hoping you could help me out. At least give me a place to hide up here." Rudy was leaning over the kitchen counter, looking out the window.

Granny Gazaway had little pity for her adopted grandson. "Boy, about all I can do for you is let you take my car. My neighbor told me at church that some laws was here last night lookin' around my house."

"Damn it! I wonder how they got onto me so quick?"

"I guess you ain't no professional criminal. And I guess them laws will be comin' up here again before long. Maybe I can buy you a little time, but that's about all."

"I'll leave your car close to the bus station in Marietta. I'm taking the bus to Canada," Rudy told her.

"Canada?" Granny asked.

Rudy nodded. "Canada won't send me back on a charge with the death penalty. They don't believe in it up there. I figure I'll live up there in the mountains and go off the grid."

Granny was incredulous. "Are you sure about that?"

"I seen it on a TV show. They've got strong opinions about such as that up there." Rudy was confident his legal information was up to date.

"You better go far and fast. Them laws catch up to you and they'll most likely fry you," Granny observed.

"Have you got a gun around here, Granny?" Rudy asked.

She stared at him for a moment. "I reckon I got a gun I can give you, if you'll use your head. Don't use it unless you have to. And then, I recommend you use it on yourself." Granny looked out the back window. "I used the gun to kill your paw-paw. That old bastard kept beating me till I couldn't take it no more."

Rudy was shocked. "You killed Paw-Paw?"

Granny squinted at Rudy. "You better never breathe it to nobody." She pointed out the back window. "I buried him back there by the old shed. I growed some really good tomatoes on that spot."

Granny climbed onto a folding step and pulled a paper sack out of the top cabinet. She stepped back down with some difficulty and passed the brown paper sack to Rudy. Rudy opened the sack and found a worn Colt .45 1911 model. There was a box of bullets with four missing rounds. Rudy gave Granny a quizzical look.

"That's all the bullets I needed. I put the ones I didn't use back in the box." Granny was unapologetic.

Rudy hefted the gun and pulled the empty magazine out. He had once handled a gun during his time in the Navy, but he'd never fired one. He worked the mechanism back and forth. Then he stuck the gun in his belt and put the box of bullets in his front pocket.

"I guess paw-paw didn't suffer much?" Rudy asked.

"Not enough, that's for sure. My back still bothers me from digging that hole I put him in. That old bastard laid on that floor you're standing on and bled all over the place. I finally put a bullet in his mouth to shut him up. A damned grown man that couldn't die like anything but a coward."

Rudy shook his head. "I guess he needed it."

Granny frowned. "I can tell you what he didn't need. He didn't need to hit me again! It took me the better part of two days to clean the blood up and get his brains out of the tile floor."

Granny gave Rudy a hard look. "And it sounds like to me you ain't no prize, your own self. Boy, I'm thinking you need to just get on out of my house."

"Granny, I just need a place to rest for a day or two. Just 'till the heat is off."

Granny spat into the sink. "Boy, what you done, the heat won't never be off."

Rudy turned toward the window again. He didn't want to face Granny when he asked her, "You know where I might get a little meth? I'm runnin' on empty and I sure could use something to pick me up."

Granny shook her head. "Boy, you shore are a disappointment. I reckon that Rutledge boy up in Hot House. That's over by Mineral Bluff. He's my daughter's boy. You and him used to play when your momma sent you here to visit."

Rudy rubbed his hands together. "I sure could use something. Do you have his phone number? Maybe I can call him and work something out."

Granny walked out of the kitchen, shaking her head. "You sure are a disappointment, Rudy."

Granny came back with the Fannin County phone book. She tossed it to Rudy. "His woman is named Joyce Rutledge. The phone's in her name."

Rudy quickly found the number. His hand was shaking so badly that he first dialed the wrong number. He got it right on the second try.

"Hello?" Rudy heard Rutledge answer.

"This is a grandson of Granny Gazaway over in Bethlehem. I hear you might be able to help a feller get his head right."

It wouldn't occur to Rutledge that he was being set up. He answered honestly. "I can get a feller a touch if you got some greenbacks."

"I got a little. I guess I can scratch up enough to get a touch. Can we meet up somewhere?" Rudy asked.

Granny tapped Rudy on the arm. "Ask him to come by the house. Tell him it'll be worth his time."

Rudy put his hand over the microphone. "What for?"

"You need a different car. That ole boy's so dumb we can talk him into a trade," Granny suggested. Rudy realized Granny was right. Her car would probably be on a lookout list along with his Jeep.

Rudy thought it over. "Can you meet me over here at Granny Gazaway's house?" he said into the phone.

"I reckon I can, but that'll cost extra." Rutledge was already counting his money.

Rudy thought it over. "I'll have the cash and I'll make the extra drive worth the trip."

Rudy hung up and then wiped his face with a towel he found hanging on the counter. *Soon,* he thought, *this will all be over.*

SUNDAY, DECEMBER 9, 2007
12:33 P.M. EST
BETHLEHEM COMMUNITY, BLAIRSVILLE, GEORGIA

It took less than fifteen minutes for Arlow to get the airplane in the vicinity of Granny Gazaway's house. Then Doc had to figure out which house it was. From the air, the little houses, built using similar floor plans over seventy years ago, looked the same.

"I can't tell which one's which from up here," Doc complained. "All these roofs look the same."

Arlow pointed at the road below them. "This is the main road off Murphy Highway. I'm going to go back to where it starts. We'll follow the road till you spot a landmark you know."

"That'll work," Doc said.

Arlow rolled the plane around slowly, conscious of the attention he might draw at this low level, and pointed the plane back toward Nottely Lake. Once over the water, he turned again and headed west.

Doc was able to follow the road and figured out which house was the Gazaway residence. Doc spotted Granny's Buick in front of Granny's house. He also saw something under the edge of her carport covered by a blue tarp.

"GBI 34 to the command post," Doc called into the GBI radio.

Tina Blackwell answered. "What do you have, Doc?"

"There is something under the carport covered by a blue tarp. It wasn't there yesterday. Can the ground troops make it out?" Doc asked.

Another voice broke in. "209 to 34, it looks to be big

enough to be the suspect's Jeep. We've tried to get more, but there's a Buick parked right in the way."

Doc tried to think of a way to get a better look, but nothing came to mind.

As the Aero Commander circled the area of northern Union County, a light rain began to fall. Arlow adjusted the engine settings and slowed the twin-engine plane to conserve fuel.

"Aren't you going to turn on the wipers?" Doc asked.

Arlow glanced over at Doc, "This airplane doesn't have wipers."

"Why not?" Doc asked.

"We're not supposed to fly in this kind of weather," Arlow said with a smile.

Doc wasn't sure if he was kidding or not.

SUNDAY, DECEMBER 9, 2007
12:48 P.M. EST
BETHLEHEM COMMUNITY, BLAIRSVILLE, GEORGIA

Jerry Rutledge made the trip to Bethlehem much more slowly than he had anticipated. There were troopers and deputy sheriffs parked all along the main highways, parked in such a way that they could examine every car coming by their checkpoint. Rutledge, under other circumstances, would have been stopped for doing forty miles an hour on a four-lane highway like the Mountain Parkway. He drove his rusty Toyota as though it were loaded with eggs. Luckily for him, every other car on the road was carefully observing the speed limit.

Rutledge stopped at a traffic light controlling the turn onto the Murphy Highway on the western edge of Blairsville. The intersection was the center for fast food for the little town, but now, along with drive-thru eateries, there were marked patrol cars on every corner. When he slowly made the turn, he saw other police cars parked along the Murphy highway.

He took the highway north for a few miles until the turnoff for Pat Colwell Road. Rutledge kept his eyes peeled for the little tar and gravel street where Granny Gazaway's home was located.

He was thirty minutes late when he pulled into the driveway. He pulled up close behind Granny's Buick. He vaguely remembered the house, though it looked much smaller, when he came here to play as a child. He remembered a redheaded kid named Rudy had lived at Granny's house a couple of summers. Rutledge's mother told him that Granny Gazaway was Rutledge's granny. They played cowboys and Indians, rambled through the woods behind the house, and rode bikes all over the community.

Rutledge smelled of sweat and meth as he climbed out of his beater and, looking all around, made his way to the carport door. He hoped all the cops would be gone when he made the trip back.

CHAPTER 15
WAITING IS THE HARD PART

Daniel Byrd sought out Tina Blackwell. He felt like he wasn't contributing to the case.

Byrd found her stooped over the county map, examining the roads in the vicinity. "Tina, I'm the case agent for this investigation. I feel like I should be doing more."

Tina shook her head. "The boss wants you out of the line of fire. Since you and Deputy Michaels have a rapport, I think it's best if you stay with her. This could go a lot of ways, and not many of them are good."

"Has anyone issued a warrant for this Grant guy?" Byrd asked.

Tina shook her head. "No. Right now, we are playing a waiting game. We wait until he leaves with the girl. Or we get word from Texas that they have his DNA at the crime scene. Either way, it's looking like a long haul."

Byrd nodded. "I understand. I sure would like to help, though."

Tina stopped talking as two suited men entered the

command post. "Shit! Looks like the FBI. There must be a press conference nearby," she observed dryly.

Byrd recognized the agent leading the way. He was from the Gainesville Resident Agency and was notorious for spending his workdays in the gym. He rarely showed up during an investigation, waiting until the state and local officers resolved the situation before making an appearance.

Tina pointed her chin at the newcomers. "Okay, case agent. Deal with the feds."

Byrd groaned. "Damn."

Byrd intercepted the two men as they looked around the room. "What's up?" Byrd said, addressing the lead agent.

"Tom Jenkins, with the FBI. We're going to need a phone line and a desk here. We'll be using it until our mobile command post arrives." Jenkins shrugged off his overcoat, and for a moment, Byrd thought the federal agent would try to hand it to him.

Byrd nodded. "We're adding lines as fast as the phone company can work. You might try getting set up over at the sheriff's office. They probably have some free phones at the jail."

Jenkins shook his head. "Kidnapping is a federal offense. We have jurisdiction. We'll be taking the lead."

"That only applies if the victim is transported across state lines. We don't have any proof that the girl was brought to Georgia. In fact, all our witnesses indicate otherwise. The suspect has family in Washington state."

"Then what is all this activity about?" Jenkins was perplexed.

"Just covering our bases," Byrd offered.

Jenkins frowned. "I guess we'll go to the sheriff's office

and call our office in Atlanta. That's not what we were told—we were told the girl is here in Georgia."

Byrd looked Jenkins in the eye. "Not as far as I know. And I'm the case agent."

"Byrd, isn't it?" Jenkins pulled his overcoat back on.

Byrd fished a business card from his credential case. "Here. This has my cell phone number. Call me anytime for an update."

The two men turned and left the building.

Tina gave Byrd a quizzical look. "What are you up to?"

"I haven't had cell service since about fifty miles south of here. They can call me anytime."

Tina's right eyebrow went up. Then, after a moment, she chuckled.

"Now," Byrd insisted, "is there anything I can do?"

Tina shrugged. "We've got most of the bases covered right now. I have a feeling that when things start happening, we'll need them all. Before all hell breaks loose, why don't you make sure our guests from Texas get some food while we wait for word?"

Byrd shook his head in frustration. "Got it." Byrd looked around the room for Major Crosby. He found him in the pilot's lounge watching Raelynn sleep.

Byrd was surprised to see Adeline Riley and Sheriff Jim Hallman there, as well. "Hey, Addy. Welcome back to Georgia. And this time you brought your boss." Byrd motioned at Raelynn. "She didn't get much sleep last night."

Crosby wasn't sympathetic. "I didn't either."

Raelynn must have heard the voices. She came around and then stood up at the sight of her boss, the sheriff.

The Texans gathered around Raelynn and Byrd. Raelynn wouldn't make eye contact with either Major Crosby or the sheriff. Crosby tipped his hat back and stood in front of Raelynn. "Ma'am, I'm not saying I condone what you did, running out like that, but I'll not say I blame you for doing it. That might be the most Texas move I've ever seen."

Raelynn met his eyes. "Thanks, Major. That means a lot."

Adeline hugged her friend. "Girl, you take the cake!" she said with a smile. "I'm sure happy to see you!"

Raelynn shrugged. "Well, at least Rudy is here close. With all the cops we saw on the side of the road, I can't imagine he'll be able to slip through."

Byrd watched the two friends. Adeline had been Raelynn's cover during the 2005 undercover operation in Presidio. Before that, when Adeline was a Texas DPS Narcotics Agent, they had been partners on a drug task force. Their connections ran deep.

Sheriff Hallman watched the interaction. Then he extended a hand to Raelynn. "Like Stetson here, I wish you hadn't run out here on your own. I admire your spunk, though." In a sign that most, if not all, was forgiven, Hallman hugged his deputy.

Adeline broke the tension. "You reckon we can find some food around here, Danny? I could eat *your* cooking right now."

"They're serving food to everyone over at the jail. If y'all don't mind crowding in my car, I can run you over there," Byrd offered, glancing at Crosby.

Crosby laughed. "I'll get in your car if I have to cut my legs off. I'm about as hungry as I've ever been."

Byrd motioned for everyone to follow. As the officers threaded their way toward the parking lot, Crosby took a look at the operation. "Why isn't this operation set up at the jail? Seems like it would make more sense."

"Visiting day, Major. With the holidays coming up, the sheriff's office will be packed. The sheriff would have liked it better, too. But there would be lots of prying eyes and ears and not as much parking." Byrd pointed to the large open lobby of the airport. "It's also hard to keep day-to-day operations going with all these extra folks in the way."

Crosby watched the beehive for a few more seconds and then followed Byrd toward the car. "Agent Byrd?"

Byrd stopped and turned to face the ranger major. "Yes, sir? And you can call me Danny, sir."

"No 'sirs', Danny. We've worked on cases together. Feel free to call me Stetson."

Byrd was apprehensive. "Okay, Stetson. What can I do for you?"

Crosby took off his western hat for a moment. He held it in his left hand by the leather sweatband. Byrd noticed the big ranger kept his gun hand free—a habit Byrd had adopted as well.

Crosby cleared his throat. "Some things I said have been blown out of proportion. I think you may have been told I didn't want you doing something to mess up this case. Does that sound familiar?"

Byrd stood his ground. "People say lots of things, Stetson. A man can't believe everything he hears. You pulled me out of a fix back in El Paso, and I won't ever forget that. If you believe I'll cause problems on this case, I'll step back and stay out of the way."

Crosby pursed his lips. "As a supervisor of people who take their jobs very seriously, I probably overstepped when I told my rangers not to touch base with you. I'll own up to that."

Byrd noticed that Crosby had begun to turn his hat around in his hand, the brim making several orbits. Crosby cleared his throat again.

Byrd stepped closer. "You did what you thought was right at the time. And you have a lot of weight on your shoulders. I'd never second-guess you."

Crosby clasped Byrd's shoulder with his left hand. With his right hand, Crosby pointed at the gold Cinco peso badge on his chest. "I took an oath, like you did, to look out for those in need. The higher you go in rank, the greater that burden becomes. You get that?"

"I do."

"I wanted to make sure nothing from this investigation got tossed out of court because a friend helped a friend. But I guess I should have thought through what I said before I said it."

"Stetson, no need for you to worry about this. I'm going to take a back seat and let others take the lead. My director has given me my marching orders. I'll keep Raelynn informed and safe till this thing is over." Byrd's voice was steely.

"Your director may have gotten the wrong message from me. I'm going to correct that after lunch," Crosby said, putting his hat on. Crosby stopped short. "What about Sheriff Hallman?"

"He partnered up with Sheriff Smith. I think they wanted to talk sheriff business."

"I guess it's 'the first hog to the trough'," Crosby remarked.

"Well then, let's go eat." Byrd pointed to his car. Addy and Rae had already climbed into the back seat. Byrd laughed. "I guess they think you need the front seat."

Crosby shrugged, "I guess I do."

Byrd chuckled. "We call that front passenger seat the death seat. If we go around one of these hard curves up here and end up down a ravine or in a tree, the one sitting in the front passenger seat is usually known as 'Victim #1.'"

Crosby thought about that as he pulled the seatbelt tight.

The only way Jerry Rutledge would agree to drive Rudy Grant's Jeep back home was if Rudy let him have a pinch of the meth Rutledge had just sold him. Rutledge crushed up the bit of crystal and then used his finger to rub the powder along his gum line. He felt the surge of energy and then leaned over the kitchen sink. The meth was strong enough that, for a moment, he thought he would throw up.

Rudy grabbed his shoulder. "This ain't hard. I just need you to wait about fifteen minutes after I leave and then drive my car to your—"

Rudy suddenly stopped talking and looked toward the ceiling. "I hear an airplane overhead!"

SUNDAY, DECEMBER 9, 2007
2:44 P.M. EST
BETHLEHEM COMMUNITY, BLAIRSVILLE, GEORGIA

The DEA Aero Commander circled under the layer of gray clouds, giving Doc a good view of the little house where Granny Gazaway lived. Arlow had circled wide for a few minutes, fearing that the people in the house might hear the twin-engine airplane overhead. The low cloud ceiling was not working in their favor.

Doc saw a different car parked at the house than during their last flyover. "GBI 34 to any of the surveillance units. I'm seeing another car at the target house. Has anyone gotten eyes on it?"

"It's a beat-up sedan," came a reply. "The driver looked like a white male. He looked like he weighed about as much as an eight ball of meth."

Doc chuckled at the description. "Could be a family member, I guess. It is Monday."

Doc watched a man walk out of the house and get in the car. "The driver came out of the house. He's wearing a baseball cap and a big jacket. Looks like he's leaving."

The radio crackled. "Should we try to follow him, 34?"

"We're here for the little girl," Doc responded. "Just hold what you've got."

SUNDAY, DECEMBER 9, 2007
3:22 P.M. EST
BLAIRSVILLE, GEORGIA

By the time Byrd and the Texans returned to the command post, the new phone lines were in and ringing off the hook. The group had rushed through a meal of sliced turkey, dressing, English peas, and mashed potatoes, appropriate for the holiday season.

Sheriff Hallman sat down with Union County Sheriff Smith as they prepared to talk about the challenges each faced. Smith spat tobacco juice into the opening in the top of a soda can. Hallman looked amused at the practice.

Tina Blackwell looked up as Byrd came through the door of the command post. "Danny, I need your help on something," Blackwell shouted across the room.

Byrd ambled over. "What have you got for me, Tina?"

She handed Byrd a typed lead sheet. "A woman from Fannin County just called and said a guy is meeting Rudy

Grant to sell him some meth. She says it's her live-in. A guy named Jerry Rutledge."

Byrd groaned. "He's a CI of mine. A worthless one, but a CI nonetheless."

Blackwell pointed to the lead sheet. "Yeah, the tipster's name is Joyce Rutledge. She said she'd be working at the Dine and Dash this afternoon. Do you know where that is?"

"Sure," Byrd nodded. "I can get over there right away."

"Where is this place?" Blackwell asked. "I've never heard of it."

Byrd pointed at the map. "The place is actually part of a convenience store right here on the Union/Fannin County line on the Mountain Parkway."

Blackwell logged the tip out to Byrd. "Run over there and talk with her. See what she might know as quickly as you can."

"Sure," Byrd said as he looked around the room for Raelynn. "I'm gonna take Raelynn with me. She needs to keep occupied. This won't take long."

Blackwell nodded. "Take her along. We're stalled out here until Texas gets a warrant or we see the girl at the house."

Byrd spotted Raelynn and Adeline talking in the pilot's lounge. He walked to where they were talking. "I have to run down the road for about ten or fifteen minutes. There's a woman who says she has information about Rudy setting up a meth buy. You up for a ride, Raelynn? We shouldn't be gone more than an hour."

Raelynn nodded. "Anything is better than sitting here watching my fingernails grow." She turned to Adeline, "Do you want to go?"

Adeline thought it over. "Sure. Let me get my big coat, and we'll take a ride."

Byrd shrugged. "We won't be gone that long."

Adeline headed to her go-bag. "You never know. This weather could get a lot worse before the day is over."

Raelynn nodded. "I wonder if I could borrow a raincoat. My barn coat is warm, but it's not waterproof."

Byrd shook his head. "We'll be in my car. You should be fine. We're burning daylight, ladies."

Adeline tugged her big coat over her shoulders. "Rae, I don't have another coat with me."

Raelynn thought it over. "They don't want me around any of the action, anyway. I guess I'll be fine."

The group headed for Byrd's car.

SUNDAY, DECEMBER 9, 2007
3:58 P.M. EST
BLAIRSVILLE, GEORGIA

It's exactly like that dip-shit Rutledge to give me a car sitting on empty, Rudy thought. Rudy began to look for a service station as he pointed the worn-out Toyota toward Marietta. Rutledge had given Rudy his baseball cap and heavy coat, helping Rudy to feel anonymous. But Rudy wouldn't truly feel better until he was out of Georgia. He figured Rutledge would only buy him a few hours, at most.

Before leaving in Rutledge's car, Rudy had carried Madison to one of Granny's back bedrooms and tucked her in. Now, Rudy was focused on his search for a fuel stop, so much so that the outline of the trooper car behind him wasn't immediately alarming. Rudy noticed the blue and gray patrol car as he found the right turn lane from the Murphy Highway onto the Mountain Parkway.

Rudy broke out into a cold sweat. As he negotiated the right turn towards Blue Ridge, he saw two more State Patrol cars sitting along the road. Rudy was about to floor the old sedan when the car behind him pulled up beside one of the marked cars at the intersection.

The momentary realization that they weren't looking for him in this car didn't stop Rudy from being drenched in a cold sweat. He used the barn coat to wipe his face. He needed to keep his cool for a little longer. *There was no way that the cops would be looking for me once I got out of this county.*

CHAPTER 16
ON THE MOVE

Granny Gazaway had no love for Jerry Rutledge. Even though they were kin, she had despised Rutledge's father. He had kept the boy away from his Granny when he was young. Granny had celebrated when the father had gone off to prison, where he belonged. She lost nothing when Jerry Rutledge's worthless father had been stabbed to death only months away from parole. She knew Jerry hadn't lost much either from the death of the quarrelsome man he hardly knew.

She could tell by the way he acted that Rutledge was equally uncomfortable being alone with her. He paced the floor, stopping occasionally to listen for the airplane Rudy had heard overhead.

"Granny, I think Rudy's been gone long enough. I'm gonna go," Rutledge declared.

"No, you ain't," Granny said. "He needs some time to get out of this area. Now you set your narrow ass down over there and watch my TV or do whatever you do. I promised Rudy a running start."

"Well, can you turn up the heat in here? I'm freezing my butt off," Rutledge whined.

"You tough it out. It's cold in here for a reason," Granny retorted.

Rutledge grudgingly took a seat in front of the TV.

SUNDAY, DECEMBER 9, 2007
4:55 P.M. EST
BLAIRSVILLE, GEORGIA

Raelynn and Adeline climbed into the back seat of Byrd's government car. They both put their booted feet onto the back of the front passenger seat and made themselves comfortable.

"Hey," Byrd said. "Don't go messing up my car. This thing is new to me, and I plan on driving it as long as it holds up. I don't want you two tearing my seats up with your cowboy shoes."

"Just drive, Danny," Adeline said. "We need to chill-lax back here for a while. That big lunch is making me sleepy."

Byrd ignored the female cops and fired up his Crown Vic. "Alright. But try not to snore. It keeps me awake." He caught Raelynn's eye in the rearview mirror.

Raelynn frowned. "It's your fault. If you hadn't gotten me drunk, I wouldn't have snored."

"Right," Byrd said as he navigated around the assortment of police cars parked along the road to the airport.

SUNDAY, DECEMBER 9, 2007
5:02 P.M. EST
BETHLEHEM COMMUNITY, BLAIRSVILLE, GEORGIA

After Rudy had been gone for about twenty minutes, Granny relented. "Go on if you want to. Rudy's had time to get out of Union County."

Without responding, Rutledge stood up and stretched. He was nervous about the prospect of driving Rudy's car. Rutledge figured it was a stolen car, and Rudy wanted to ditch it somehow. Rutledge expected the cops to stop him and maybe lock him up for a day or so. The cash Rudy had given him would cover that, he figured. And he'd get to meet some potential meth customers in the county lockup.

Rutledge wrapped his old coat around his middle and headed to Rudy's Jeep. He pulled the blue tarp off the vehicle, climbed in, and got the old SUV running.

SUNDAY, DECEMBER 9, 2007
5:27 P.M. EST
BETHLEHEM COMMUNITY, BLAIRSVILLE, GEORGIA

"GBI 34 to base. It looks like our boy is getting in the Jeep," Doc announced over the radio. He had been in the airplane long enough to get comfortable with the controls.

"Is the girl with him?" Tina Blackwell responded over the radio.

"I'm not positive. He looked to be alone, though." Doc leaned out the window and tried to get a better look as the Jeep backed out of the driveway.

Doc thumbed the mic button. "He's on the move. He's backing into the street and facing back towards the Murphy Highway."

Doc watched as the Jeep started back toward Blairsville. Arlow was holding them at an altitude and speed that allowed Doc to keep the SUV in sight.

"We have eyes on him," Doc called over the radio. "I don't see any reason to be subtle at this point."

Arlow took the hint and dropped the airplane lower. The weather had cleared enough for the DEA pilot to be able to negotiate the mountainous terrain. "Doc, tell the base we'll have overwatch for the marked car stopping him."

Doc chuckled. "I don't think they'll need it. There are about a dozen cars lined up on the road waiting for him. He's about to meet a whole passel of troopers and deputies. I see them cutting on their blue lights." Doc watched as the Jeep neared the Murphy Highway and a small caravan of State Patrol and Union County deputy cars was lining up behind him. "We've got a ringside seat!"

SUNDAY, DECEMBER 9, 2007
5:36 P.M. EST
BLAIRSVILLE, GEORGIA

Trooper Troy Clifton barked, "Driver! Step out of the car with your hands up! Do it now!"

Clifton watched as the driver stared at the side view mirror. Clifton had his patrol rifle pointed at the driver's head. He wondered if he should adjust his aimpoint to account for the safety glass in the side window. The driver was still staring back at him in the mirror.

As the other troopers and deputies crowded around, Trooper Clifton tried to make eye contact with the driver. "Hey, I'm talking to you. Step out of the car! Now!"

While the driver continued to stare at them, Clifton assessed the situation. "I need a couple of you troopers to get back in your cars and be ready if he floors it. I want a couple of you to form up on me, and we'll move up on the car. Everyone, be aware that the young girl may be inside. Don't shoot unless your shot is clean and your life is in danger. Everyone understand?"

While two troopers climbed back into their cars and positioned them to chase, the rest of the assembly of troopers and deputies slowly moved forward a few feet at a time. No one rushed the car.

Troy Clifton was nearing the rear corner of the car when the driver's door sprang open. He saw a scrawny man lean out of the door. The driver asked, "What's wrong, fellers?"

Clifton took two giant steps and dragged the driver out of the car and onto the ground. "Mr. Grant, you're under arrest."

Jerry Rutledge tried to crane his head around as the trooper and a couple of deputies applied handcuffs to his wrists. "I ain't Mr. Grant, sir."

Clifton pulled the photo he'd been given of Rudy Grant. The photo was of Grant in his guard's uniform and was not the best copy. Clifton wondered how old the picture was as he rolled Rutledge over to compare the faces. Clifton was immediately concerned that the man didn't look much like the photo. "If you're not Grant, then who are you?"

"My name's Jerry Rutledge, sir. I'm working for GBI Byrd. He has me signed up as a helper." When the trooper didn't respond, Rutledge continued. "You ought to remember me, trooper. You ran me down and did one of them pits on me." Rutledge squirmed and tried to sit up.

"Just stay where you are," Clifton ordered.

Clifton grabbed the radio microphone from inside his patrol car. "420 to the Command Post. We've got a problem. This bird says he's Jerry Rutledge, not Rudy Grant. And, unfortunately, I think I recognize him."

Tina Blackwell called back on the radio. "Is there any way to confirm, 420?"

Clifton leaned out of the car. "Can one of you guys see if he has a license on him? I need to look at it."

When the deputy came back with Rutledge's license, Clifton was disappointed. "420 to command post. It's confirmed. He has a valid Georgia License in that name."

"Hold him there to be interviewed. Use the remaining units to block the roads on either side of the target house. Establish roadblocks about a quarter mile from the residence so we don't alert anyone in the house. We'll have agents on the way to execute a search warrant." *Tina Blackwell sounded frustrated*, Clifton thought.

SUNDAY, DECEMBER 9, 2007
5:48 P.M. EST
MASHBURN MILL COMMUNITY, BLUE RIDGE, GEORGIA

Rudy Grant nursed the worn-out car along, looking for a service station without any cops sitting in the driveway. He found one at the intersection of Loving Road. He whipped the old car up next to a pump and used his credit card to pay. He didn't want to go inside, where he was sure he would be caught on their surveillance system. He stood in the cold as he pumped a full tank of gas.

He was sweating profusely as he stood under the awning, waiting for the tank to fill. The wind had begun to whip around the station, and the cold wind was bitter, but he was sweating anyway. He touched the pistol in the pocket of the barn jacket he'd taken from Rutledge.

This will all be over soon, he reminded himself.

He was heartened that he hadn't seen a cop car since leaving the Blairsville area.

SUNDAY, DECEMBER 9, 2007
5:55 P.M. EST
MASHBURN MILL COMMUNITY, BLUE RIDGE, GEORGIA

Byrd was in no hurry to find Jerry Rutledge's wife. He had been ordered to stay away from the action.

While he drove, Raelynn and Adeline caught up with each other. After some small talk, Raelynn asked Addy, "Do you know Ranger Chandler?"

Addy was leaning back with her hat over her eyes. "Sure. He works out of Van Horn. He's a good ranger. Why?"

Raelynn was non-committal. "What do you know about him? He's running the investigation into my mom and my sister's deaths. I was just curious."

Adeline didn't sit up. With her hat in her face, she said, "He's a good troop. Was a trooper in Fort Stockton. Good reputation. Why? Are you worried he won't do everything by the book? That's not him. He lives by the book."

"Anything else you can tell me?" Raelynn asked.

Adeline tipped her hat back and sat up. "Are you wondering if he's single? He is."

Daniel Byrd slowed the Crown Vic as he saw cross traffic ahead. The conversation on the police radio indicated Rudy's Jeep had been stopped as it left Granny Gazaway's house. He listened to the tense exchange of information between the command post and the officers on the traffic stop.

Byrd was startled when an old Toyota shot out from Loving Road onto Highway 515. Byrd shifted to the passing lane as the little car got into the slow lane and righted itself.

"Ladies," Byrd interrupted, "I hate to interrupt this social event in my back seat, but it sounds like on the radio that Rudy is on the shoulder. In a minute, we should know if Madison is in the car with her father or back in the house."

Byrd was continuing to watch the Toyota as he listened to the police radio. The troopers were searching Rudy's car. As Byrd eased back into the slow lane and adjusted his speed, something about the rusty car caught his attention.

Byrd was only half listening to the radio as he focused on trying to remember where he had seen the old car. In the background, he heard Trooper Clifton mention the name Jerry Rutledge over the radio. Byrd's eyes went wide.

Byrd pulled alongside the old car and got a look at the driver. The man was looking straight ahead. Byrd was certain the driver wasn't Rutledge, but he certainly met the description of Rudy Grant.

Byrd let the car slow and drifted back behind the Toyota.

"Ladies, I need some help here," Byrd said as he nudged the nearest boot. "We may have a situation."

Adeline sat up. "What is it?"

"Hide the hats and try to stay low. I need Rae to take a

look at the driver of this car ahead of me. I think we might be following Rudy." Byrd said calmly.

SUNDAY, DECEMBER 9, 2007
6:03 P.M. EST
BETHLEHEM COMMUNITY, BLAIRSVILLE, GEORGIA

GBI ASAC Lamont "Monty" Davis led the charge as a specially trained team of GBI agents rushed up to the door of Granny Gazaway's house. The agents were wearing black tactical vests with the letters GBI in gold on the front and back. Tactical helmets, boots, and M4 rifles completed the ensemble. Davis used his left boot to kick the door under the knob and throw it open.

Davis stepped aside as the door slammed back into the wall. The agents making up the rest of the stack shouted, as they rushed into Granny's home, "GBI Agents with a search warrant! Anyone inside the house, show me your hands!"

Monty Davis encountered Granny sitting in her kitchen. He pointed his rifle at her for a moment before deciding the woman wasn't a threat. She was sipping a cup of coffee as she watched the agents rush through her house. Davis ambled over to join Granny. "Ma'am, are you the homeowner?"

Granny looked amused as she responded. "I shore am, son. And I might as well tell you that the girl y'uns are looking for is in my back bedroom."

Davis needed to watch Granny, but he shouted to team member Jamie Abernathy, "Look in the back bedroom. This lady says the girl is back there."

Davis heard the bedroom door being pushed open. Then, for several seconds, no sounds came from the back of the house. Davis glanced at Granny, who kept sipping her coffee.

Abernathy walked into the kitchen to join Davis. Abernathy, a seasoned investigator for the GBI, was pale, Davis noted, as she pulled off her ballistic helmet. Her long blond hair tumbled down as she set the helmet on the kitchen table. Next to the helmet, Abernathy tossed down a dirt-worn, homemade doll.

"Are you Granny Gazaway?" Abernathy asked.

Granny nodded without looking up.

"What's your true name, ma'am?"

Granny glanced up from under hooded eyes. "My given name is Bernice."

Jamie Abernathy grabbed the old woman a little more harshly than Davis expected. "Bernice Gazaway, you're under arrest," Abernathy pronounced. "Get to your feet. We need to search you, ma'am."

Davis helped Abernathy stand the old woman up. Abernathy frisked her from top to bottom. "What's this all about?" Granny asked.

Abernathy's eyes went dead. She leaned into Granny's ear. "You old crone, you know exactly what you're under arrest for. And I hope the judge throws the book at you."

"I want me a lawyer," Granny pronounced. "Y'uns can't ask me no questions without one here."

Abernathy was more agitated than Davis had ever seen her. "You better find a damned good one, lady," Abernathy said.

She turned to Monty Davis. "You probably need to go back there and then call the command post on Granny's landline."

David turned to the hallway. "Radio's faster."

"People all over can hear that radio," Abernathy countered.

Davis was curious as he headed for the hallway. He noticed the air in the hall was much colder than the kitchen. *Granny left a window open*, he thought. *But why?* Then he caught the smell that every criminal investigator recognizes immediately.

SUNDAY, DECEMBER 9, 2007
6:11 P.M. EST
BLAIRSVILLE, GEORGIA

Tina Blackwell was listening intently for any information on the radios when the on-duty analyst called her name. Blackwell looked up, annoyed. "Can it wait?"

The analyst shook her head. "It's Monty Davis. You're going to want to take this."

Major Crosby and Director Hicks moved closer to the phone bank as Blackwell answered the phone. "Blackwell. Is there something you couldn't put out on the radio?"

Blackwell's eyes dropped to the floor as she listened to Davis. Blackwell could only stand, shoulders drooping, and shake her head. "How long ago? Can you give me a guess?"

She listened to Davis explain for a moment. Then she turned to Hicks and Crosby. "They found Madison. She has been stabbed to death. It looks like she's been dead since Thursday night or Friday morning."

The air seemed to escape the room as the word was passed around to the law enforcement team. The command post had gone quiet as Tina Blackwell glanced back. "We're going to need a crime scene unit at the Gazaway house." Blackwell turned to Sheriff Smith. "Sheriff, we're going to keep the road blocked to the house for the time being. Is that okay with you?"

Sheriff Smith was somber. "Do what you need. I'll notify the jail to expect Mrs. Gazaway and have the coroner on the way."

Blackwell turned to Stetson Crosby. "What will your DA in Texas need? Anything he needs, we'll make sure our crime scene techs handle."

"I'll make some notifications, and then I'll consult with the DA. But I'm sure your people will do everything we need anyway." Crosby headed to an unused phone to start making calls.

"We need to keep this off the police radios right now," Blackwell announced to the room. "The media will be here soon enough. Let's give our agents some time to work."

She would later find out her admonishment came too late. A twenty-year-old jailer had posted the information on a social media page. Atlanta media outlets caught wind of the information before Stetson Crosby could pass the information to the Texas DPS Director.

Crosby's next call was to Ranger Steve Chandler. "Take a warrant for Rudy Grant. We found Madison Grant's body in Georgia. He hauled her across the country after he killed her."

CHAPTER 17
ON THE HUNT

Adeline and Raelynn kept low in the back seat. They tucked their western hats into the floorboard and crouched on top of each other, trying to be invisible.

Byrd maneuvered to get close alongside the rusty car again. As they pulled near the old car, Raelynn exclaimed, "That's Rudy."

Byrd took his foot from the gas pedal and let his car drift and then slide over behind Rudy's car. "You're one hundred percent on that identification?"

Raelynn nodded. "That's him. What are you going to do?"

Byrd pulled the radio microphone up and called for assistance. "GBI 89 to the command post."

A voice came back over the radio. "Go ahead, 89."

"I am behind Rudy Grant on 515 toward Blue Ridge. I need some marked cars over this way to make a traffic stop," Byrd requested.

Tina Blackwell must have taken the command post radio microphone away. "Danny, what's your 10-20?"

"We're on 515 coming up on Highway 60. Do you have anyone close?"

"I'll start uniforms your way, but most of the troopers are close to the CP. I'll let Fannin County know and try to get Doc and Arlow headed that way."

SUNDAY, DECEMBER 9, 2007
6:17 P.M. EST
MORGANTON, GEORGIA

Rudy Grant couldn't believe his eyes. He had just seen his bitch sister-in-law in the back seat of the car that had pulled up beside him. He tried to convince himself he was imagining things. He noted that the vehicle was a sedan similar to those used by Texas DPS. It was a plain car, and the driver looked neatly trimmed, like he was wearing a tie. If it was Raelynn he saw, she was now crouched in the back of the car.

Rudy decided to make the next left. He saw Highway 60 coming up ahead. The traffic light was red. He stayed in the right lane until the last moment and then shifted to the left lane and turned on his signal. The Crown Vic pulled up alongside the beater Rudy was driving.

Rudy tried his best to keep his eyes straight ahead. As he waited for the light to change and give him a chance to make the turn, Rudy tried to examine the car beside him casually. The driver of the car was a cool customer. He was driving with his left arm, with his shoulder held high, leaning against the door so that Rudy had a hard time getting a look at him.

When the light changed, Rudy was focused on the car beside him. A car behind him honked the horn.

Rudy's head was pounding as much as his hand as he waited for the Crown Vic to make a move. When it didn't, he shot across 515 and turned onto Morganton Highway. He had traveled a short distance when the road came to a T intersection. Highway 60 was to the left, and Rudy took the turn to the left. Rudy was afraid to get off the main highway for fear of being lost in the mountains.

He followed the signs for Highway 60, even as it wound again to the left. He passed an outfitter shop, a pizza place, and then the Morganton Post Office. The route made a hard right. Rudy made the turn and then started traveling on one of the most dangerous roads in Georgia. He accelerated the old Toyota as the road seemed to straighten out. He was doing sixty when he went into a hard left curve, running off the pavement and then overcorrecting into the oncoming lane. His heart was pounding as he got the car under control.

SUNDAY, DECEMBER 9, 2007
6:24 P.M. EST
MORGANTON, GEORGIA

Byrd couldn't make the turn and opted to continue toward Blue Ridge. As soon as he saw a break in traffic, Byrd turned on his blue lights and pushed the government car through the tall grass of the median and out the other side. He used his momentum to sling the car back to the left and into the lane of eastbound traffic. Byrd talked on the radio as he straightened the car out and prepared to turn onto

Highway 60. "Tina, he just turned onto Highway 60 towards Dahlonega. Do you have any kind of ETA on help?"

"Stick with him if you can, Danny." Tina Blackwell encouraged. "Texas is preparing felony warrants on Rudy. Don't let him get out of your sight if you can help it."

"What about air support?" Byrd asked as he turned off the lights and siren and wheeled onto Highway 60. "If he sees me behind him, he will run for sure."

Byrd jammed the accelerator to the floor as he swung his car onto the familiar route. The state highway had many hairpin turns with rock walls on one side and sheer drops on the other. He knew Rudy would have a hard time getting away if he stuck to Highway 60. He flicked off the blue lights as he tried to catch up to Rudy. This wasn't the time to spook him.

"Arlow is on the ground refueling, and the GSP Aviation unit has been over the house during the search. GSP is going to need fuel before they can head your way. Arlow says he can be airborne in five minutes." Blackwell sounded tense.

Byrd was grim. "This had better be over in less than five minutes. He's headed down the mountain."

SUNDAY, DECEMBER 9, 2007
6:26 P.M. EST
BLAIRSVILLE, GEORGIA

Tina Blackwell was surrounded. Buster Hicks was on one side; Major Stetson Crosby was on the other. Everyone could feel the tension.

Blackwell propped her head on her left palm, her elbow on the table. "Rudy's going to run. I think we've got to put every resource we can toward Highway 60." She turned to see Hick's response.

Hicks closed his eyes for a second. Then, glancing at Major Crosby, Hicks said, "Let's make it official. He's a murder suspect. I think we have probable cause to arrest him for the murder of his daughter." Hicks motioned to the GSP radio operator sitting at the command table. "Call 10-3 on the radio and let's get people moving his way."

The GSP radio operator, a veteran with the GSP named Jessica Porter, leaned into the radio microphone. "Blairsville Command Post to all cars and stations. 10-3 10-33. GBI 89 is behind the murder suspect. Any unit available, respond to Highway 60 southbound from 515. Units responding, please acknowledge."

Troy Clifton came on the air. "420 to the CP. Alert Fannin County and Lumpkin County. He's headed to an area with no cell phones, and the radio coverage is very spotty. See if either county can provide support."

Blackwell glanced back at Director Hicks. "Any ideas, boss?"

Hicks shook his head. It seemed that, no matter how carefully a plan was laid out, something unexpected jumped out at you. "No. We have to play the cards we've been dealt."

Hicks and Blackwell paused to watch the DEA Aero Commander roll down the runway and leap into the air.

SUNDAY, DECEMBER 9, 2007
6:29 P.M. EST
MORGANTON, GEORGIA

Byrd checked for Adeline and Raelynn in the rearview mirror. "You ladies need to buckle up tight. We're in for a roller coaster ride."

Raelynn was more concerned about the moment Rudy came to a stop. "Addy, do you have an extra gun on you?"

Adeline shook her head. "All my equipment is back at the motel. I . . ." Suddenly, the female officers were thrown into the side of the car as Byrd made a tight turn, braking hard and then shifting the car into second gear.

"Damn! What was that?" Raelynn asked.

"An easy curve. They're going to get tighter." Byrd lightly rode the brakes through another curve and then accelerated out the other side. He would try to apex each turn, but the fear of oncoming traffic forced Byrd to stay as close as possible to his lane.

Adeline spotted a road sign she hadn't seen in Texas. It was a yellow caution sign with an arrow surmounting a zig-zagging line. "What does that sign mean?" she asked, concerned.

Byrd pressed the brakes hard. The Texans were thrown against the front seat. Byrd fought the wheel as he downshifted again, struggling to keep the car under control. Through gritted teeth, Byrd remarked, "It means lots of curves ahead. Hold on!"

As Byrd pushed his car out of the curve onto a long straightaway, he activated his lights and siren. Byrd wasn't under any illusion that Rudy wasn't aware of their presence. Byrd grabbed the microphone and tried the radio. "GBI 89 to the CP. We are 10-80. Rudy is running south on Highway 60."

There was no response on the radio. Byrd pressed the microphone button briefly and listened for the repeater to kick back. The radio was silent. He wasn't getting out. Byrd knew from experience that the mountains on either side of them would block any radio signal for long stretches.

Adeline tried dialing the command post number on her work cell phone. She got an odd sound out of the phone. It was then she saw the phone display reading "No Service."

SUNDAY, DECEMBER 9, 2007
6:30 P.M. EST
BLAIRSVILLE, GEORGIA

Doc Farmer watched the rainwater pour off the wings as the DEA airplane crawled into the air. "GBI 34 to GBI 89. Can you copy me, Danny?" Doc started calling as soon as the plane took off. There was no answer. Doc tried the same call on the GBI car-to-car channel.

"Go ahead, Doc. I can copy you on channel two," came the answer.

Doc was relieved. "I've got you, Danny. What's your 10-20"

"We're about five miles out of Morganton, southbound on Highway 60. We've lost cell phones and the repeater system. Can you relay to the CP?"

Doc relayed the information to the command post.

"Danny, we're coming to you," Doc assured Byrd. "We're

having to keep low because of the weather. While we're on the way, let me relay your location. We've got help coming your way."

"Got it," Byrd's words were distorted. "We're passing Old Dial Road."

Byrd could see Rudy ahead, now. The beater still had some life in it. Byrd wound the engine of the Crown Vic until it was howling, then threw the car into a tight curve. He used the transmission to control the speed into the bend without overloading the brakes. He doubted Rudy would know how to take these tight curves.

Byrd's car couldn't have responded any better. The heavy Police Interceptor Package car excelled at the straightaways and could hold its own in the serpentine roads of southern Union County. Byrd glanced at the instruments, noting there was plenty of fuel to stay on Rudy's tail, and was pleased the car was performing perfectly.

In the next straightaway, Byrd handed the microphone to Adeline. "Tell Doc we're just past Hoot Owl Hill Road."

"Seriously?" Adeline asked.

"I'm just reading the signs. Doc knows this area like the back of his hand. He'll know where we are." Byrd saw Rudy fishtail up ahead as he overtook a camper. "Tell him we're not far from Skeenah Gap."

Adeline followed instructions.

"Danny, we're having trouble getting to where you are," Doc came over the radio. "The clouds are beginning to settle in over these mountains," Doc had a tone in his voice that Byrd didn't like.

Byrd glanced in the rearview mirror. "Tell Doc not to let Arlow crash that plane. They're going to be our only way to communicate."

The answer from Doc was garbled.

Byrd pushed the accelerator hard. They were coming into one of the few long straightaways on the route. The Crown Vic engine responded quickly, pushing the car past 90 mph in seconds. Byrd was closing in on Rudy. The little beater looked like it was straining to continue. There was smoke boiling out of the exhaust.

Byrd had to brake hard as they came into a left-hand curve. He felt the rear end of his car getting light and compensated by shifting gears. Byrd saw Rudy struggling to keep the little car on the road. Rudy was braking hard, too, and Byrd used the opportunity to close in on Rudy's back bumper.

Adeline kept trying to reach Doc on the radio to no avail. "I guess we're no longer on the planet Earth," she remarked. She sniffed the air for a moment. "Danny, what's that smell?"

Byrd frowned. "That's our brakes."

Rudy had negotiated the last couple of curves without losing control. Byrd was now inches away from Rudy's back bumper, steadily applying pressure. Byrd considered trying a PIT maneuver, but there was no way to be sure Madison was not in the car. Suddenly, Rudy's brake lights flared, and the nose of the car dipped.

"Put on the air that he's turning on Doublehead Gap Road," Byrd told Adeline. Then, as he watched Rudy make the turn, he exclaimed, "His left front wheel separated from the car. He won't be able to go far in this country on three wheels."

The left front wheel of Rudy's car bounced along ahead of him as Rudy plowed a furrow with his brake drum. Rudy's car began to swerve from side to side on the rough county road. Rudy swung to the right to avoid a pothole, and the front brake drum scraped the road, flipping the old car. Rudy hit a shelter near the road where kids wait for the school bus, and then the car stopped on the roof. Steam was pouring out of the engine bay as Rudy scrambled out of the wreck and ran across the road into the woods.

Byrd skidded to a halt along the roadway and jumped from the driver's seat. Adeline and Raelynn were climbing from the back when Byrd ran to the overturned sedan.

He fell to the pavement, using his hands to maneuver, and looked for Madison in the car. He quickly checked the front and the rear seats. Then he pushed up from the ground and forced the trunk open. He didn't see any sign of the little girl.

As he stood to look where Rudy had run into the woods, he heard the first 'pop,' then a clang as the bullet struck the overturned Toyota.

Byrd crouched behind the front fender of his car. "Shots fired," he shouted.

Adeline and Raelynn scrambled for cover. Byrd pressed the remote trunk release for the Ford and reached in for his go-bag and M4 rifle. He brought the rifle up and scanned the tree line for Rudy.

Byrd crouched beside the car for a second to catch his breath and slow down his breathing. "I'm going after Rudy. You two stay here with the car. Help is on the way."

Adeline shook her head. "Not happening. We're going, too."

Byrd saw the determination on both cops' faces. He shrugged. "Okay. Don't bunch up once we're in the woods. We'll make easier targets. But stay in sight of each other." He looked at the sky. Heavy drops of rain began to fall, plopping around them rhythmically. Byrd knew it was a precursor to heavier rain. "I'll grab some rain gear and my overcoat from the trunk before we start. We may be in the woods for a little while."

"What's that on the barrel of your rifle. Looks like a silencer," Raelynn wondered.

"That's because it is a silencer. Technically, a suppressor. I talked Staff Services into issuing it to me to protect my ears. I don't think they've stopped ringing since Mexico."

"I'd rather Rudy hears a bullet coming," Rae remarked with feeling.

Still crouched behind the G-ride, Byrd tossed a raincoat to Raelynn and then tugged on his overcoat. He waited for the others to do the same. He slung the rifle across his back and led the way into the woods.

CHAPTER 18

TURNING OVER EVERY ROCK

SUNDAY, DECEMBER 9, 2007
6:38 P.M. EST
MORGANTON, GEORGIA

Trooper Troy Clifton was pushing his blue and gray patrol car as hard as he ever had. He considered Daniel Byrd a friend. The marked Charger was first in a veritable parade of law enforcement vehicles as they turned onto Loving Road, taking a shortcut to the Morganton Highway. Clifton unclipped his radio microphone and held it to his lips.

"GSP 420 to GBI 34, can you copy?"

Clifton recognized Doc Farmer's voice. "GBI 34, go ahead, Troy."

"Doc, I got a line of cars that looks like a procession turning onto the Morganton Highway. Have you heard any more traffic from Danny?"

Clifton was intimately familiar with the curvy road to Dahlonega. He'd had his first patrol car accident chasing a drunk down the mountain pass. He did not take the route for granted. He slowed to begin the looping turns that defined the trip. He reminded himself of the refrain from Trooper School: "If you don't get there, you can't help."

"We heard some broken transmissions and now there is nothing," Doc responded. "The clouds are right down in the mountains now. We can't see anything either."

"Do you have any idea where he was the last time you had contact?" Clifton asked, taking care to have a firm grasp on the steering wheel as he talked.

"It sounded like he was getting close to Skeenah Gap. He'd had enough time to get that far."

Clifton thought it over. The trip to Dahlonega was about twenty-five or thirty miles from where he was. Even at 'trooper speed,' it would take forty-five minutes on the treacherous snake-backs of a highway. As he felt his brakes get soft in a curve, he realized the caravan must slow down and start looking for any signs of an accident.

"Thanks, Doc. We have a unit from the Cumming Post coming north to head them off."

"Y'all be careful. That road will eat your lunch, 420," Doc cautioned.

"Yes, sir!" Clifton replied as he took a particularly sharp turn.

SUNDAY, DECEMBER 9, 2007
6:40 P.M. EST
SKEENAH GAP COMMUNITY, FANNIN COUNTY, GEORGIA

The group had been in the woods long enough for their eyes to adjust to the dim light. Byrd could see Rudy ahead, climbing slowly up the mountain ahead of them. As they passed a large rock outcropping, Byrd noticed a blood smear.

It was fresh, so it had to be Rudy's. Byrd wondered if he'd been injured in the crash.

Byrd motioned for the Texas officers to get behind a tree.

"Do you see him?" Adeline asked.

Byrd shook his head, "I lost sight of him. Since we know he has a gun, let's not take any chances. He can't be far ahead of us."

Byrd cupped his hands around his mouth, letting his rifle hang at his side. "Rudy," Byrd called. "Give it up. You've got nowhere to go."

Rudy snapped off six quick shots. Byrd could hear at least one close enough to his head to make him duck. Adeline pointed her service pistol into the woods, but couldn't see anything.

"We'll have to wait for movement," Byrd called to Adeline. "Rae, you need to stay well back. No point in letting him get lucky."

Byrd heard the movement on the hillside above him. He looked around the tree and could see Rudy running. Byrd couldn't see Rudy well enough to take a shot.

Adeline had heard the movement, too. A rustling sound as Rudy scampered over the rocky mountain face. She stepped out from her cover and saw Rudy chugging up toward a clump of small pines. Adeline fired a single shot as Rudy puffed up the mountain. "Missed him. Are you not going to try with that long gun?"

Byrd thought it over. "If I get a clear shot, I plan to put him down, but I don't want to be slinging lead all over the mountains. We could be up here for a while, and I only have thirty rounds to work with. In a few minutes, there will be more cops here than you can shake a stick at. We need to keep him on a short leash."

Adeline nodded. "That's what I was doing." The broad grin gave her away.

Byrd began to trudge up the mountainside as the Texans followed behind. He wanted to conserve his energy for when Rudy gave up the climb and decided to shoot again. The dried leaves beneath his feet made a crunching sound as he started uphill. It was the same sound Rudy had made as he ran.

They continued uphill for a quarter mile, stopping to rest and hearing Rudy's steady progress up ahead of them. A slow, steady rain had started to fall. Rudy was stumbling often on the rain-slick leaves and pine needles. Byrd let him climb. He wondered if they were going in a straight line or a wide circle. He'd seen people lost in the woods cover the same ground several times.

They were closing in slowly on Rudy's position when they heard the distant sirens. There were so many sirens wailing that they sounded like one constant moan.

Byrd stationed himself behind a giant maple tree and shouted. "Rudy, the cavalry is on the way. You might as well give it up."

The answer was seven shots from a pistol. Byrd was confident Rudy was armed with a semi-automatic pistol based on the number and sound of the shots. The bullets were heavy and struck the occasional tree with a hard "thunk." He guessed it was along the lines of a Model 1911. That would explain the volleys of six or seven shots at a time.

Adeline and Raelynn had found a large granite out-cropping, one of many that littered the mountainside, and hunkered down while Rudy popped off shots.

Byrd's legs were complaining from the hill-climbing. He decided to rest until the uniforms arrived.

The sound of the sirens was getting closer. Byrd looked back the way they had come but couldn't see his car. They were probably several hundred feet off the road by now and maybe that much higher up the mountain.

As the sirens neared the road they were on, Byrd took a chance and moved closer to where he thought Rudy was. He trudged carefully along a deer trail, being careful not to make any noise, and scanned the area ahead.

When the sirens indicated the patrol cars were passing their location without stopping, Rudy called out. "Sounds like the cavalry is going somewhere else."

Byrd could make out Rudy's head. The M4 was fitted with an EOTech optical system, and Byrd brought the red dot into line with Rudy's hairline. Rudy was hunched behind a rock about seventy-five yards away. Byrd decided it was time to end the hunt.

Byrd braced himself, gripping the gun tightly as he squeezed the trigger. The rifle bucked slightly, and the bullet, traveling at almost three times the speed of sound, cracked loudly.

A big hawk, startled by the shot, screeched, spread its wings to their full five-foot width, and took flight. Byrd glanced toward the big predator as it caught an air current and soared.

Rudy dived behind the rock. Byrd couldn't be sure if the bullet hit anything or not. He scrambled behind a solid hickory tree and waited. He didn't have to wait long. Rudy fired off seven more shots in the general area. None of them came close to Byrd. Byrd rolled from behind the tree in time to see Rudy scampering up the mountainside.

Byrd clawed the ground to get to his feet. Rudy was close, and Byrd wanted to close the gap. As the group of cops struggled up the rocky mountain face, Byrd saw

Raelynn slip on a protruding rock. Her hands flew up as she tumbled a few feet down the side of the mountain.

Byrd grabbed her arm and helped her to her feet. "Are you okay?"

She nodded and bent over at the waist. "I'm good. I was afraid I had wrenched or broken my ankle, but I think I'm good." She tested her legs by taking a few careful steps as Byrd held her arm.

Byrd looked her over for a moment. He reached up, touching the side of her head, and felt warm blood on his hand. "Shit!" Byrd exclaimed.

Adeline saw Byrd's bloody hand. "Rae, are you okay?"

Byrd pursed his lips. "I banged up my head a little. Nothing serious."

Adeline pulled her head forward and took a look. She used a small LED flashlight to examine Raelynn's cranium. "It's gonna bleed, but it doesn't look too bad."

Raelynn frowned. "That's all we need, one of us walking wounded. This climb is going to get tougher in the dark."

"Right," Adeline said. "We need to be careful. Once it gets dark, we may be stuck up here till daylight."

Byrd looked around at the fading light. "I think we're past that point."

As they waited for Raelynn to gather herself, Byrd considered their circumstances. They need to be careful as they climb higher in the mountains, or Rudy might double back and ambush them. There would be no more chasing him after dark.

SUNDAY, DECEMBER 9, 2007
6:59 P.M. EST
SUCHES, GEORGIA

The line of patrol cars was crossing the Lumpkin County line when Trooper Clifton realized they had come too far. The GSP car from the Cumming Post was sitting in their path, waiting. He slowed his Charger and nosed off the highway.

"649, did you see them?"

The reply over the radio was quick and clear. "No sign."

Clifton's voice was tense as he pressed the radio mic button. "We need to circle back. They didn't have time to get this far anyway."

A family in a minivan waited patiently, and incredulously, as the dozen State Patrol and Union County SO cars performed three-point turns, blue lights flashing, and headed back the way they had come.

"420 to all units. Let's work our way back up toward Skeenah Gap. Check all the side roads and look for any signs of a car off the roadway. Skid marks, pushed over foliage, anything that might indicate a crash." Clifton led the line of cars back up the mountain.

SUNDAY, DECEMBER 9, 2007
7:01 P.M. EST
SUCHES, GEORGIA

Rudy sat on the damp ground beside a giant rock, loading bullets into the only pistol magazine he had. Granny hadn't offered another magazine, and Rudy hadn't thought to ask. Each time he tried to squeeze rounds into the old rusty magazine, his injured hand would throb from the effort.

He wasn't sure how to use the pistol's sights and was forced to point the gun at the cops and "spray and pray."

He'd wrapped his bleeding paw with a clean white cloth before he left Granny's house, but the effort of holding the steering wheel in the chase had reopened the wound. With hands slippery from blood, sweat, and rain, he had dropped a couple of bullets onto the wet ground, and the forest was too dark for him to find them.

He tried to control his breathing as he sat waiting for the law officers to come into sight. The ragged breaths made it hard for him to hear the cops coming after him.

Rudy assessed his circumstance. He didn't have food or water. He was steadily running out of ammunition and energy. In the crash, he'd managed to lose the pain pills and the meth he had. All in all, the day hadn't gone as he had hoped.

SUNDAY, DECEMBER 9, 2007
7:04 P.M. EST
SUCHES, GEORGIA

Byrd motioned for Adeline and Raelynn to follow him as they continued to trudge up the mountainside. He kept his rifle ready as he worked his way from tree to tree about a hundred yards behind Rudy.

"You think he has any idea where he is?" Raelynn asked. "He did stay somewhere near here a couple of summers when he was a kid."

"I don't see how he could," Byrd remarked. "I've been in this area for the last four years, and I don't have a clue where we are."

Adeline stopped for a moment. "That's not encouraging."

Byrd paused his climb as well. "I hear the sirens coming back."

The trio looked back in the direction they thought the road was. The marked cars continued past Doublehead Gap Road, Byrd thought. He wondered how long they would be able to keep chasing Rudy without food or water if the backup didn't locate Byrd's car.

Then Byrd smiled as he heard a single siren come closer and then stop. "They found my car."

SUNDAY, DECEMBER 9, 2007
7:19 P.M. EST
SUCHES, GEORGIA

The gouge mark in the asphalt caught Troy Clifton's attention. He slowed his patrol car and looked down the side road. His heart raced when he saw Byrd's government car.

"I see GBI 89's car down there on Doublehead Gap Road," Trooper Clifton shouted into his radio mic. Clifton's radio was silent as the caravan of marked cars pulled to a stop and disgorged their occupants. The troopers and deputies rushed to the GBI car and then, finding it empty, rolled over the sedan. There was blood on the pavement near the side door of the rusty car. Clifton stood up and looked at the mountains to his left and right.

"They've got to be close, surely," Clifton said.

The officers were looking all around when they heard the pistol shots. The mountains made the sound echo around. "Could anybody tell which direction those shots came from?" Clifton asked the assembly. No one could.

"Can anybody get out on your radio?" the trooper asked.

When consensus was that they had no radio contact, Clifton began to examine the area. He saw lights on in a small log house with a gravel driveway. "I guess I'll see if these folks will let us use their phone." He headed for his patrol car. "We put a man on the moon, and we can't talk ten miles in the mountains," Clifton said, shaking his head.

Clifton carefully maneuvered his patrol car around the GBI car and the crashed sedan. He pulled his patrol car into the driveway of the lighted home near the crash site. The homeowner, a man of about fifty, stuck his head out the door and watched the trooper approach. Howard J. Mauldin had to admit he'd never seen a Georgia trooper up close. His newly constructed mountain home was his escape from an accounting practice in Miami.

Clifton climbed the front steps and stuck out his hand as the homeowner stepped out. The men shook hands. "Sir," Clifton started. "Sorry to bother you, but if you don't care too much, I'd like to use your phone."

"I told my wife it sounded like a car had crashed down the road here." He motioned Clifton into his home. Clifton took off his campaign hat and stepped inside.

The homeowner pointed to an old-style phone on the wall. "No bother at all. Go ahead and use the phone and whatever else you need."

"You may regret making that offer, sir. I'm about to bring a large contingent of officers here near your house. We have a murder suspect on the loose in the area."

Mauldin put his hands on his hips. "I moved up here to get away from such foolishness. You do what you need to do."

SUNDAY, DECEMBER 9, 2007
7:35 P.M. EST
BLAIRSVILLE, GEORGIA

'Damn it!" Tina Blackwell exclaimed. It was inevitable that the media would get a fix on their operation, but now was probably the worst time for the satellite trucks to come rumbling up the airport access road.

She waved to the GBI Public Information Officer, Bob Bankston, to come over. "Grab a trooper or two and make sure those knuckleheads from the media don't block us all in."

Bankston, a large man with glasses, was a veteran reporter for many years before coming to the GBI. He had been hired for exactly these kinds of events. "Got it. I'll put up a tent over to the side of this building. They'll be pissed that they'll have to stay outside, but I can give them enough details to keep them happy for a while."

Bankston started out the door, then he turned back. "Tell the director and the sheriff they might want to get with me before they get cornered. I don't want anyone saying anything that might hurt the investigation."

"They're on the phone with the governor. I'll let them know what's going on." Blackwell turned to head for the private office off the main room.

"Tina? I have one question," Bankston asked.

"Sure."

"Was Byrd alone in the car? They'll want to know who we're looking for. I can give them information on the suspect, but the search for the missing agents will be a headline, too."

Blackwell recited the names and spelled them for Bankston. "I don't have a picture of the Texans, but we'll probably have to give up Danny's credential photo."

The desk phone beside Blackwell rang. "Blackwell."

"This is Trooper Clifton. We've found Danny's car. The suspect wrecked out, and Danny is parked in the roadway behind him. No sign of any of the agents or the suspect, but we can hear shots from up on the mountains."

Blackwell stood up. "I'll start rolling help your way. What else will we need?" Blackwell asked.

He could tell Clifton was thinking it over. "It just started raining up here. You might want to see if Emergency Management or the Fire Department can supply us with some portable lights. It's going to get dark up here soon."

"Give me a location."

"Doublehead Gap Road off of Morganton Highway. You can't miss the road. In fact, we need to find a way to get some of these patrol cars off this side road in case we need to get an ambulance in." Clifton was thinking several moves ahead.

"On it," Blackwell said as she hung up the phone.

The rain had started as a gentle patter. Now the rainfall was steady and drenching. Byrd pulled his heavy overcoat tight as water dripped from his hair. Rae and Adeline, missing their hats left in the car, pulled the collars up on their heavy jackets. The canopy of trees provided some protection, but it seemed the rain might be settling in for a while.

Byrd was leaning against a granite chunk, watching the last place they'd seen Rudy. His legs were burning from the climb. He guessed they had climbed over a hundred feet. The crash had been in a valley, surrounded by mountain peaks. Byrd knew the peaks could reach well over three thousand feet.

Byrd glanced at the sky. It was already so dark in the woods that Rudy could get out of the area without them seeing. Byrd also recognized the heavier the rain came the harder it would be to hear him trying to maneuver near them.

Adeline crouched next to Byrd. "Are we in deep shit?"

Byrd shrugged. "He can't see us any better than we can see him. On the other hand, the three of us will naturally make more noise as we try to stay on his trail. How many rounds do you have for your pistol?"

"Two mags on my belt and what I have in my gun. How about you?"

Byrd shook his head. "I have a thirty-round mag in the carbine and I have a spare mag for my pistol in my go-bag. Not enough to hold off the Mexican Army, but this isn't the Alamo."

Adeline looked all around at the dark forest. "Should we try to make it back to your car?"

"That's a good idea," Byrd said. "There's just one little problem."

"What's that?" Raelynn asked.

"I don't know which direction to start in. There aren't any stars to be seen nor a house in sight. We could wander around these woods all night and end up in the same fix. Or one or more of us could fall in a ravine we can't see in the dark and break a leg. Or our neck."

Adeline nodded. "You're a regular fountain of hope."

Byrd grunted in response. He knew there wasn't a happy answer.

SUNDAY, DECEMBER 9, 2007
7:41 P.M. EST
SUCHES, GEORGIA

Arlow stared at the sky. Between the darkness and the rain, he wondered if there was any point in launching the Aero Commander. He had called the National Weather Service. The weatherman said most of the rain was over, but that pop-up thunderstorms were still possible until daylight.

His FLIR system was better than most law enforcement versions, surplus from a Navy F-14, but the cold rain would seriously impact the system's ability to pick up the heat of a human body among the sun-heated rocks in the area.

Doc joined Arlow as the attendant finished topping off the gas tanks of the DEA airplane. "What do you think, Doc. This weather service says we have a fifty percent chance of their forecast being 100% wrong."

Doc looked up, too. "I don't know," he finally said. "But I do know this; those folks out there in the woods need as much help as they can get. I reckon if you can't fly, I'll grab my car and help search on the ground."

Arlow met Doc's eyes. "You know I won't give up on them." Arlo glanced back at the sky. "Give me thirty minutes for the worst of this weather to pass, and then we'll get back in the air. I need somebody to run the FLIR."

Doc sighed deeply. "I was hoping not to have to do that again. Flying scares the hell out of me."

Arlow scowled. "I thought you were in the Air Force."

"I was. I was always in the back. With you, I'm sitting right at the windshield. That's a lot closer to the action than I'd like."

Arlow nodded. He looked over his shoulder once more as the dark clouds continued to hurl rain at the ground. "Let's get in the dry and choke some coffee down. This front seems like it's moving pretty fast."

Doc flexed his shoulders and turned for the FBO. "If I drink much more coffee, I'll be needing you to land on the highway and give me a pee stop."

Arlow looked at Doc's dark jeans. "In those pants, you can just pee on yourself. Nobody will notice."

Doc thought it over as he walked. "Arlow, you're scaring me so bad I might not ever pee again."

SUNDAY, DECEMBER 9, 2007
7:44 P.M. EST
BLAIRSVILLE, GEORGIA

The talking heads stood all around the parking lot of the Blairsville airport. Each found a small piece of grass where their camera operator could get their report without any other reporters in the background. One local reporter from the Chattanooga station had to put his camera on a tripod and record himself.

Arty Winters got prime real estate in front of the airport FBO door. An up-and-coming reporter for an Atlanta station, Winters had nosed his way to the front of the line. His camera operator shot inside the building, giving a glimpse of the command post, and then pulled back to show the newsman. "Law enforcement is reporting that officers involved in a chase with a triple murder suspect are missing somewhere in the wilderness of the North Georgia mountains. We are covering the story from the command post outside the city of Blairsville. At least one of the missing officials is an agent with the Georgia Bureau of Investigation. GBI spokesman Bob Bankston says GBI agent Daniel Byrd and two officials from the State of Texas are missing and are believed to be actively pursuing a fugitive. We have been told by our sources that he is a suspect in the killing of his entire family in Montana, Texas, a city about halfway between Fort Worth and El Paso. We hope to have more information soon, but now I'll turn it over to our network affiliate in Montana, who will tell us what we know about those tragic murders alleged to have been perpetrated by this suspect on the loose."

Once the light on top of the video camera went off, Winters dropped his microphone near the tripod, exhaling. "Looks like we may be here a while. Can we get that video to the affiliate in Atlanta so New York can run it tonight?"

The camera operator pulled a cartridge from the video camera. "The satellite link should be able to get this direct to New York if the rain doesn't interfere."

The reporter perked up. "So, we might be able to do a live feed back to the network?"

The camera operator was non-committal. "I'll let you know as soon as I know."

Winters scrounged a cup of coffee from another network affiliate. By the time he'd finished the cup, his camera operator was headed back to him. "I sent the video to the network, and they love it. They're running it right now as a "breaking news" on the seven o'clock. They want you to do a live standup at eleven."

CHAPTER 19
FEELING HELPLESS

SUNDAY, DECEMBER 9, 2007
8:25 P.M. EST
SUCHES, GEORGIA

Tina Blackwell got out of Director Hicks' Tahoe and opened the rear door for Major Crosby and Sheriff Hallman. Her stride was long as she fought the urge to run to Danny's car. Blackwell looked inside the GBI car for any clues. Danny had stopped long enough to take the keys. *That's so Danny*, she thought.

There were fire engines, an ambulance, and over a dozen police, sheriffs, and state patrol cars parked on the road. Every agency in the area was represented.

Hicks joined Blackwell as he tugged on his fedora. The rain was steady and cold. Blackwell pulled on her blue wool ball cap with the gold letters "GBI" across the front.

"What do you think, Tina?" Hicks asked.

"No bullet holes and no obvious blood in the car. I'm guessing they are now in foot pursuit."

Hicks looked around. There were steep mountains on each side of the country road. "Can any of these country boys pick up their trail. We need to do something before it gets too dark."

Tina motioned Trooper Clifton over. She had to shout to be heard over the diesel generators powering the big lights pointed toward the mountain to her right. "Troy, is there anybody in this group who might be a tracker?"

Clifton shook his head. "Not in the dark. We might be able to see where they went in the woods, but we'd never be able to track over this rough ground. We might try getting a dog out of one of the state prisons?"

Hicks liked the idea. "Is there a phone around here? I'm guessing phones and radios don't work here."

Clifton laughed. "Director, the sun doesn't work up here. Come with me and I'll introduce you to Mr. Mauldin. His house has become our new command center."

As the two walked off, Tina Blackwell stared at the mountains around them. She dreaded the idea that a real rescue mission couldn't be conducted until daylight tomorrow. *A lot of bad things could happen tonight*, Blackwell thought.

She was still staring up at the mountain when she heard the first shot. The echo off the mountainside made it difficult to pick out the direction. It was followed quickly by six more shots, as she instinctively counted them. They were followed by a ripping sound she recognized. Surprisingly, the sound of the sonic boom was easier to locate.

Danny has his rifle. At least that's good news, Tina thought. *And we know which direction they went.* Tina leaned on Danny's car for a moment. She hadn't eaten anything today and had been existing on coffee. She wondered how much longer she could stick with this job.

SUNDAY, DECEMBER 9, 2007
8:45 P.M. EST
SUCHES, GEORGIA

Director Hicks sent some of the troopers and deputies to get some rest. The valley they were in, guarding Byrd's car and the rolled-over Toyota, was now covered in a blanket of fog. Hicks wondered if the visibility was as bad up on the mountainside.

He tried his best to get Tina Blackwell to go back to the shelter of the command post, but she wouldn't entertain the idea. Sheriff Smith hung in there, as well. The sheriff had arranged for a truck with food to come to the scene. Aluminum foil-wrapped burgers were passed around to those who were weathering the rain and waiting for daylight.

"Tina, it's after one," Buddy Hicks said. "The dogs will be here around daylight this morning. Why don't you climb in my Tahoe and nap?"

Blackwell sighed. "I'll go sit out of this rain for a little while, but I want to be here. He's my agent," Blackwell said. "And those folks from Texas are my guests."

"At least eat one of the burgers and get something to drink," Hicks said. "There's not much we can do now."

"I left the Mauldin house a little while ago," Blackwell replied. "I talked to Doc. He said the clouds are lifting. He and Arlow are going to get out in the next twenty minutes. The National Weather Service says the whole front is lifting and we should have clearer skies by daylight."

Hicks grunted. "Clearer? Not clear?"

Blackwell pursed her lips. "Why can't things like this happen in the summer?"

Hicks stared through the fog at where he thought his agent might be.

SUNDAY, DECEMBER 9, 2007
8:48 P.M. EST
SUCHES, GEORGIA

Byrd might as well have been blind; the darkness was complete and overwhelming. The last volley of shots had been near the summit of the mountain they had been climbing, or maybe the summit of a ridge, but Byrd couldn't tell anything else about where Rudy might be.

He had fired a shot in frustration and had immediately regretted it. An advantage of the suppressor was that the normal fireball coming out of the end of the weapon was mitigated. However, it was not the proper procedure to fire when you could neither see the target nor the background. Byrd doubted there was another person in these mountains at night, but rules were rules.

On the plus side of the ledger, Byrd could hear a generator running, and he thought he could make out lights off to his left. He hoped it was a command post. It would offer a direction for them to walk if they were still here at daylight.

Byrd took deep breaths to get his temper in check. "Addy? Where are you?"

"Here, behind you." The stage whisper made Byrd jump. She was less than three feet away and was invisible in the dark, rainy night.

"We've got to stay on our toes," Byrd said. "Rudy might be smart enough to circle back around behind us. He could get the drop on us pretty quickly."

"Danny," Raelynn called. "Can I have your pistol? I want to be able to defend myself."

Byrd thought it over. "There are plenty of rocks up here. If he gets close, you can take him out with one of them. Hell, you probably have a better chance with a rock than a gun right now."

Raelynn didn't answer.

Byrd felt sorry for the El Paso County deputy. "We need to keep this on a professional level," he reminded Raelynn. "Don't worry, we're going to get him."

Byrd's words were met with silence.

MONDAY, DECEMBER 10, 2007
7:11 A.M. (2:11 A.M. EST)
CREDEN HILL, HEREFORDSHIRE, ENGLAND

Omar Warren poured a cup of coffee for himself and a tea for his companion in his little apartment. The British government had allocated the space for his temporary use over a year ago, with the promise of better accommodations in the future. His new fiancée, Matilda, was on the couch waiting for her first tea of the day. She absentmindedly turned on the TV.

Omar asked her to turn to the BBC West Midlands, his favorite of the few stations available. He preferred the news readers from the BBC to most others he'd seen in his travels.

The screen was filled with shaky video of a mountainside where a car had crashed and was resting on its top. The sound was turned down, but Omar noticed the banner running across the screen. "American Officers missing after chase with murder suspect. Officers feared dead outside North Georgia city."

A captioned photograph of Daniel Byrd was projected on the screen. Omar stopped sipping his coffee. He held the cup suspended in space near his lips. Even without the caption, he remembered Byrd.

"Turn it up, Tilly. I want to hear this." Omar called.

Matilda glanced at him. "Don't call me Tilly." She was smiling as she used the remote to increase the volume.

A talking head on the screen looked concerned. "An agent of the Georgia Bureau of Investigation and two Texas law enforcement officers are missing this morning after a chase with a murderer." The cameraman zoomed in on a photo of several law enforcement cars sitting on the road near a crashed car. "The GBI agent, a deputy sheriff from Texas, and a Texas Ranger were attempting to capture a murderer who is alleged to have killed an entire family in a small Texas village." The camera pulled back to show a picturesque view of downtown Blairsville. The BBC man continued. "In this idyllic mountain setting, the officers went missing last night and are feared dead. Nearby residents heard gunshots and shouting, but the area is far too mountainous to marshal a search until dawn."

The camera zoomed in to a close-up of the newsman. "American authorities are planning a massive ground search when there is light, but a storm front passing through the area will hamper the operation," the reporter solemnly intoned.

Omar picked up his phone and dialed a number he knew by heart. Matilda watched, curious about what had seemed to fill her man with such urgency.

"Loftus," came the answer on the phone.

"This is Kleinman from Creden Hill," Omar said.

"I know. To what do I owe this call so early in the morning? We government types are not early risers."

Omar put a fist on his right hip, stared at the ceiling, and compressed his lips for a moment. "The situation in the US. Georgia, to be exact. Do you know about it?"

"Let me see." Omar could hear Loftus searching through papers. "My morning brief from the office is here on my printer." He heard Loftus mumble something and then stop. "Here it is. Our friends with the FBI included the information in a Five Eyes synopsis. A Georgia Bureau of Investigation agent and a Texas deputy are missing in the North Georgia Mountains. GBI reports they were in pursuit of a murder suspect when, it is believed, the officers were involved in a car crash."

"Is that it?" Omar asked.

"The names of the agent and a picture are included. And the latitude and longitude of the crash. Not much else. Why are you interested?" Loftus paused. "Oh, I see. The agent is Byrd. The one who arrested you."

Omar lowered his voice. "Aren't the boys in North Georgia? The Army Rangers training camp? I supplied them with some cold-weather gear last month."

Loftus could be heard rustling papers again. "Here it is. E Squadron is training with the American Delta Force in a place called Dahlonega, Georgia. But you know we can't task them with something that would blow their covers. The Prime Minister would have my balls if I activated them for something like this."

"What are your balls any good for if you don't use them?" Omar asked. "You know they have all the toys and the skills to find Byrd. Why not make the search a part of their training?"

There was a long silence on the line. "Are we trying to make amends for past sins?" Loftus asked.

"Something like that," Omar offered honestly. "He was fair with me and never mistreated my family when he searched our house in Fitzgerald. I feel like this is a situation that will draw a bright line between Omar Warren's past and my future."

"He'll never know you had a hand in this, anyway it goes," Loftus replied. "It's after 2 a.m. in the States. If the boys can do their work and get out before the sun rises, we might be able to do something. But no promises."

Omar smiled. "My dad kept a self-defense trainer at his old camp in Fitzgerald, Georgia. He was quite a character. A big ballsy Brit who'd served in the SAS. He kept getting into trouble of every sort, and my dad would get him out of it. Do you know who he was?"

"Who did your father *say* he was?" Loftus asked. But Omar could tell Loftus knew the answer.

"He was your brother," Omar remarked. He hoped he hadn't overstepped.

Loftus sighed. "Well, we can do little to control who our relatives are. I'll make some phone calls." Then the line went dead.

Matilda had been watching and listening with great interest. "What in the name of heaven was that all about? You are certainly asking a lot of Mr. Loftus. Is this Byrd a friend from your childhood? And who is Omar Warren?"

Omar tilted back his drink. Then he met his future wife's eyes. "No, quite the opposite. But I owe him this."

"Maybe you can open up to me when I'm Mrs. Kleinman," Matilda remarked. She watched her future husband over the top of the teacup.

"I guess there *are* some things I should tell you about my past," Omar mused.

"Bad things," Matilda asked with a hint of concern.

"Not bad, I guess, but certainly unconventional. I guess I'm having some pangs of conscience."

Matilda stood up and joined Omar. She clinked her glass against his. "To your conscience. May the dreams that wake you up at night go away."

Omar held her tight. "All those dreams aren't bad," he said as he leaned in to kiss her.

MONDAY, DECEMBER 10, 2007
3:53 A.M. EST
SUCHES, GEORGIA

Byrd hugged his rifle to his chest and tried to find a position that allowed him to blend into the trees. The rain had slowed, but the temperature had dropped in the last hour. He knew it would only get worse between now and daylight. Those were the coldest hours of the night.

"Ladies?" Byrd whispered. "How are we doing?"

"Cold and wet and hungry," Adeline responded. "How long until daylight?"

"About three more hours," Byrd guessed. "If we're still stuck up here after daylight, we may have to come up with a plan to get word to the cops back down on the road."

"How long do you think Rudy could hide out in these woods?' Raelynn asked.

"Eric Robert Rudolph was able to hide in these very mountains, about ten miles from here on the North Carolina side, for about seven years," Byrd observed.

"Who?" Adeline asked.

"The Olympic Park Bomber during the 96 Olympics," Byrd explained. "I hope that's not Rudy's plan. Was he in the military?"

"Yes, in the Navy," Raelynn said.

"Not a SEAL, I hope." Adeline hadn't seen his background package before they left Texas.

"No, he was a mechanic of some kind. I don't think he even had to carry a gun." Raelynn leaned back on her tree.

Adeline was concerned. "I've never had to chase anyone through terrain like this. Will we hear him in the dark if he were to try to sneak up on us?"

Byrd's response was a whisper, "I sure hope so. If I knew where he was, I'd try that myself."

"This mountain will be crawling with cops as soon as the sun comes up. We have to hunker down and wait," Adeline observed.

MONDAY, DECEMBER 10, 2007
4:02 A.M. EST
SUCHES, GEORGIA

Rudy rocked back against the boulder he was partially protected by. His left hand was throbbing, and his thumbs were so sore he didn't think he could reload the pistol magazine. The wet fingers forcing ammo into the mag had begun to bleed along with his hand.

But Rudy knew he wasn't out of the fight. He had spent the last three days running from the police he couldn't see. Chased across the country by his own conscience. Now his pursuers had a face or, more correctly, faces. His bitch sister-in-law and the man and woman with her. Rudy felt a deep-down fear and a kind of sadness. He was sorry his life had changed. If only he hadn't been so panicked by all that had happened to him that day and the bad luck of his daughter getting in the way.

Rudy shook his head and almost cried when he realized he would not likely get away. Even if he were able to kill the cops on his trail, he would have a hard time getting away. Not impossible, he thought, but difficult.

He had accidentally chosen a spot with an acoustic anomaly. Maybe it was the rocks, perhaps they reflected the sound waves, or the wind that allowed him to hear the cops talking.

He recognized his sister-in-law's voice. He was right when he thought he saw her in the cop car. She wasn't alone. There was another female voice and a man, talking low, about fifty yards away, he guessed.

He could hear the tone of their voices, but was only able to understand some words. They were grumbling about being wet and cold, it appeared to Rudy. The man said he could find their way out in the daylight, but the weather and the thick tree cover made it difficult right now.

The man was saying, ". . . plan to get word to the cops back down on the road."

Rudy heard Raelynn mention his name and strained to hear more.

The man asked if Rudy was in the military. Raelynn was talking, but Rudy couldn't make out the words till she said, "He was a mechanic."

Rudy heard the other woman ask, "Will we hear him in the dark if he were to try to sneak up on us?"

The man said something, and the other woman responded, "This mountain will be crawling with cops as soon as the sun comes up."

Rudy didn't like the sound of that. He decided the best defense would be a good offense. He reloaded the pistol magazine with some considerable effort. He slammed the freshly filled magazine home, and then he pushed himself up from behind the rock. He planned to work his way carefully toward the voices.

The ground was wet and covered with slick leaves. Where there were no leaves, there were unyielding granite outcroppings. And the trees at this altitude were scrub pines and something that reminded Rudy of a Christmas tree. He figured he could walk right up to the cops and not see them. He hoped it worked the other way around.

CHAPTER 20
CHARGE OF THE LIGHT BRIGADE

MONDAY, DECEMBER 10, 2007
4:11 A.M. EST
CAMP MERRILL—US ARMY RANGERS TRAINING CENTER
DAHLONEGA, GEORGIA

Camp Frank D. Merrill, named for Frank Dow Merrill, a United States Army general honored for his command of Merrill's Marauders in World War II, is the second phase of ranger training in the US Army. The ranger candidates are challenged by the mountainous terrain, frequent waterfalls, and deep ravines.

Outside the barracks of Camp Merrill, eight men stood in a circle. They were dressed in worn blue jeans, work boots, and heavy, dark-colored coats. On top of the coats were rifle-grade body armor and various pouches with specialized gear. Each man was armed with a slung Mark-18 Mod-0 CQB rifle. The men were doing a final check of each other's gear before they loaded onto the MH-6 Little Bird helicopters. The compact yet powerful army choppers received *their* final check on the asphalt landing pad by their pilot team from the 160th Special Operations Aviation Regiment, on the west side of the training camp.

Each of the elite soldiers tugged on their partner's equipment and tried not to think about the weather front moving in. They had the best rain and cold protection money could buy, but the ride outside of the light, maneuverable helicopters would be miserable. And every minute, a misstep by one of the veteran pilots could end in a fireball on the side of a North Georgia mountain. They were hardened veterans of armed conflict on six of the seven continents.

Once the checks were done, Major James Broadmoor addressed the men gathered. The scruffy-looking group, when viewed up close, didn't look like traditional soldiers. And they weren't.

Broadmoor was the only member of the team without facial hair, but his long brown hair, beginning to have the occasional touch of grey, was not regulation. "Gentlemen. We came here to train. This is just another training mission. For this one, however, we will be carrying live ammunition."

Sergeant Major Graeme Sutherell stepped forward. "Boss, what are the rules of engagement for this, uh-hum, training?"

"There are three American law officers in the forest northwest of us. They have been battling with a murderer who is on the lam. The officers are a man and two women. The male officer was last seen wearing a business suit. The suspect is in jeans and a barn coat. That's a kind of heavy work coat. If the man in the coat is aggressive in any way, we will engage to protect the police officers."

Sergeant Sutherell nodded and then looked all around. "Why intervene in this situation? Not that it matters."

Broadmoor looked around at his men. "I learned as we were getting ready to brief that this murderer has killed his wife, mother-in-law, and his daughter. I believe the young girl was twelve."

One of the men almost made a joke about wanting to kill his wife and mother. The last statement had brought a sudden silence over the group of men.

Broadmoor cleared his throat. "We don't want to alarm the local population, so suppressors will be utilized. This drill is not on the books. We have about three hours before sunup. If we haven't found the coppers by then, we are to head back to the camp." Broadmoor looked over the faces of the soldiers he led. "Let's go do what we do!"

"Right, boss," Sergeant Sutherell said. 'How's the weather? Can the Little Birds get us in, or is this a hike?"

Broadmoor looked at the bleak sky. "The pilots say this isn't the worst they've flown in."

In pairs of twos, the men climbed onto the seats fixed outside the body of the US Army Special Operations MH-6 Little Birds. The benches could seat three fully armed and equipped special operators. Tonight, with the rain and wind moving in the area, Broadmoor opted to use seven operators and himself on the chancy operation.

Once each soldier had given the thumbs up, the helicopter blades roared as the machine lifted into the mountain air. The world around them was suddenly dark; the helicopters completely blacked out. "NOD's deployed," Broadmoor said into the encrypted radio. Then he pulled the bulky set of scopes attached to his helmet into place. Civilians refer to them as night vision goggles, but in the military, they were known as Night Observation Devices. He could already see heat signatures from animals in the woods.

Broadmoor's face already felt frozen solid as the helicopter picked up speed. The boys would be told, once the mission was over, about the killer and all the things he had done. They didn't necessarily care about such things; orders were orders, but the fathers in the group, of which there were seven, wouldn't mind so much having spent a cold night hanging from a helicopter once they knew the objective. Broadmoor was a father. And his daughter had recently turned twelve.

MONDAY, DECEMBER 10, 2007
4:35 A.M. EST
SUCHES, GEORGIA

Rudy shuffled toward where he thought the cops were. His only hope was to kill them and then try to find a place to hide out. Maybe an empty house or someone's barn. He carefully stepped forward; his gun extended in front of his face. The ground was slippery, and the night seemed black as pitch.

He was working his way higher up the mountainside as he crept closer to his goal. Then he slipped.

Rudy's feet slipped and he pitched onto his face. Suddenly, he was flat on the uneven ground, and his breath had been knocked out of him. He lay still for a moment, listening for the cops to rush over and put him out of his misery.

Once he was able to breathe again, he realized he had lost his pistol. In a panic, he felt around in the wet ground nearby.

Thank you, Jesus, Rudy thought as his fingers brushed the big automatic. He used his right hand to wipe mud and pine needles off the gun and then sat back against a sapling.

Rudy waited, listening, as he regained his equilibrium. He shook his head for a moment. "I never did like Georgia," he mumbled as rain dripped from his forehead.

MONDAY, DECEMBER 10, 2007
4:35 A.M. EST
SUCHES, GEORGIA

The DEA Aero Commander was slowly circling the mountains. The airplane had been specially fitted to loiter over a target location for several hours. The biggest risk to the twin-engine plane was the winter weather. Arlow Turner was fully aware how the slightest mistake or miscalculation could result in the airplane flying into the weather phenomenon pilots call a cumulous granite cloud. In other words, a cloud with a rock in it. He had explained these things to Doc as the plane thundered down the runway at Blairsville.

Doc seemed to have given up being scared. Arlow watched Doc's face as the airplane bounced around like a paint can in a shaker he'd seen at a hardware store. Doc looked resigned to whatever fate had in store for him, keeping his eyes locked on the green screen, which displayed the images of the heat signatures on the ground. He had seen activity from deer and other small mammals, but no green blobs he could identify as human. "How much longer can we stay in the air?" Doc asked. "I can see that weather screen of yours, and it doesn't look promising."

Arlow scanned the gauges. The plane was running well, and both engines were feathered back to extend the plane's available flight time. Then he looked at the color weather radar. The screen displayed a weather front moving into the area. The blob was dark green with some large blobs of yellow and red. Doc knew it was bad news.

"Doc, we'll have to get on the ground in the next hour or we'll be looking for another spot to land."

Doc glanced over. "You mean another airport? I can't think of one close."

"We may have to land on the Appalachian Highway. It's not that dangerous." Arlow projected confidence he didn't feel.

Arlow had split his time between struggling with the controls in the bumpy air to glimpsing at the FLIR screen. Doc was holding up well as the plane rocked left and right.

Arlow was adding power when Doc called out to him. "I see something! It's coming toward us."

Arlow pulled the airplane into a climb as he glanced at the screen. He saw a nest of infrared beacons flashing from a single location. The speed of the moving flashes had to be military helicopters. There was no other explanation for the lack of white light coming from the aircraft.

Arlow switched on his military radio and rolled the dial to the UHF channel designated for coordination. "Omaha flight to helicopter at latitude 34.78 by 84.17. Reply on guard."

"On guard," the muffled voice backed by the steady beat of rotor blades replied. "State your agency and intentions."

"Flint 355, DEA Airwing on a search for missing police officers." Arlow was curious what a military training flight was doing up in this weather, but the Army Rangers were known for training in horrible meteorological conditions.

"Flint, this is a training flight from Camp Merrill. We'll be orbiting in the area as part of the op. We request that you give us plenty of room. Over."

Arlow glanced over at Doc. "No worries. We are not able to get as low as you. In fact, I'm climbing out of this hole as we speak. I'll be loitering at six thousand feet."

Doc was checking the aviation map. He pressed the intercom button. "Arlow, we're over the Morganton Highway at about Skeenah Gap Road. That's pretty close to where they went in the woods."

Arlow nodded. "They're not telling us any kind of call sign. I'll bet it's a Special Ops helicopter. Those brightest beacons we can see are the aircraft, and the smaller beacons are the operators. Pretty ballsy to be operating up here at night, blacked out."

"Flint, we'll be loitering in the area as well. Please be aware of our operation as you conduct your search."

Arlow shrugged. He glanced over at Doc. "What choice do we have?"

Arlow leveled the Aero Commander off at fifty-five hundred feet and, once at his cruising altitude, settled into a long, wide orbit. As he held the twin-engine airplane steady over the search area, Arlow muttered to himself, "Odd though. Those guys usually confine their operations to areas closer to Dahlonega at night. I wonder what they are doing up here?"

MONDAY, DECEMBER 10, 2007
4:37 A.M. EST
SUCHES, GEORGIA

"What's the problem?" Broadmoor asked over the private radio channel.

"Police aircraft looking for the missing officers," the pilot responded. "I asked them to give us some room. They are orbiting at six thousand feet. No more issues."

The Little Bird was flying much slower than its maximum speed of 152 knots. The FLIR was more effective at the reduced airspeed. Both pilots were fighting the rough air as the helicopters plowed along treetop level in the mountains. The machines were buffeted and twisted in the air as the pilots fought to maintain course and altitude. The pair of pilots in the helicopters trained constantly for this sort of mission.

"Any sign of our targets on your FLIR?" Broadmoor asked. The FLIR on the Little Bird was far superior to the unit Arlow had hijacked from the Navy.

"So far, all the contacts have been wildlife," the FLIR operator replied. "And we're too low to get a good look for more than about five clicks. We've got our eyes peeled."

Broadmoor chuckled. "Work your magic, boy-o. We need to get on the ground."

"Roger that!" the pilot came back. "If this rain keeps up and the temperature drops ten more degrees, we might be taking up temporary residence in one of these hollows, anyway. Then we'll all be on the ground."

Broadmoor worked his jaw back and forth. His lips were so cold he wasn't sure he could talk. "We're freezing back here. I hope our team can last long enough to find these cops."

The pilot double-clicked the transmit button. "Yes, sir. We understand. In a gesture of solidarity, the crew has turned the heat down in the cabin."

"Thanks," Broadmoor laughed. He knew the crew was as cold as he was—one of the side effects of flying without doors.

MONDAY, DECEMBER 10, 2007
4:43 A.M. EST
SUCHES, GEORGIA

Byrd recognized the sound of a twin-engine airplane overhead. He listened as it turned away, and the engine pitch changed as the plane climbed.

"I'll bet that's Arlow. Nobody else would fly in this kind of weather," Byrd observed. As the plane flew away, Byrd heard rustling in the woods near them. "Shit, I think Rudy is close!"

The sound of a pistol shot proved he was correct. The sound was close. Instinctively, all the officers hugged the rugged ground. A bullet struck the mountain behind the cops as a shower of granite slivers rained down on them, and the bullet zinged off into the side of the mountain.

"Rudy!" Byrd shouted. "You're not giving us much choice. Daylight is coming sooner than later. I'm coming for you."

"I guess you'll have to come. I can't go back to Texas," Rudy responded.

"You just wait and see," Raelynn shouted. "I'm planning on watching them stick a needle in your arm."

The reply was swift and clear. The pistol boomed twice. Neither round came close to the law officers. Byrd felt a surge of adrenaline as he realized how close Rudy was to them.

"I've had enough of his shit. I'm about to rock his world." Byrd raised his M4 rifle and pointed it at the location where he had seen the flashes from the pistol shots. Byrd let out a deep breath and squeezed the trigger.

The sound of the rifle bullet, even with the suppressor on the gun, was deafening in the wet forest. BOOM-BOOM-BOOM! The cops were showered with dead leaves and pine needles as the concussion of the shots spread around them.

He touched Addy on the shoulder, fumbling in the dark. "We've got to move. If he gets close to us, we could all be goners."

Quietly, the trio moved deeper into the woods. Byrd glanced around as they searched for a safer location to wait out the night. The rain had slowed to a gentle patter on the dead leaves carpeting the ground and would help mask the sounds of the officer's movement. Byrd knew from experience, however, that the slowing rain would soon usher in colder air.

The three soaked cops needed to find a place sheltered from the wind to wait out the coldest part of the night. Byrd wondered for a moment if they had more to fear from Rudy or the elements.

Byrd strained to see Rudy in the murky forest. The granite outcroppings were lighter areas in the night. Byrd shuffled toward a large mass he could barely make out in the darkness. Each step was a potential disaster on the slick leaves as Byrd did his best to herd the two Texans toward a rock outcropping he hoped would offer some shelter.

MONDAY, DECEMBER 10, 2007
4:59 A.M. EST
SUCHES, GEORGIA

The soldiers felt the helicopter tip to the left and pick up speed. That was a good sign. "What do you have?" Broadmoor asked over the private radio channel.

"Pistol and maybe a rifle flash at our ten o'clock," the pilot responded. "I'm looking for a place to put you on the ground. I see a pasture about a quarter click from the action. I'll set you off there and then guide you in."

"Will that be close enough to spook them?" Broadmoor asked.

The Night Stalker pilot came back on the intercom. "The rain and wind will muffle our rotor noise. We should be good."

Broadmoor double-clicked his radio microphone.

Each of the eight soldiers tried to peer into the night. They felt the sensation of a roller coaster going over the top as the helicopter floated up to lose airspeed. The pilot began circling the potential landing zone. It would ruin the night if the aircraft landed on a cow or a horse.

Broadmoor could make out the trees around them as the chopper settled above a grass-covered knoll. Once the helicopter was low enough, the men unbuckled and dropped to the ground. It was too risky to land completely on the ground, which could be hiding ditches or stumps.

The pilot expertly hovered less than a foot from the blowing grass as the men worked their way out from the down-blast of the rotor blades. As quickly as he had stopped, the pilot pulled up on the collective and rocketed back into the air.

The action was repeated by the second pilot, who hovered long enough for the four men on his bird to drop to the ground, and then the second bird was quickly back in the dark sky.

"Move on my marker. I'll take a high orbit around where the shooting took place." The pilot knew from experience that the soldiers would be hustling to keep him in sight. On the same channel, he called to the pilot of the other bird. "Roco, find us a good place to pick our men up. I think I saw a church parking lot on the way in. Take a look at it."

"Affirm," was the only response.

Broadmoor followed the Little Bird helicopter; its infra-red beacons were visible in his night vision. He waited as the pilot activated the compact laser designator.

"Look for the 'Finger of God,'" the spec ops pilot announced over the radio. "We love to give bad guys the finger!"

Broadmoor saw a bright green laser beam marking a line from the helicopter to the ground. The "finger" was a military-grade laser designator emitting at a special wavelength, not visible to the human eye. A military grade imaging sensor is needed to "see" the LD spot on the target. Broadmoor could see the beam as it pointed toward the place the gunshots had come from. He motioned for his men to follow. No one spoke as they quietly entered the deep, wet forest in the North Georgia Mountains.

The night observation devices the men wore over their eyes made the forest seem to glow. The ambient light was almost non-existent in the rough terrain, but the soldiers had the very best equipment money could buy. The special NODs could see in the deep woods thanks to the helicopter-mounted spotlight broadcasting on an invisible spectrum of light. Broadmoor led them deeper into the tall pines and hardwoods as the helicopter marked the goal.

Broadmoor stumbled as the red clay beneath his feet was replaced by granite outcroppings. The scrub underfoot would snatch at his jeans and wool sweater as he muscled along. The helicopter, a few thousand feet above his head, crept along almost soundlessly as the soldiers assumed an arrow formation beneath it. The chopper would have to be hovering directly over anyone in the mountains for them to detect the rotor sounds. Thanks to the finger, that wouldn't be necessary.

Broadmoor tugged at a clinging vine and then leaned against an ancient pine tree. "One to the Bird. How much farther?" His voice was barely a whisper.

"The rifle shots came from about 100 meters from your current position. The pistol shooter is right off your left shoulder. You are close." Broadmoor acknowledged the message with two clicks of the microphone.

With the information, Broadmoor was able to pick out the cops dead ahead. They were lying flat on the ground near a large boulder. He motioned for the second element of the team to move toward the shooter. Using his left hand, he motioned to the area to his left.

Sergeant Major Sutherell nodded once, acknowledging he saw the target, and moved his element quietly toward Rudy's position.

CHAPTER 21
SOMEONE TO WATCH OVER ME

The forest seemed lighter to Byrd, but his eyes were so tired he could have been imagining it. The waking forest, with rain still coming down, was a noisy place. Owls hooted in the distance, and other animals, everything from squirrels to coyotes, were moving along the mountainside. Byrd thought he'd heard a helicopter. But it didn't sound close.

Byrd was wet and miserable, as were the Texans, he assumed, from resting on the cold, wet ground. He knew there were at least a couple of more hours until sunup. Byrd was stretched out on the ground in a tumble of rocks to break his outline, his M4 sighted in on the last place he saw Rudy's pistol shots. He was listening intently for any sound of Rudy moving and trying not to shiver in the unrelenting cold. The background noise had been constant, yet it changed every second. Byrd was not a hiker or a hunter. He couldn't read the sounds, no matter how much he tried.

Byrd heard Adeline whisper. "If he rushes us right now, I'm afraid we won't be able to react in time. My hands are numb, and my right leg is cramping."

We need water and heat, Byrd thought. He couldn't come up with a plan to get either.

Byrd decided he needed to force the situation. Byrd kept his eye on the target location and said, "Rae, you and Addy make some noise. Stay behind the rocks but make some rustling in the dead leaves or something."

Byrd felt a hand on his shoulder. Byrd's heart leapt into his throat. An unfamiliar voice, barely a whisper, said, "Don't do that, ladies."

Byrd rolled over on his side to see a group of men, or at least that was all he could guess they were, huddled near them. They were dark shadows in the night. "We're here to help," the same voice said.

Byrd strained to make out the figures. They each had a long gun and a ballistic helmet similar to what he wore on raids. The helmets had a binocular device on top, which Byrd assumed were night vision goggles. Some of the men were looking through the goggles as the others set up a protective perimeter around the cops.

"I'm with the GBI. The man out there is a wanted felon," Byrd offered in a whisper.

The man who was kneeling beside Byrd said, "We know. Just stay low and wait."

Byrd tried to make out the clothes the team around him was wearing. He could tell they were wearing ballistic plates and helmets. They had long guns, which he thought were similar to his M4. And each of the long guns had a fat cylinder suppressor on the barrel.

"Call to him," the man kneeling directed Byrd.

Byrd raised an eyebrow, but he did as he was told. "Rudy! Give it up, buddy. It'll be daylight soon! This is not going to go your way!"

MONDAY, DECEMBER 10, 2007
5:59 A.M. EST

He didn't see anything. Rudy raised the .45 Colt Commander and pointed into the darkness. Rudy's pistol was shoved skyward by an unseen force as it boomed twice. Rudy was surprised to see a man standing near him in the bright flash of the Colt.

The last thing Rudy saw was a small flash of light. He felt something hit him in the chest, almost like he imagined being stabbed would be like, and then his left lung exploded.

MONDAY, DECEMBER 10, 2007
6:01 A.M. EST
SUCHES, GEORGIA

Rudy must have stood. Pop-pop. Bright flashes came from about four or five feet above the ground, about fifteen yards away. The night lit up, and for a moment, Rudy was a dark silhouette.

The shots were followed by a sound Byrd recognized—the distinctive sound of suppressed fire. Three shots. There were no flashes, only the crack of a supersonic bullet traveling from gun to target. And it was a short trip.

Dim lights came on in the area where Byrd thought Rudy must be. He could see men outlined in the light, and he could see Rudy lying on the ground.

Byrd stood and helped Addy and Rae to their feet. "What just happened?" Rae asked.

Byrd waited for the man beside him to answer. Without replying, the man walked toward Rudy's body. Byrd and the Texans followed.

One of the soldiers was using a low-power flashlight to examine the downed fugitive. Rudy was lying on his back, mouth and eyes open, with several wounds bleeding through his shirt. His face was slack, and his eyes were already clouding up.

The man who spoke motioned at Rudy. "Is he the one who killed his little girl?"

Raelynn screamed as she felt her heart breaking, still clutching the hope that Madison would be found alive. "Madison is dead!" Rae pulled her right foot back and kicked the body on the side of the mountain. "You bastard. Why did you do it?"

The man turned to Byrd. "I'm sorry, mate. I thought you knew the little girl was dead."

Raelynn kicked Rudy's body again as she stood in the cold and dark. She couldn't take the fear and the dread she had been wearing like a jacket anymore. Adeline grabbed her in a bear hug and pulled her close.

Byrd stepped between Raelynn and the body. "Rae, there will be an autopsy. You've got to stop."

The men had circled Byrd and the Texans. "Are you guys cops?" Byrd asked.

The man who had whispered in Byrd's ear, and the only one to speak that night, said, "Just concerned citizens. Are you the one called Byrd?"

"I am. What's your name?" Byrd asked.

"Think of us as your guardian angels. We came down from heaven and put the bad man down."

Byrd shook his head. "You killed a man. Admittedly, a man who wanted to kill us, but a man nonetheless. We'll have to do a report. What are we supposed to tell our bosses?"

"Our medic has checked him out," the man said. The man with the flashlight stood up. He glanced back at the body and then gave a thumbs-down motion.

"He's gone. We use frangible bullets so there won't be any ballistics in case any part of a bullet is left in him, which I very much doubt. We note you are armed with a .223 rifle. The medical examiner will not be the wiser. I'd say your best bet is you, Mr. Byrd, take credit for our friend here."

Byrd shook his head. "Credit or blame. I didn't do it."

The man shook his head. "Then you have a problem. We aren't here and never have been. You will not be able to identify us later. We will be long gone when your help arrives."

Byrd considered the circumstances. "You aren't going to take us out of here?"

The man shook *his* head. "Not enough room in our extraction vehicles. But we'll let your people know where you are. You'll be fine. We can leave water if you like."

Byrd shook his head. "We can make it a little while longer. So, you're not cops. Who are you?"

The man shook his head again. "You're a smart man, Mr. Byrd. Smart enough to know that's a question that will never be answered. But you're alive and he is dead. The rest is up to you."

Byrd looked at the Texans. "Are you guys okay with this?"

"Hell no! I wanted to shoot him. If it was up to me, I'd shoot him right now," Raelynn said as she reached for Byrd's rifle.

Byrd pulled the gun away as Raelynn tried to pull it from his shoulder. "Rae, if he's shot when he's on the ground, even if he's dead, you and I will have to answer for it. The pathologists will play it right down the middle. We can't do it."

"Maybe you can," the man said. "Boys, lean our departed friend against this tree."

The men dragged Rudy's body upright and propped him against a massive oak. "Mr. Byrd, give her your rifle. But one shot only, madam."

Raelynn looked at Byrd, confused by what was happening. "What should I do?"

The man pulled Byrd's M4 from his shoulder and handed the gun to Raelynn. "You get a free shot at this man. I understand he wronged you and your family. You may take a single shot if you would like."

Raelynn raised the rifle to her shoulder and fired a single round into Rudy's chest. The body jerked and fell over to the ground. "Damn, that felt good!" Raelynn exclaimed.

Byrd took his gun back. "You're suggesting we tell our bosses, who are no doubt somewhere out there waiting on us, that I shot Rudy in a gunfight?"

The man nodded as the group gathered around. "That would be what I'd say, if I were you. No issues with ballistics. The rounds are through and through. You happen to have a gun of the same caliber as the fatal wounds. It will all fit—if you want it to."

"And if I don't want to? You shoot us to keep us quiet?" Byrd asked.

The man, the obvious leader, shook his head. "No. I guess in a spy movie or something, that might happen. No, we were tasked with keeping you from being killed up here. We have accomplished that mission by neutralizing the suspect, and soon we'll be calling in your location. Officially, this group doesn't exist. There'll be nothing to prove we were ever here."

"So, if we claim we were rescued by soldiers wearing blue jeans, we'll sound like people who say they were kidnapped by aliens?" Byrd wondered.

"Or Bigfoot. I hear he roams the forest around here. Something like that," the speaking soldier said.

The leader of the group handed Byrd a package of glow sticks. "This will help your people find you."

The group of men started walking away and in seconds had disappeared into the night.

Addy stood beside Byrd. "Danny, did that just happen? I have to be dreaming."

Byrd turned to the Texans. "Beats the hell out of me."

Byrd slumped against a granite rock and laid his rifle across his knees. He systematically broke several light sticks and placed them around them. Byrd was struck by the surreal shadows cast by the chemical sticks on the ground as he looked to his companions. "Are both of you okay with what just happened?"

"I shouldn't have done that," Raelynn blurted out.

Adeline was more pragmatic. "If we get out of here, I think we have to stick to their story. That you shot him in a gunfight. Otherwise, they might put all of us in the loony bin."

Byrd sat back and closed his eyes. "I can't lie under oath, but I guess in the long run, nothing is going to trial. Since Rudy was a clear danger and couldn't contradict our story, we went with the official version. I sure would like to know how they found us."

Raelynn sat beside Byrd on the ground. "Does the military train around here? They were definitely soldiers of some kind."

Byrd nodded. "The Army has a Ranger Training Center close to here. They run training ops out of a camp near Dahlonega. That's about ten miles as the crow flies."

Adeline slumped beside the others. "I don't think they got here by crow. I assume they came by helicopter. But I damned sure didn't hear one."

Byrd looked for a dry place to sit. He moved to an overhanging rock where the ground wasn't as damp. He felt the moisture in his underwear as he dropped to the ground. He tried to pick Raelynn out of the gloom.

"This is a hell of a way to spend the night," Byrd said, chuckling as he leaned back on the rock. His winter overcoat was ruined, he thought.

CHAPTER 22

LOWDOWN ON THE SHOWDOWN

MONDAY, DECEMBER 10, 2007
6:43 A.M. EST
SUCHES, GEORGIA

The Aero Commander was being buffeted by the winds as colder air rolled into North Georgia. Arlow had given up on the autopilot and was hand-flying the orbit they had established near the site where Byrd's car had been found.

Doc Farmer was alternating between watching the blips on the screen move through the woods and praying for this night to be over. Doc had tightened his seatbelt until he was surprised blood was still flowing to his feet. He had tried closing his eyes, but if it were possible, that seemed to make it worse. Under other circumstances, he might have asked to be taken back.

"Doc, can you make anything out of those beacons. Can you tell what they're up to?" Arlow was curious about the nighttime operation going on under them.

Doc shook his head. "No. A while ago, they were spread out in the shape of an arrowhead. They huddled up around a spot in the woods, and there was some flickering, like little lights going off. Now they are all walking toward a church on Doublehead Gap Road. It looks like the choppers are landing behind the church in the parking lot."

"Ranger training flight to Flint unit on guard, over."

Arlow looked at Doc, illuminated by the gauges of the DEA airplane. "Something's up!" He switched the UHF radio to the guard channel. "Flint 355, over."

"Understand you have FLIR? Can you confirm? Over."

"That's affirm, ranger training. We can see you moving southeast." Arlow watched the green screen.

"You should see glow sticks on the ground where your people are, Flint."

Doc focused on the screen. He saw the glow of the light sticks scattered over an area near the crest of the mountain and pointed them out to Arlow. "Affirm. I see them," Arlow replied.

"A little birdie is telling me you need to send help to that location ASAP, Flint."

Arlow felt a surge of adrenaline. "Are any of our side hurt? Do we need a Medivac?"

The calm voice over the guard channel comes back. "Your people are good, but there is one confirmed casualty."

Arlow was relieved. "Thanks. Who do we send the thank-you card to?"

"No idea. I'm not here and haven't ever been here. And neither has anyone else I know. Good day, Flint." The channel was silent.

Arlow switched over to the law enforcement radio channel. "Flint 355 to the GBI Command Post."

Arlow recognized Tina Blackwell's voice. "Go ahead, Flint 355."

"I have a location on the missing agents. I have a lat/long of 34.7531 by 84.1932. They look to be about a mile off Doublehead Gap Road. They are north of where Grant crashed the car. I believe all the agents are good, but our suspect is down."

"Do you mean down as in 'needs medical attention', Arlow?" Blackwell was tentative.

"I can't be one hundred percent. Based on what we know at this time, he is down. We'll need fire and EMS for the agents involved. I still don't have communications with them on the ground." Arlow was matter-of-fact.

"We're rolling everything we've got. We have DNR game wardens with ATVs. I'll have them on the way. If you can stay in the air, be prepared to guide the ground teams in."

Arlow looked over at Doc. "Sorry, Doc, but it looks like we'll be on this roller coaster a little longer."

Doc kept his eyes on the ground. "It'll be worth the ride."

MONDAY, DECEMBER 10, 2007
6:44 A.M. EST
SUCHES, GEORGIA

Tina Blackwell stood on the side of the blocked roadway. It seemed surreal to be standing on a public roadway with no traffic. She had been considering her options for the morning and how to start a search in these mountains.

She slumped on the hood of Byrd's car. Then she took a deep breath and looked for Director Hicks and Major Crosby. "We have a location," she announced when she found them talking in the rain.

Hicks, Crosby, and Blackwell began to walk toward Troy Clifton's patrol car, idling to maintain power for his blue lights and radio.

Troy Clifton shouted at them, "Doc and that DEA pilot have found them! Doc says our guys are okay."

Blackwell smiled. "We heard, Troy. Thanks. And pass the word on how much we appreciate everyone's help. They can all go home."

Clifton grunted. "We ain't leaving till they're out of the woods." The trooper's jaw clenched for a moment. "I mean that literally."

MONDAY, DECEMBER 10, 2007
6:51 A.M. EST
SUCHES, GEORGIA

Byrd huddled against the cold as Adeline and Raelynn wrapped their arms around each other to share the heat. The wait seemed interminable after the adrenaline of the chase had dissipated.

"Rae, are you doing okay?" Byrd asked.

Raelynn gingerly touched her head. The bleeding had stopped. "I'm freezing, but other than that, I'm fine."

"I mean with all this," Byrd explained. "I know you're going to have to go back and bury your mom, sister, and niece. So, are you okay?"

Raelynn thought it over. "Yeah. I've got family back in El Paso. Aunts and uncles who will help out. And I'm sure there'll be more tears. But taking Rudy sure makes me feel better."

"Good," Byrd said.

Byrd saw the headlights of the four-wheelers before he heard the buzzing sound of their approach. He, Adeline, and Raelynn were huddled underneath the rock overhang, doing their best to avoid the rain. It seemed to Byrd they had been waiting a long time in the rain and dark. He prodded Adeline, who was closest to him, with his foot. "I think we're about to be joined by some game wardens or a bunch of rednecks looking for a place to drink."

Both women sat up. "I see a light way over there," Raelynn said as she pointed.

Bryd took a deep breath. "Are we all together on this? Raelynn, it's your family. Any second thoughts?"

Raelynn shook her head. "I shouldn't have shot him, even if he was already dead. I know that as an officer. But it sure made me feel good. I feel the best I have since Friday morning at my mama's house."

Byrd looked at Adeline. "How about you, Addy? Will you be okay with this? Speak now or forever hold your peace."

Adeline laughed. "Rudy would have killed us if he got the chance. I know what he did to Rae's mom and sister. And I have an idea what happened to Madison. Nope, no worries."

Byrd sat forward and stood his rifle in front of him on its stock. "I guess that leaves me."

Adeline rolled upright. "Danny, you know what you can handle. If you need to confess to your bosses, tell us before we get separated."

Byrd shook his head. "Can doing bad be good?"

Raelynn raised her voice. "Danny, we didn't do anything wrong. What we did was our jobs. If you're having second thoughts about protecting those men who saved our lives, well, I suppose I can understand that. But we did nothing wrong, except maybe me shooting Rudy."

The ATVs were getting closer. Byrd looked toward the headlights, making their way toward them. Byrd stood and waved a light stick at the game wardens.

He turned back to the Texans. "No, I guess I needed to convince myself. I'm good."

Raelynn stood beside him. "It's not too late. We'll back your play, either way."

Byrd leaned against Raelynn. "It's almost over."

The game wardens, four in all, made a beeline for the cops when they saw Byrd waving the glow stick. Byrd raised his right arm to signal they were alright.

The lead game warden, Sergeant Pete Haney pulled up alongside them. Anyone hurt?"

"Deputy Michaels here has a scrape on her head, but I think it can wait till we get to paramedics," Byrd said as he got to his feet.

Haney looked the group over, noting the dried blood on the side of Raelynn's head. "Nobody else hurt, then?"

"Just the suspect," Byrd replied calmly.

Haney examined the dark woods. "Where is the suspect? Do you know?"

Byrd pointed into the darkness, and another warden saw the body slumped against the tree. "I got him over here, Sarge. He's down." The warden lit Rudy's corpse with a powerful LED light. It was apparent Rudy was dead.

"Jim, you stay with the body," Haney ordered. "We'll get them out to the ambulance and then bring the crime scene folks back for the body."

Haney looked at the waterlogged cops. "Come on. Let's get you guys out of here, and then we'll worry about our child killer." They paired Byrd and the Texans with a game warden. Byrd climbed across the four-wheeler and sat behind Haney. Haney revved the engine, and the four-wheeler surged toward Doublehead Gap Road. Byrd slumped on Haney's back.

The game warden turned his head and shouted at Byrd, over the roar of the engine, "I guess y'all are ready to get to some food and shelter."

Byrd thought it over. "Some hot coffee sure would be nice. And maybe a place out of this damned cold rain."

MONDAY, DECEMBER 10, 2007
6:57 A.M. EST
BLAIRSVILLE, GEORGIA

Arty Winters had dreamed of this moment for all of his professional life. At thirty-five, he didn't have much longer to break out of an affiliate news role into the national spotlight. This morning, he was about to go live on the network's 7 a.m. news show with "Breaking News." He had spent the night doing research, using a payphone to run down information, and wrote a dynamite story the network agreed to let him offer. Winter was taking a calculated risk. The allegations he planned to make would result in a national story that would thrust him into the spotlight. By the time authorities were able to confirm or deny the details, he would be on his way.

From the satellite truck's connection, he could see the hosts in New York as they did sound checks and reviewed the stories for the first thirty-minute segment. Winters watched and listened as the stars made small talk. When they mentioned his name, Winters worried he would lose control of his bladder.

Buck up, son, Winter thought, *this is your break.*

Winter quickly freshened the light makeup he had applied himself. He double-checked his microphone and then waited for the red light on top of the camera to go on. He had chosen a spot near the Blairsville Airport's sign for the background of the shot, where he'd stand with rain peppering his face, to add to the local color.

The producer in New York came over Winter's earpiece. "Winter, we'll be tossing to you in two minutes. Everything ready on your end?"

"Ready to go," Winter responded with enthusiasm. He moved in front of the camera, giving his camera operator time to perfect the framing of the picture.

Winter flexed his feet, a practice he had learned from a veteran street reporter. The stars in New York were teasing the guests for today's show. Suddenly, Winter heard the producer's voice from the ether. "Go in three, two, one!"

Winter saw the light go on, and he gave the camera his best serious look. The voice of the producer in his ear was replaced by the morning show lead anchor. "We are going live to our network affiliate from Atlanta. Arty Winters has been on the scene since early yesterday following a manhunt for a suspected killer who, authorities believe, traveled from Texas to Georgia with the body of his twelve-year-old daughter. Arty, what can you tell us about the situation there in Georgia?"

Winter lowered the tone of his voice. "Thanks, Chet. I'm here outside a command post in Blairsville, Georgia, where I have been reporting since yesterday. As you said, a man named Rudolpho T. Grant is alleged to have killed his estranged wife and her mother in Texas. Authorities believe that Grant then brought his twelve-year-old daughter to Georgia to connect with someone described by law enforcement officials as Grant's extended family. Authorities, tragically, discovered little Madison Grant's body late yesterday afternoon."

The network talking head in New York had been told there was more to the story. "I understand you may have uncovered some details that make this story less straightforward. What can you tell us, Arty?"

Winter took a breath. "I have information that a Georgia Bureau of Investigation agent engaged in a reckless pursuit of the alleged killer of the Grant family. Our sources have told me that Grant, a much-loved member of the Hispanic community in his hometown of Montana, Texas, was pursued with aircraft, dogs, and ATVs by the Georgia officers. There are allegations that Grant was shot to death by Georgia officers without a chance to surrender."

The star from New York had questions. "Arty, these are serious charges, and if they are true, I suspect the authorities will take swift action against the officers involved in any sort of racially motivated acts."

Winter nodded seriously. "I am told that this information is so new that the Georgia authorities haven't been able to confirm the assault. I have asked Bob Bankston, the public information officer for the GBI, to respond to these allegations."

Bob Bankston stepped into the frame. "Thanks, Arty."

"What can you tell us about these charges?" Arty thrust his microphone into Bankston's face.

"The GBI takes any allegations of wrongdoing very seriously," Bankson said, maintaining a blank expression as he stared into the camera. "A complete investigation will be made into your allegations. However, I must correct some of your information."

Bankston held up a photo of Rudy Grant from his employee ID. "This red-haired white male, identified as Rudolpho Grant, was killed last night when he engaged in a gun battle with law enforcement officers. GBI Agents, along with Union County deputies and troopers, discovered a body we believe to be Grant's daughter. The body was recovered at the home of an acquaintance of hers in Georgia after, we believe, Mr. Grant brought her here from *Monahans*, Texas, a city between Fort Worth and El Paso. That friend, Mrs. Bernice Gazaway, has been charged with Party to a Crime and Concealing a Death. GBI agents and local officers arrested Mrs. Gazaway yesterday afternoon at her home in Blairsville, where the young girl's body was found."

Winter's face was red. "Have you confirmed that the picture you have is Rudolpho Grant?"

"We have," Bankston said without looking towards Winter. "It's an ID photograph from his former employer, the Texas Youth Commission. We'll be doing a press release once the results of the autopsies are in, but that will be sometime tomorrow," Bankston concluded as he stepped out of the frame.

Winter opened his mouth to speak when he heard the star say, "Thanks, Arty. And now let's switch to our weather team tips to help you prepare for the coming snowstorm across the northern tier . . ." The earpiece audio feed went dead. He saw the camera operator make a thumbs-down motion as the camera's red light went off. Winter knew his career had taken a turn . . . off a cliff.

CHAPTER 23
WRAPPING UP

MONDAY, DECEMBER 10, 2007
8:22 A.M. EST
SUCHES, GEORGIA

The ambulance with its back doors open was parked behind all the police, sheriff, and trooper cars along the road. Most of the officers who had spent the night on the road were waiting by the ambulance for the game wardens to bring Byrd and the Texans to the makeshift command post. The overcast was clearing, and the temperature was dropping.

The game wardens drove the buzzing four-wheelers up to the rear doors of the ambulance and helped Byrd and the two Texans climb down on rubbery legs.

Buster Hicks stood at the back doors, watching like a mother hen as the officers were helped into the ambulance. "I sure am glad to see you three," Hicks said.

Byrd slumped on the bench as Adeline and Raelynn shared the gurney. An EMT checked the area where Rae's head was bleeding and cleaned it with a bandage.

"This scrape on your head might need stitches. We need to take you to the ER," the EMT declared.

Raelynn brushed her curly blond hair and touched the wound. "It'll be fine."

Adeline nodded. "She's got a hard head, for sure."

Hicks looked somber as he eyed Raelynn. "Deputy, I hate to be the bearer of bad news. Lord knows you've had enough in the last few days." Hicks swallowed hard. "Your brother-in-law killed your niece, I'm afraid. He brought her body here with him."

Raelynn sighed. "I had guessed that."

"If there is anything you need while you're taking care of your family here in Georgia, be sure to let me know." Hicks offered her a hand, squeezing Rae's firmly, before climbing down from the ambulance.

Hicks pulled his hat back on. "If you all need anything, be sure to let someone know. You've had a rough night, I'm sure."

"We're glad to be back in civilization. Any chance we can get something to eat?" Byrd asked.

Hicks looked around for someone to grab the trio some of the leftover burgers. "We'll see to it."

Byrd closed his eyes for a moment and enjoyed the warm air blowing from the ambulance's heater. A female EMT passed out blankets and towels before she began the process of documenting their vital signs.

The Texans had drifted off to sleep in the warm ambulance.

Stetson Crosby leaned out of the rain. Byrd thought his eyes looked sad and weary. Byrd nudged Raelynn and Adeline with his foot. The women jumped and straightened in their seats.

He sought out Raelynn's eyes. "I understand you already know about your niece?" Crosby asked with trepidation in his voice.

Raelynn nodded. "I do, Major." Raelynn sighed heavily. "And I appreciate your kindness. Maybe on the way home, if you'll let me ride back to Texas with you, I'll be ready to hear more details. But for now, knowing that everyone tried so hard to rescue her is enough for me."

Crosby squeezed her hand. "Well, we will certainly want you to fly back with us. The State of Texas would expect nothing less."

Raelynn's eyes teared for a moment. "I sure do appreciate what everybody did."

Crosby looked at the floor of the ambulance.

A deputy extended burgers and canned drinks to Byrd to give to the rest of the team. Crosby waited until they unwrapped their burgers and began to eat.

"Ranger, are you good?" Crosby asked Adeline.

Adeline turned his way. "Yes, sir. I'd say I'm right as the rain, but I don't think I'll use that expression again for a while."

"Were you involved in the shooting?" Crosby asked. "We'll need to figure out how to conduct an investigation, if you were."

Adeline answered honestly. "Major, I fired a few rounds during the chase through the woods, but I didn't hit anything."

Crosby gave the matter some thought. "I'll make sure the GBI knows we have exemplars for your firearms back at the lab in Austin. If they recover bullets they can't identify, we can help them out. As far as an investigation goes, we'll be in Georgia long enough to give statements to the GBI for their investigation. If the governor wants something more, we can deal with that later."

"I'll give the GBI whatever they need for their investigation," Adeline affirmed.

Crosby nodded. He looked at Raelynn. "How about you, Deputy Michaels? Did you fire any shots?"

"I left all my guns back in Texas, sir." Another honest answer.

Crosby glanced at Byrd. "So, I guess that leaves you, Danny?"

Byrd smiled. "Me or Bigfoot, Major."

Crosby chuckled. "I don't believe in Bigfoot."

"Do you believe in guardian angels, Major?"

Crosby wasn't sure what to make of the question. "I guess so. Why?"

Byrd looked far away for a moment. "I guess they can take lots of different forms."

Crosby wasn't sure what to say. After a moment, he said, "I'll get word to Sheriff Hallman that you're okay, Deputy. He's been worried sick, but we made him stay at the command post. I think he's coming down with something, maybe the flu."

Raelynn touched Crosby's sleeve. "Thank him for me. And thank you."

Stetson Crosby carefully climbed out of the ambulance. He pushed his western hat down on his head as he dialed Sheriff Hallman's cell phone.

The trio of cops unwrapped the cold, soggy burgers. "Not much to write home about, but they'll do in a pinch," Byrd offered.

Byrd had emptied a cup of sweet tea and was finishing work on the burger when Buster Hicks climbed in beside him. Hicks looked more tired than Byrd had ever seen him. His face was drawn and pale in the harsh light in the back of the emergency vehicle.

"Danny, can you tell me what happened up there? Just a thumbnail so we know what we're dealing with. The GBI still has the job of finishing out this investigation."

"Ladies," Byrd said with his eyes closed, "we call this a 'Public Safety Statement.' I'm quoting from the GBI Use of Force Investigations Manual. The officer should be advised that these questions are in the interest of public safety. The officer's response to these questions is voluntary and the officer will not be required to answer these questions. The purpose of these questions is to determine the safety and well-being of the officer and the general public."

Buster Hicks chuckled. "That is accurate. However, since I don't plan to write a report, it's even more informal. I want to know what happened so I can brief the governor and the director of the Texas DPS."

Byrd opened his eyes. "We chased Rudy down the mountain out of Morganton. You probably already know he was in my CI's car. He crashed out somewhere around here, and then we followed him into the woods. We exchanged gunfire several different times, but neither one of us hit anything as far as I know. Then, I guess around six, we cornered him on a ridge, and he shot at me. I shot back, and then he went down. Raelynn didn't have a weapon, and Addy had a pistol but wasn't involved in that exchange of gunfire."

"Neither one of them fired a shot?" Hicks asked.

Byrd looked into Raelynn's eyes. She met Byrd's questioning eyes with a look of determination. "No, sir," Byrd said. "Just me. I think I fired three or four times. In the heat of the moment, I'm not sure. Ranger Riley did fire once or twice up on the mountain when Rudy was firing wildly.

But the final gunfight was me against him. That about covers it."

Hicks nodded. "Region Ten is here to work the shooting, but you go and get some rest. We'll want to have the autopsy this afternoon to confirm there aren't any other bullets in the body, and then the Texans can head back home if they like."

Byrd glanced over at Hicks. "Director, that man deserved to die if anybody ever did."

"You'll get no argument from me, Danny."

"Director?"

"What, Danny?"

"Do you ever wonder why God lets bad things happen?" Byrd mused. Byrd knew Hicks to be a man of faith.

Hicks looked thoughtful. "I guess we won't know the answer to that on this side of the forever. But I know he put us here to do a job. People like you and I, these folks from Texas, and every man or woman who puts on a badge and gun exist on Earth to fight evil. That's in our DNA."

Byrd nodded. "I think so, too. I really do."

Vince Atkins, one of the Crime Scene Specialists from GBI Region Ten, stuck his head around the door frame. "Excuse me, Director. I need to ask these folks to step out so we can do the photo thing before they get out of here."

Hicks nodded. "I understand."

Hicks extended a hand to Adeline and then for Raelynn to climb down from the rear of the ambulance. "What are we doing?" Raelynn asked.

Byrd spoke up. "It's standard procedure in an officer-involved shooting. Any law enforcement personnel involved will be photographed—front, back, and sides, as well as close-ups of any noticeable injuries. Also, I'm guessing they'll want to take my gun to the lab and maybe our clothes."

Atkins readied his camera. "Danny, the Director said we could skip the clothes under the circumstances. Particularly, the out-of-state officers. But we'll need to go through all the rest of the steps."

"Thanks," Byrd said as he stood beside the ambulance for the photos to be taken. Adeline was next, and then Raelynn stepped up.

While Atkins was taking photos, a second agent from Region Ten walked up. Jack House was a widely recognized expert in crime scene investigation. A crusty older agent, who smoked constantly, except when examining a scene. "Danny, I need to collect the gun you used."

"Sure, Jack." Byrd grabbed the rifle from the floor of the ambulance. "I took the magazine out already and ejected the live round from the chamber."

Byrd handed House the gun, magazine, and the ejected round. House documented each one separately and then had Byrd sign a receipt as he puffed away on a cigarette he somehow managed to keep alive in the rain.

Byrd was climbing back into the warm ambulance, trying to keep his blanket dry, when Sheriff Smith approached him. "Daniel, I've arranged for motel rooms for all of you to get in the warm and dry. And your car is at the front of this pack. If you keep on going down this road, just take every right till you get to Dial Road. That'll take you back to Highway 60, and you know how to get to town from there."

"Thanks, Sheriff. I think we'd all like to get out of these clothes."

"Do you have dry clothes?" Smith asked.

"I keep a bag with three days' worth of clothes in the trunk. I don't know about the ladies, though."

Sheriff Smith put a wad of chewing tobacco in his mouth. "We'll get them something if they don't have anything clean and dry to wear. We've got a Walmart down the road. You just let me know."

Byrd shook hands with Sheriff Smith. "Could you get word to the GBI folks where we'll be. And tell Major Crosby that Adeline will be going there as well."

The sheriff gave Byrd a thumbs-up as he walked away to handle another issue.

Byrd motioned to Adeline and Raelynn. "The sheriff has arranged for us to have rooms. We can shower and clean up if you'd like."

Raelynn wrapped her blanket, which was slowly becoming sodden, around her shoulders. Byrd was struck by the sadness in her blue eyes. "Let's go."

Byrd pulled Raelynn into a hug. "I don't think I told you how sorry I am about your family."

Raelynn hung her head for a moment. Then she met Byrd's eyes. She held them for a flash and then headed for Byrd's car.

Adeline followed behind. "Should I tell Major Crosby where I'll be?"

Byrd shook his head. "That's handled. So, let's make like the good shepherd."

Adeline frowned. "What does that mean?"

"Let's get the flock out of here," Byrd said over his shoulder.

As they walked toward Byrd's car, a Union County Sheriff's car pulled in front of Byrd's Crown Vic. Byrd motioned for the marked car to back up, but the deputy only stopped long enough to disgorge Arlow and Doc.

Doc rushed to Byrd and threw his arms around him. "Son, I thought you were a goner this time."

"Hell, Doc," Byrd retorted. "When I found out you were with Arlow flying around in this weather, I thought *you* were a goner."

Doc slapped Byrd on the back. "I did, too," Byrd noted that Doc looked tired. His curly, iron-gray hair was wet, and his clothes looked like they'd been slept in.

Byrd turned to his companions from Texas. "Adeline Riley of the Texas Rangers and Raelynn Michaels of the El Paso County Sheriff's Office, I want you to meet Jackson Farmer, or Doc as we all call him. These ladies just spent a luxurious night in the mountains with me. Now, we're headed to dry out and get some food."

"Can we hitch a ride?" Doc asked. "That deputy said he could bring us up here, but we'd have to get back on our own."

"We'll be packed like sardines,' Byrd remarked. "Climb on in. You look worn out, Doc."

Doc shrugged. "I probably am. I won't know till I get feeling back in my legs. I had the seatbelt in that airplane on so tight it acted like a tourniquet."

Byrd fired up the blue Crown Victoria, which had served him well. He turned the heater on full blast as his friends piled into the car. Byrd waited for Addy and Rae to buckle up.

"Safety first!" Byrd announced as he watched everyone get buckled and sorted. Then he pulled the shifter into gear and navigated around the wreckage from Rudy's crashed getaway car.

Byrd knew he'd be on administrative leave through the rest of the holidays and maybe into January—at least until

Region Ten wrapped up its report. And then he'd be offered more visits to Anne Kuykendall.

That thought made him smile.

MONDAY, DECEMBER 10, 2007
1:42 P.M. EST
BLAIRSVILLE, GEORGIA

Byrd heard the soft tapping on his motel room door. He rolled off the bed and pulled on a dry pair of pants and a shirt.

"Who is it?" Byrd asked.

"It's Tina and Sheriff Hallman," came the muffled reply.

Byrd pulled the door open a crack. Blackwell and Hallman stepped into the room.

"I came to check on you," Blackwell said. "The command post is breaking down, but the Region Ten folks will be working the crime scene for the rest of the day and into the night."

Byrd pointed to a pair of chairs. "I'm okay. Just a little waterlogged. Sheriff, we heard you were under the weather. Are you feeling any better?"

Hallman nodded. "Sheriff Smith got me into his doctor, and I got a shot of some kind. Whatever it was, it did the trick. I feel a whole lot better. How about you? Have you been able to get any rest?"

"I was able to get a nap earlier. Is everyone satisfied with the outcome?"

Blackwell shrugged. "A dead suspect has its upside and its downside. We'll probably all get sued by Rudy's family. But the folks from the Rangers are telling me there is plenty of evidence to prove Rudy was their murderer."

Byrd dropped onto a corner of the bed. "It would have been nice to try him and then let Texas give him the needle, but he decided things would go another way."

Blackwell leaned back in the chair. "Speaking of the Texans, they are going to be heading back home tomorrow morning, right, Sheriff?"

Hallman stood behind the cheap motel chair. "That's right. We need to get back to our jobs and . . ." For a moment, Hallman's voice faltered. "And I need to make sure Deputy Michaels and her family are tended to."

Byrd frowned. "Will Rae be in any trouble, Sheriff?"

Hallman chuckled. "Officially, she violated several of my policies. Practically, however, she did what any good Texan would have done. No elected official wants to stand on policy when the interests of the people are served. Her punishment, in my eyes, was spending the night in the woods, unarmed against a killer."

Byrd hung his head. "What Rudy did was bad business. I'm sorry for anyone to have to endure that much violent death at one time."

Hallman sighed. He looked ready to go, but Byrd had noticed Blackwell glance in his direction.

Blackwell leaned forward in the chair. "Can I ask you something? Off the record? Just us three."

Byrd nodded. He trusted Tina more than anyone he'd worked for.

"How did Doc find y'all? Did it have anything to do with the helicopters we heard down on the road?"

Byrd kept his eyes on Blackwells. "I don't know about any helicopters. After I shot Rudy, I grabbed some glow sticks from my go-bag, broke them, and tossed them on the ground around us. I figure that's how Doc saw us."

"You carry glow sticks in your bag? When did you start doing that?" she asked.

"Any good agent would have an emergency supply with them. You never know when you might need to mark something at a crime scene," Byrd lied.

"What are you not telling me? I have a feeling there is more to this," Blackwell persisted.

"Tina, we all got lucky. We brought a family annihilator down. Raelynn has some closure on her loss, and the rest of us are happy to have been able to sacrifice for the greater good." Byrd stood and walked to the window and pulled back the curtain.

"Is it still raining. Seemed like it might rain right through Christmas?" Byrd mused.

"It's clearing up. We may get a few days with some sunshine." Blackwell stood up. "Danny, get some rest. The Crime Lab will be doing Madison's autopsy this afternoon. I'll send someone else to cover it."

Byrd hung his head for a moment. Then he scowled as he looked into Blackwell's eyes. "No, I'm the case agent. And I owe Raelynn and her family that much. I'll get dressed and head to Headquarters."

Blackwell shook her head. "I'll make sure they wait on you to get there. Get some more rest if you can before you take off."

"I'm awake," Byrd said with finality. "It's part of the case agent's job to be at the postmortem. Even with all the evidence we already have, we should touch every base on the investigation of her death."

"You're a good man, Daniel Byrd," Hallman observed.

Byrd half-smiled. "I guess Rudy will be there too."

Blackwell frowned. "I'll make sure the lab finishes him before you get there. Wouldn't do for you to observe his autopsy."

Byrd glanced at his watch. "Tell the lab I'll be there by four. I should be able to make that."

Blackwell shrugged. "Handle your business, but don't plan on coming into the office for a few days."

Blackwell and Hallman made their way to the door. Hallman reached out and patted Byrd on the back as he picked up his hat to leave.

Byrd turned to face Blackwell. "I opened a twenty-six case against Rudy. Should I change the case code?"

Blackwell nodded. "You opened it as an Assistance Rendered case, and that's what it was when you were helping an out-of-state agency on their investigation. Since he won't be prosecuted, you can leave it that way if you want."

Byrd shook his head. "The case in Georgia might have started as an assistance case, but we have to carry it on the books as the highest crime we have."

Blackwell shrugged. "I can approve the change, if you want. Technically, it could be a twenty-six, a zero three, or a zero one."

Byrd's lips were pressed firmly together. "I want to change it to a zero one. The little girl deserves that. A kidnapping—a zero three—isn't high enough. It needs to go on record as a zero one. It should be designated as the highest crime we investigate."

Blackwell moved to the door. "Yep, although she'll never know."

Byrd held the door for Blackwell. "I'll know."

EPILOGUE

When Byrd stopped, Judge Jerry Mason rocked back in his chair. He steepled his fingers as he rested his arms on his stomach. "I do remember the incident. A very tragic set of circumstances. And all completely out of this court's jurisdiction. But how does it affect Mr. Warren, and what interest does the British government have?"

Omar's attorney, Lane Sims, looked to Consul General Rahway. "I think our guest from the UK may want to offer something on that, your honor. That's how I understood things."

The Consul General looked to General Carleton-Smith, who stood and addressed the room. Both Rahway and the general were noticeably uncomfortable. "Much of what I am about to tell you is top secret. It is being offered to clarify some circumstances which are even unknown to Agent Byrd and Sheriff Michaels."

Then Carleton-Smith addressed the judge. "I believe you are a military man, Your Honor?"

Mason nodded. "United States Army. I came out of the reserves as a colonel after twenty years and two tours in the Middle East."

Carleton-Smith smiled ruefully. "Have you ever heard of a military unit in Britain that is unofficially known as 'the Increment?'"

Mason shook his head. "No. Should I?"

Carleton-Smith chuckled. "I should be relieved that you haven't. They are one of Britain's closest-held military secrets. Officially, the group is known as the E-Squadron of the Special Air Service. Unofficially, they are the Increment. Either name is still considered a secret by the British government. They are a secret force loosely attached to our MI-6."

Mason nodded. "I've heard of the SAS. What's an MI-6?"

"MI-6 is the British Secret Intelligence Service. Like our CIA," Byrd injected.

Carleton-Smith stood beside Byrd and addressed his comments to him. "E-Squadron is a highly secret special force that penetrates deep behind enemy lines and conducts sensitive operations on behalf of allied governments, including your own. They are, as I said, the action arm of our Secret Intelligence Service. Our friend, Omar Warren, as you know him, has provided them with many secret tools and special equipment."

Byrd shrugged. "Your man with MI-6 alluded to that when I met with Omar in London last year."

Carleton-Smith pulled out a chair and sat beside Byrd. He leaned back. "They frequently train in America with your special forces. Green Berets, SEAL Teams, and your Delta Force, among others."

Byrd was non-committal.

"In fact, you might have some knowledge of their expertise and training."

Byrd frowned. "Not that I'm aware of."

"You spoke of the search for the young girl's killer in the mountains of North Georgia. And about the oddly dressed soldiers who came to your aid."

Suddenly, Byrd had a chill. "The guys from the Ranger Camp?"

Carleton-Smith nodded. Then the soldier raised an eyebrow. "No ordinary military team could have performed that mission in the weather that night. Our boys were lucky to have been training with your American Night Stalker pilots."

Byrd nodded slowly. "Not ranger trainees then?"

Carleton-Smith chuckled. "Highly skilled men who happened to be in the right place at the right time. Small world, what? Mr. Warren prevailed upon the highest authorities in the British government for a favor. A move that could have caused . . . problems for many people if the truth had been uncovered."

Judge Mason frowned. "You Brits came a long way, at least the general did, to tell us next to nothing."

Byrd leaned forward in his seat. "Your Honor, I think they told me a lot."

Mason sat forward. "They were talking about those men who saved you that night?"

Byrd nodded slowly. "That's the way it sounds. Without the help of those men that night, we would probably have died of exposure up on that mountain. As you said, they came a long way to tell us that."

Carleton-Smith motioned toward Omar. "It is indicative of our relationship with this man that our government is willing to disclose its involvement in this matter. I trust the people in this room will treat this information accordingly."

Byrd looked at Omar Warren. "You called them in? You used your contacts to come to our aid?"

Omar took a deep breath. "I did."

"How did you know what was going on?" Byrd wondered aloud.

"The BBC actually carried the story when you and the others were lost in the woods."

"Well, I owe you for that," Byrd remarked.

Omar nodded. "Even back then, I felt like I owed you, Agent Byrd. My life had changed trajectory."

Byrd sighed. He leaned forward on the big table and steepled his fingers. "That explains some things."

Mason stared at the ceiling. "And I understand, now, why it can't go on the record."

Byrd leaned to his left and moved his gun back an inch on his belt. The pistol was bothering his back. "Thanks for understanding, Judge."

After a full minute of examining the ceiling, while he digested the implications, Mason turned to Sheriff Raelynn Michaels. "Do you have anything to add, Sheriff?"

She shook her head. Her eyes were red and her face was flushed. "I'd hoped never to relive those days. But based on the totality of the circumstances, I agree that Mr. Warren should be afforded all the mercy Your Honor is willing to offer up."

Mason pursed his lips. "Mr. Warren. Do you have anything to add?"

Omar hung his head. "No, sir. I appreciate you hearing all this and taking it into account."

British Consul General Gail Rahway waited for the appropriate moment to speak. "On behalf of the British government, I simply want to say thank you for your consideration in this matter. Some lines were crossed that morning in the North Georgia mountains. Our government regrets stepping over those lines, but the Crown is satisfied with the outcome."

Major General Carleton-Smith stood and addressed the judge. "Your Honor, I have personally investigated the events of that day. We, of course, will never reveal the details of that morning to anyone. We soldiers in the United Kingdom are bound by the Official Secrets Act. But to a man, the members of that group are proud of their part in this manhunt. Mr. Grant deserved what he got."

Raelynn Michaels slapped the table. "Amen!"

Consul General Rahway rose and began shaking hands all around. "We thank you for your time. I believe Agent Byrd has all the pieces to the puzzle now, and he can offer facts the Crown would prefer not to be party to."

Judge Mason looked around the room. "This could have ended much differently without your men." Mason stood behind his desk. "I feel like I need to express my appreciation to the British contingent. Much of this story was cloudy, at best."

Mason reached out to shake hands with Carleton-Smith and Rahway.

Once the general and the consul were out of the room, Judge Mason looked around at all the faces around the table. "I guess I don't have to say this was all off the record. But I'll say it anyway."

Byrd stood uncomfortably and helped Raelynn to her feet. "Is Steve still with the rangers?"

"He's going to have to hang it up in a couple of more years," Raelynn said. "I guess that's the only good thing to come out of that night. Meeting the man I love."

"I noticed you didn't take his name."

Raelynn frowned. "Sheriff Chandler doesn't have the right ring. And most people don't know Texas Ranger Chandler is my husband. It makes it easier for him to work around El Paso."

"I'm happy it worked out," Byrd offered.

Judge Mason gave the pair a look. "You two can catch up later."

Mason motioned toward the door and waited as everyone filed out. "All right, Mr. Warren, now that your hearing is over, are you ready to hear the court's determination?"

Omar stood and faced Judge Mason. "Yes, Your Honor. I'll take my medicine."

Mason cocked his head toward Byrd. "It's time for me to dispense some justice."

ACKNOWLEDGMENTS

I can't imagine how any of these books would have been completed without the love, patience, and commitment of my family. Thanks to Grace, Emma, Zack, Erika, Adeline, Raelynn, and Stetson—and to the Hodge family, Mark and Shelia.

I must thank my sounding boards and first readers—Mark Hodge, Mike Crosby, and Jess Hampton—as well as the fans, many of whom I have never met, who give me the confidence to move these characters forward.

I've also been blessed to work for the best state law enforcement agency in America—the Georgia Bureau of Investigation—and to work alongside many other dedicated state and local cops from across the US. I hope I've given readers a taste of what the job involves—though with mixed success.

Unlike Daniel Byrd, I have friends. I wouldn't have had any success without the career-long—and in some cases, lifelong—friendship of so many patient individuals.

Trust me when I say, I have been blessed beyond my due.

Phillip W. Price began his law enforcement career with the City of Canton, Georgia, Police Department in late 1974 (at the age of nineteen). On January 1, 1976, Price was hired as a radio operator for the Georgia State Patrol assigned to the Headquarters Communications Center. On January 8, 1978, Price transferred to the Georgia Bureau of Investigation (GBI) as a special agent. Price retired as a Special Agent in Charge (SAC) in 2006.

After a stint as a traveling consultant, conducting training on methamphetamine manufacture, Price was hired as the task force commander for the Cherokee Multi-Agency Narcotics Squad (CMANS) in May of 2010. Price retired on December 17, 2021.

In 2021, Price completed his first novel, *Mountain Justice*. The setting for the story is the North Georgia Mountains, and the story follows a young GBI agent, Daniel Byrd, who uncovers corruption and murder in the otherwise idyllic setting.

Price followed the first novel with *A Little Bit Kin*, the tale of a methamphetamine cook who gets in over his head. The drug distribution scheme spirals out of control, and GBI Agent Byrd is left to pick up the pieces. Much of the novel revolves around the world of methamphetamine abuse and the lifestyle that goes with it.

Price's third novel, *Self Rescue*, follows Byrd around Georgia as he pursues a CIA contract officer who dabbles in methamphetamine smuggling from the Mexican border to the Peach State. Soon, Byrd ends up on the Texas/Mexican border in a fight for his life.

Price's fourth novel, *Asphalt Blues*, continues the investigation into the drug enterprise that the GBI and Texas authorities uncovered between El Paso and Atlanta. *Asphalt Blues* received the Literary Titan Gold Award in 2024.

Drawing from real events and his own professional career in law enforcement, Price delivers authentic, lived-in portrayals of police work—capturing how officers think, speak, and operate with a level of accuracy rarely seen in the genre.

Price has an associate in arts degree from Reinhardt University, a bachelor of science degree from North Georgia University, and a master's degree in public administration from Columbus State University.

Price has appeared on One America News Network and Salem Cable News Network.